"A FRESH AND ORIGINAL TALENT . . .
A DIFFERENT KIND OF STORY"

—*Washington Star*

"All the anger of a black youth in a white
society is here, but Barry Beckham has
wrought from his material a tale that would
be moving and dramatic in any society, in
any century. He has given us a character who
is a black man and yet Everyman, and this
tour de force of a novel is rendered with an
imaginative eye, a perfect ear, and a feeling
heart. MY MAIN MOTHER is the best first
novel I have read in years."

—Charles Bracelen Flood,
author of *More Lives Than One*

"A tale of death, black pride, a search for
love and the quest of a young man for
respect . . . a novel of penetrating insight."

—*A.L.A. Booklist*

SIGNET Titles of Related Interest

MY MAIN MOTHER

Barry Beckham

A SIGNET BOOK from
NEW AMERICAN LIBRARY
TIMES MIRROR

Published by
THE NEW AMERICAN LIBRARY
OF CANADA LIMITED

This is an authorized reprint of a hardcover edition published by Walker and Company. The hardcover edition was published simultaneously in Canada by The Ryerson Press, Toronto.

FIRST PRINTING, JANUARY, 1971

 SIGNET TRADEMARK REG. U.S. PAT. OFF. AND FOREIGN COUNTRIES
REGISTERED TRADEMARK—MARCA REGISTRADA
HECHO EN WINNIPEG, CANADA

SIGNET, SIGNET CLASSICS, SIGNETTE, MENTOR AND PLUME BOOKS are published in Canada by The New American Library of Canada Limited, Toronto, Ontario

PRINTED IN CANADA
COVER PRINTED IN U.S.A.

To the good-doing
Sidney Offit

MY MAIN MOTHER

1

SO IT'S ALMOST TIME.

I've been coming here for several days now to proofread my history I started writing almost a month ago, and tonight I should finish it off. Tonight should be my last night in this old, wooden station wagon ensconced in the Maine woodlands.

Listen, this old Ford wagon was presented to me by my late Uncle Melvin, who died before I killed my mother. Good-doing, wine-drinking, pipe-smoking Uncle Melvin knew that no one else could possibly love the old Ford more than I. Even as the rain patters on the roof above me now, I love it. She has only two wheels—both on the right—so that when I pretend to drive it, I am always cutting a sharp corner on my left. A hole in the floor through which eager weeds grow up and stretch toward the dashboard. Also: three doors that won't open; a fat, dead worm found once in the yellow foam of the cut-up back seat; and a hood that refuses to shut. To see ahead of me, I must lean my head out the driver's side window.

You might call my story a confession of the soul, a revealing of the mind's construction or a proclamation of my own emancipation. I come here from my room in town, come here to this Ford leaning on its side across the road from the old, gray house. I keep my manuscript in a box near my drumsticks on the back floor and Jeff, strong boxer of mine, guards it all. He sleeps lightly under the porch of that grand, gray, monstrous-looking castle that has been the source of so much grief for me; and paradoxically, so much happiness. These things—the house, the car, the drumsticks, the manuscript and Jeff—they are the stuff of my life.

If you please, my credentials: black, beautiful, man of many moods, genius, hero of sorts.

Jeff now sits in the back seat on his haunches. He licks drops of rain that creep through the fogged windows' edges. I talk a lot about Jeff, my fine boxer, tan with a large diamond of white on his chest and spots of white on his ankles. He is my only living companion. If you could see how he stands sometimes: butt of a tail wiggling, hind legs bent perfectly, head stretched forward with his large black mouth closed (for a change). I used to call from a distance and he'd pivot quickly, and like a single horse in his own stampede, bound toward me. A little old now, Jeff is still solid. Slap him on his shanks or on his side and it's all meat you feel, solid flesh. I'll allow him to lick my face with that dripping red tongue of his, or I'll put my fist between his sharp whites, or, before I put him out here to guard the property, I'd let him sleep at the foot of the bed with Uncle and me, glad to have his comfortable solidness next to my feet, and sleeping easier with the sounds of snorts and sneezes. And Jeff does not play. He showed me that during the first week I had him. I saw him grab a stray cat by its neck and wring the life out of it. Jeff.

They told me officially at the funeral two weeks ago in Boston that Uncle Melvin had left me this beautiful rusting auto with the rotting, wooden sides. This lovely old station wagon he left for me; lovely old conveyance that now conveys only the love that I hold for it.

At his funeral, arriving late, I threw off my coat, rushed toward the white casket, without even seeing the

10

thirty or so people sitting on folding chairs with their hands correctly in their laps, poor imitations of mourning relatives.

I started to ask who it was in that casket. Who was it in that five-foot casket with his hands folded, looking like a doll trying to smile? Who was this doll who couldn't have weighed more than twenty pounds, whose legs were as thin as my arms, whose shoulders weren't as broad as a ballerina's waist? Surely not Uncle, who had stood tall in his blaze-orange hunting cap, who would hold the leash to five hounds in one hand and who shook the old castle when he had trampled through it?

"Cancer," said one of the ushers, as if I hadn't known about the suffering. And then, "Here, step this way, sit down please." He handed me a clean-smelling mimeographed sheet: MELVIN PIP. LIVED 70 YEARS. A GOOD MAN WHO LIVED WELL AND LEFT MANY FRIENDS AND RELATIVES BEHIND HIM. WAS A MEMBER FOR TEN YEARS OF FIRST BAPTIST'S USHER BOARD. MAY GOD REST HIS SOUL, FOR HE WAS ATTENDING CHURCH REGULARLY IN HIS EARLY DAYS.

I thought it would be best to begin at the beginning, from the nascent stages of my hatred for Mother to where I am now. None of that *medias res* stuff for me, although this report may well be an epic. And the story begins in the summer.

2

I WAS SEVEN YEARS OLD.

The day even began wrong: rain in the morning and then cloudiness and later an adhesive, wet hotness about the air. I had been shooting beer cans lined along the road in front of the house with my BB gun when I saw the bad sheen, the very, very bad convertible rocking and rolling up the road toward the house. It was a moving nightmare of shining red and chrome.

After he had parked his car next to Uncle's station wagon, out jumped big Larson. He sported a dark, double-breasted vine and one of those hanging bow ties the same color as his black ten-gallon hat. I leaned on my rifle—next to the gate—and watched him as he kicked a beer can out of the way and sauntered toward me.

I said, "Even-nen, pardner."

"Hey, kid," he said, and put his hand that smelled of Lifebuoy soap on my head, and, ring scratching my scalp, rubbed my head as if he were a pitcher just in from the bullpen. There should have been something in the way he shook my head back and forth to warn me. There should have been a raven fluttering around his black sky. Or he should have come masqueraded in borrowed plumes. But there was nothing to warn me of what would happen later that day. Not a thing.

The words of his second sentence hit my face in

small blasts of wine scents. "Where' your mother?"—still walking, past me and up the steps: slide, slide, creak, creak, slide, slide. I should have shot him in the ass with my rifle at that very moment when he rang the bell and pulled open the screen door as if he were Uncle, the owner.

Mother must have seen him coming from one of the front windows. She met him at the doorway. Wearing a plain pink dress, "Hello," she said: "hi, did you have trouble finding the place? Hot, huh?" The door squeaked, then slammed him inside. I jumped onto my long tan stick of a palomino horse and went shooting for buffaloes (when I should have been shooting at a skunk), for the bad sheen parked next to Uncle's station wagon made me lose interest in driving the old Ford.

When I got back, there were the three of them in the side yard with the bulky, portable record player and a radio—neither turned on. Uncle, Mother and big Larson just sat, drinking beer, not talking, but rocking in the porcelain chairs. I, steadying my palomino, watched from the side of the road.

"Where you say you used to live, Elvin—Massachusetts?" Uncle was unshaved, wore wide, pleated wool pants and a long-sleeved red hunting shirt (checked).

"Yeah." Big Larson, waving his ten-gallon sky back and forth in front of his high-yellow face, used a tone suggesting he had told Uncle twice or three times before.

"I knew somebody who lived in Massachusetts before . . . on Fourteenth Street . . . in Massachusetts," he said.

"Um hum," answered Larson.

"Ain't been there for a long time," said Uncle, adding, "Don't many of us live there."

Nobody spoke for a time. It was as if they had all glimpsed the Gorgon and were petrified. Mother cleared her throat, rubbed her nose. Uncle fanned at a fly. Larson crunched his can with one hand, and it popped. No breeze at all, and we don't live that far from the coast.

Suddenly big Larson rose from his red chair. He said, "This record player work?"

"May be too hot," said Uncle. "Records might melt, needle might bend."

Larson went over to the box and threw on five or six ashen-colored 78's. The first was by Billy Eckstine: slow, bassy and soft. Then he went over to Mother's seat, swept his brim in an arc before him and bowed, said, "May I have this dance, lovely lady?"

After two dances, Larson took off his jacket, exposed his yellow suspenders, pulled up his sleeves. The two were very, very close: their legs, hardly moving, were pinned one-to-one as their hips twisted circularly into each other; perspiration even on Larson's hairy arms which squeezed Mother's waist in toward him.

When the last record plopped down and the needle fell on the record and it played and the two of them began their dance again, Uncle spotted me by the fence and came over and watched with me. They finished dancing but stood together whispering until Uncle interrupted them. "Let's take a ride in that sportin' car you got there, Larson. How about it, huh?"

And soon the four of us were riding down Columbus Street with the top down. It was my first time in a convertible; Uncle and I in the back, and cool daddy, extra-special big Larson (now that he was behind the wheel) with his arm around my young and lovely mother. The breeze was drying our brows faster than we could perspire. I'd like to say that my hair was all over my face, but you'd know better than that. Soon Larson opened her up. But the cool daddy swung around the corner without braking, and all of us except him were thrown to our elbows. As we straightened up, I noticed that Uncle was not smiling, was looking at the back of Mother's head. Mother, with a beer can high in the air, had her other arm around big Larson, and I wanted to grab it and say, "Whatch you doing?"

We got back and had a boss dinner of Mother's specialty, fried chicken and potato salad, plus plenty of iced tea with lemon.

Now, after dinner, Uncle turned on the Emerson radio, and the three sat at the dining-room table for a game of whist while I played with my baseball cards. They played over a dimly lighted table, cards sliding here and there, a cigarette and a pipe hanging out of the mouths of the two men smokers.

After a while, from my seat on the worn Oriental rug, I saw Uncle stop playing. Because he did, I put down my Jackie Robinson. He put his hands into his pockets, and I did mine also. Then he yawned, stood up and spoke. I stood up, yawned and listened.

"Damned heat," he said, for I can see him standing there now. "Boy"—he was pointing at big Larson—"I sure wish I was back in your convertible again, like the ride we took this afternoon, Larson. That breeze was just blowing all through the car. Man, it was cool then."

Larson looked at my mother, who was smiling at him with her face of sharp features, lipstick and cheeks made up. Then she stood, the round of her stomach outlined by the plain but tight-fitting pink dress, her eyes moving over big Larson's face; she stood in a lazy fashion, picking up her pocketbook by the strap from off the back of the chair and throwing the strap over her shoulder and just standing there moving her eyes over me, over Uncle and over Larson. My tall, lovely and young mother stood, watched, smiled—like a judge at a beauty contest.

She spoke in a soft whisper of a voice, a voice that could have convinced you to stop what you were doing and come running to her, a voice that almost persuaded me to love her at one time: "Why don't you give Uncle

15

the keys to the car, Elvin? He's a good driver. Let him take Mitchell with him. They can go by themselves. We're not real hot, are we?"

In all that tall loveliness—the pink dress, the makeup—Mother still looked too sinister as she tottered and held on to the tabletop for balance. And her head wavered from side to side as if she were trying to deny a grogginess. Sign that she had been drinking more than beer.

Big Larson almost stumbled over himself, almost knocked down the chair as he stood up, thrust a hand in his pocket, jingled many coins, handed the keys to Uncle.

"I don't care," he said, "if you don't want to go with them. Here, take them. But watch out for that accelerator, she's fast pop," laughing with yellow teeth and punching Uncle on the shoulder.

So we left the two of them in that grand house by themselves. Alone.

After Uncle had started the motor, I remembered that I had left my rifle in the bathroom. So I jumped out.

"You don't need it, Mitchell," Uncle yelled—but I was up the steps.

When I opened the door, the two of them loomed forward. You could have stuck Rodin's *The Kiss* in front of my face and it would have been the same scene, except that these two were human, not stone. They were in that position on the couch, and they were frozen by my sudden entrance. And what should I have done?

I became one of them at first. That is, I froze too, like a statue, my hand still on the doorknob, my mouth open, my heart dissolved somewhere in my stomach's pit. Then my sneakered feet rushed me past them toward the back, toward Uncle's room, as if I had not

16

seen the closed eyes and—and those big, big hands of big Larson weighing my mother's breasts.

He went right on with his business. The dress had been unbuttoned down to her waist, the bra off and thrown somewhere—I didn't even see it near—and his hands fumbling, weighing, squeezing. Although her head was thrown back, I'm sure she saw me enter—she at least had to hear the door open—and only chose to ignore me. Her decision.

Well, I wasn't going to watch from the doorway to Uncle's room all night, so I ran through the living room a second time. I probably could have floated through, there was so much air in my stomach. And wouldn't you know that I'd forget the rifle? So I had to turn around again at the door and run back to the bathroom, get the BB gun, and step rapidly through the same scene again with my head down this time—like a *deus ex machina* chased off the stage.

In the car again: I turned the radio knob far to the right so he wouldn't talk to me. I was shaking like an epileptic. As we pulled off, Uncle proved he was used only to standard-shift autos, for the long convertible lurched. And I deliberately banged my face against the dashboard. Feeling my lip push in against my upper teeth, I knew that I was bleeding, and I cried for joy. I cried for myself, I cried for Mother and I cried for the mere joy of crying; and all the while sucking and swallowing the blood from my freshly cut lip.

Of course Uncle was fooled. He was sorry for having jolted me like that, and he cursed the nightmare, new-fangled, too modern sheen. For the remainder of the ride, he talked while I cried with my head back on the leather seat.

He said, "You know, your mother wants so much to be a famous singer. I hope she makes it. She tries so hard. She's had such a time of it, that's why we must help her with her problems."

Past the Living End, where Mother sang part-time on Saturdays and Sundays: cars parked in the spaces like boats in slips; blues blaring into the summer night; black couples leaning on car hoods, and a man pulling up his fly, advancing out of the woods on the other side of the road.

"That girl is good, your mother, Mitchell. She just needs understanding, I guess. It may be too much for you though, you're so young. Things shot to hell ever since your father left."

After we got onto the freeway, Uncle could drive with one hand, he could prove to me that he knew how to handle the bad sheen. He kept talking until he saw the neon of liquor-store lights. He pulled over and got out.

Coming back toward the car, with the wine in a wrinkled brown-paper bag, just the wet nozzle showing, Uncle got in and turned the key.

"Your father and me used to drink a lot together, Mitchell," he said, pulling onto the road. "He was okay, but couldn't understand your mother's problems, couldn't face facts like a man, like we all have to do sooner or later. Stayed with your mother until you were about three, then took off to God knows where, and ain't nobody seen or heard from him since," said Uncle, light-red wine dripping from his lips, face brown (I sneaked a look at him), with fuzz of gray outlining his face because he hadn't shaved. He continued, "When you get older, Mitchell, there are things I must talk to you about—but not now. Now we'll go back to the house and get a good night's sleep."

That was a laugh.

Past Sears Roebuck's all-night lights, and then curving the bend, on the corner of which stood the Esso station that Uncle always used and where Tony, the owner, still limped as a result of a bad fall from a horse. The same station where I used to take my one

18

week's fifty-cent allowance and spend it in one minute on a cake, a soda and five candy bars. And Tony told Uncle a lot of dirty jokes in the little gas station. Once we were past the landmark station, it was straight uphill for a half-mile, and then a turn into the rough road to the house.

So I could have got a good night's sleep, had I been deaf, dumb and blind. They were sitting on the porch steps when we got back, supposedly watching the stars, or maybe listening to the crickets.

"Did you two have a nice ride?" asked Mother in a voice similar to a "May I help you?" in a department store. I nodded and went straight to bed, not wanting to listen to more of Larson's big mouth than I had to; besides, my eyes were swollen.

I had trouble kiffing off. The Z's just wouldn't come.

While I was under those cold, white sheets, I longed for Mother to hurry, say good-bye and get in the bed with me. Those Maine summer nights can get pretty cold, but they can be bearable with a mother's warm body next to yours.

Soon my thoughts eased out into the suburbs of my mind. I was in the twilight zone of sleep and wakefulness, not perfectly lost to either state, when a shoe dropping on the floor jolted me awake. Quick, short words whispered around me.

"You shouldn't have come in here; Mitchell might be awake."

"He shouldn't be awake at this time of the night."

"Get out of here, Elvin Larson. Come on, out."

"Not hardly, baby, good as you look."

Next, the sound of rough hands sliding over smooth clothing and my mother saying, "Elvin, stop . . . please . . . don't"—the same words repeatedly, but with less emphasis each time. Feet stumbled over the hardwood floor. A zipper ripped. "Elvin, please stop."

And they got in bed—with me. Big Larson was on

my side. I knew that immediately because I almost bounced off the bed when he got in, and he had the nerve to shove me over with his hard, corny foot. Must have been a size fourteen. I lay on my back with my mouth open and arms spread, pretending sleep.

The rest was part dream, part real: big Larson with his hairy leg and sweaty ass and side pushing against me; the bedsprings squeaking, moving up and down; trees rustling outside; groaning and slapping, scratching and twisting; an airplane droning above it all; no's and ooh's and more ooh's; gasping breath, indrawn breath, sighs, squirming and kicking; a cricket proclaiming his happiness; an elbow in my stomach; total darkness except for a window full of stars; then trembling, more trembling, a very reluctant end and a close, embarrassing odor; and I there during it all.

After a while, lover Larson threw his heavy, hairy arm on my forehead, and I knew he was asleep. I should have bitten him.

Probably I couldn't cry anymore that night; that is why I didn't, but then all I wanted was to get away, escape from that stinky, hot room of circumstances beyond my control.

I eased the arm off my face, became startled when Larson flinched, snored, smacked his wide lips, then I rolled out of bed and hurt my toe on his big shoe. I dressed quickly, and finding his black hat on the windowsill and taking it with me, went into the night.

I sailed that hat perfectly into the middle of the road, then I ran down the porch steps and jumped on that wide-brimmed sky as if I were a human pogo stick. I kicked it away and ran toward it again and kicked it some more and spat on it and dug my heel into it and stomped and stomped on that black felt and then went over to get my stick of a horse, held it high, and rammed it also into that black Stetson brim until there were enough holes and tears to satisfy me.

Out of breath, I went into the old station wagon and lay in the back seat. I went into the same station wagon that I am sitting in now. And since that night, since I used it that night as a refuge from my mother's casual nefariousness, it has, as I said, been very dear to me. Since then, it's been more than a source of vicarious trips.

So, seven years old. Not eight or nine or ten, now, but seven. Are you with this? Are you checking it out? Seven years old and sleeping in a station wagon on a cool summer night. In bad shape from the get go.

3

ON TO THE NEXT WEEK.

We woke up about nine that morning. Mother was walking around in her pajamas, she was counting the dead mosquitoes dotting the bedroom walls. She was humming, and I knew that she would probably be in a good mood that day.

"That's one of my favorite tunes," she said. "Your father used to sing that to me a lot." The mattress went down when she sat on the side where I lay, and I eased my legs against the warmth of her back. And my mother hummed the song to me and smoked on the edge of the bed. "Uncle's probably out walking the dogs, probably won't be back until lunchtime," she said. She eased her hand over the back of my neck, for I was now sitting with my knees up and my arms around them.

Jumping up, Mother went to the window and put her head out, breathed in the air, turned to me with a big smile, her head to the side, her voice fresh and her eyes bright and prancing.

"Looks like a nice day, Mitchell. What a beautiful, quiet, nice day. What shall Mommy and you do today, huh? What shall we do to enjoy this day? We'll get washed up and take a walk. Just you and I," she said, clapping her hands and showing all of her perfectly white teeth.

She pulled me out of the bed and shooed me to the bathroom. I washed hurriedly, splashing the cold, sudsy water over my face, thinking of Mother's smile and vivaciousness. I brushed my teeth, remembering Mother's sweet fragrance and her soft hands on the nape of my neck—those long, thin fingers playing over the back of my head. And I hummed the tune that she had been humming; was humming and waving my head back and forth when she pushed the door open so hard that the mirror hanging on it by a string rang and scratched against the wood. Mother's hair was in her eyes, and she was holding the brown pint bottle of bourbon in one hand, turning the doorknob impatiently with the other, tapping her bare foot to a fast rhythm. And the bottle's label seemed to be standing on my nose, seemed to have jumped in front of my face. It's the bottle that I found way in the back corner of the bedroom closet a couple of days ago, I said to myself.

"You no-good brat," she screamed, the words bouncing against the tiles and the tub and then reverberating against my eardrums. Her breasts were jumping up and down, her lips were pursed. "What did you do to this bottle, Mitchell?" I was in a recording studio and she was shouting at me through some tunnel and using an echo board at that. "What the hell did you do?"

At first, the tears just fell. Then the wild, terrorlike expression on Mother's face, the feeling of being trapped in that bathroom, the knowledge of what I had done—these things made me break down, and I turned toward the toilet seat, sat on it and cried.

"Now, that's stupidity for you. I spend good money on a good—this ain't cheap stuff—on a good bottle of whiskey because my nerves are bad and this helps me calm down and you—you, mister grown-up, mister snooping-around, you go and mess with my liquor. I ought to give you the beating of your life! You're just like your father—no damned good!"

23

I was shaking convulsively, out of fear, guilt, shame. The cold water was splashing in the bowl, the mirror was still scratching, Mother was staring at me.

"What did you do to this whiskey, Mitchell?"

And I burst out louder, remembering how I had sneaked down in the cellar with the bottle. Mother stepped foward and turned off the water. Silence. She unscrewed the bottle's top, put her nose to it.

"I don't want to believe what it smells like. Nobody could be that nasty, not even you. Just tell me what you did to it, so I'll know if I should drink it or not."

So, with my voice falling, spurting unintelligibly, my eyes closed and my breath coming not fast enough, I told my mother that I had pissed in her bottle of bourbon. She threw the open end at me, and that smelly yellow liquid ran over my forehead and cheeks. I threw up my hands, tried to turn my face too late. She walked out, left me there sitting on the toilet's top.

When I went out toward the bedroom, I heard her in the kitchen. I was shuffling along the dining room's fading carpet when she called out from the kitchen.

"Mitchell—what do you want for breakfast?"

"Nothing—I'm not hungry." I had to keep my cool.

"Come on in here and get your breakfast, boy," laughing witchlike, cackling. "Aren't you hungry? You should be. Get your clothes on and come in here."

In the kitchen, whose white walls still showed some of my black fingerprints from an earlier age, Mother's flat sandals clapped against the linoleum floor. The sunlight had percolated through the curtains and was wavering all over the walls and floor. Mother poured coffee in my cup and spilled grits, slid two eggs on my plate. We ate in silence. Just Mother and I, eating as fast as two soldiers in a ditch, as quietly as two lovers dining together for the first time over candlelight. My tears had dried and stuck to my cheeks, but my hand was still trembling.

"Now, you just eat your food and relax, Mitchell," she said, and she was suddenly beautiful again, but without her makeup, with only the unhandled loveliness still in her face of darting eyes. "Your Mommy doesn't stay angry with you. And I don't believe in upsetting anyone at the table. Let's play a game. We can pretend that we're a couple out on a date. The music is soft, the lights are low; candlelights, violins, good wine." And Mother had left me, she was in the twenties of her life of sometime back there, no longer digging the present with me. "Shall we dance?" She extended her tender, untrembling fingertips across the table in front of my eyes. Above the fingers I could see her eyes fixed on my face, but not seeing me, looking instead through me at the back of my head where some screen, some playhouse of old was flashing scenes from her youth.

"Uh huh," I said, not the most elegant, suave or debonair partner in my Wranglers, armless T-shirt and high-top sneakers, not certain of the circumstances, of the duration of her mood.

The both of us—Mother and Son—rose from the table at once, and she pulled me toward her cotton nightgown, my cheek lay against her warm stomach and one hand rested against the top of her buttocks, the other held her fingers. She swung me around in a wide circle, she was smiling, her eyes were wide, she had the wholesome, clean smell of soap, and a chickadee was crying outside for us. And didn't I forget that I had just been crying, had been only minutes before that afraid of Mother's rancor? Wasn't I plain damned glad to be sharing her good humor, to be close to her, to touch, feel, imbibe all of her sudden, radiating affection?

"Just like the good old days at the Spotlight in Philadelphia, Mitchell." Then she eased out and away from me, held me by my hand only, started her sandals clapping louder and faster over the linoleum. She was

25

doing some fancy steps, and I found it hard to keep up with her. "Oh, we had fun. The band played all night, the drinks were cheap and Danny and I . . ." That stopped the dancing and it stopped the humming too. Mother was no longer the gay *danseuse*. That name— the first time I had heard her call my father's name in the house—clamped, quenched her spirit. We were facing each other like bull and bullfighter. She was about to stick the sword. "Sit down, Mitchell. This is no way to be carrying on."

So I sat, looked at the hard yellow on my plate and the untouched, warm coffee.

"Aren't you going to drink your coffee?"

I put the cup to my lips, closed my eyes, sipped, then blew, just about sneezed the nasty concoction out. Frowning. Rubbing my tongue against my teeth. Mother roared, slapped her thighs.

"I put," laughing so hard that the words choked, "I put salt in it. You should have seen your face," poking out her lips and widening her eyes in mock imitation of my surprise. "What'd you think it was, huh, Mitchell?" Laughing louder and louder until her voice was a chamber of horror echoes.

"You want me to wash the dishes, Mother?" What else could I say?

"Yes." Walking out of the kitchen. The sun had gone down, the kitchen seemed dark and lonely, the chickadee had stopped, probably frightened by the loud laugh. She returned with her change purse. "I want you to run to the store for me, Mitchell. We need some sodas—ginger ale." And she handed me a perfumed, balled-up dollar bill, told me to get the bottles from the back yard. Hurry back.

My trusty palomino was tied to the fence. He was a little wet from the dew, but I jumped on him and held the reins with one hand, and the carton of empty bottles which had corners of soda in them was in my other hand. I galloped that wooden stick down the road. Maybe Mother is watching, I thought, maybe she'll see me. So I ran faster, whipped my horse's hind legs, clicked my tongue to make him go faster. I'd show Mother how I could hurry back. I thumped down the road from the house like a knight-errant, the white pines flashing past me. I know I left a cloud of dust behind me—just had to have left it, fast as I was going. And when I pulled up to Tony's garage, my sneaks scraped over the gravel-lined cement entrance. I slid, stumbled and almost fell against one of the gas pumps, for I had come roaring in like a posse leader, and it's hard to stop on a dime when you're really smoking.

Leaning on one of the gas pumps, Tony's T-shirted, helmet-shaped stomach was the first thing I saw emerging from the dark rectangle of a doorway. As he came out from the station house, the light moved up to his chest and face, spread down to his baggy, greasy mechanic's pants, and soon he was out of the door completely, fully illuminated by the sunlight, limping, leaning on his cane, holding a can of snuff in his other hand.

"Mitchell?"—meaning, "What do you want?" Looking at my carton of bottles. "Sodas, huh? Those my bottles?" The nearest store was miles away. He took the carton from me, held it high above his head. "I'll take 'em this time, but don't bring me no bottles from another store. I don't have room for 'em, Mitchell." Tony took the carton, turned, spat, and went inside for my six sodas. "Here," he said, returning and handing me the sodas, the carton of six dripping wet bottles taken from his box cooler. They were as cold as Jeff's nose. "Your mother home?" Mouth mumbling because it was full of snuff. Black, slick hair parted and combed to the side.

"Nope." Then I paid him, waited for his thin, grease-covered white fingers to fumble out the change, and I

27

galloped away before he could start on a story "about the time when." I galloped along the highway, turned up the road toward the house. But I turned so fast that I slipped on a stone. The carton fell from my hand, the bottles broke on the hot cement, the cool ginger ale squirmed and oozed in the dirt on the road. In a world of trouble. My ass was grass, and Mother would be the lawn mower.

Mother was still in her robe and sitting at the dining-room table when I came in with empty hands. A bottle of liquor was her companion. I started to ask her where she got it, but so much of Mother was clandestine, I decided against it. Her hands, over her mouth, were folded so that her arms formed an isosceles triangle with the table. No smile from her face, partially hidden by her hands.

"Where're the sodas, Mitchell?"

"Beg pardon?"

"Was Tony's closed?"

"No."

"Did you lose the money?"

"No, Mommy."

"Then, where are the sodas?"

"I dropped them."

"All of them? You couldn't even save one? Six grand sodas you dropped, and here I am waiting to use some in my drink!" Then, standing up very slowly, putting her hands on her hips, and the dining room so dark because of the closed curtains that I could barely make out her eyes, she said, "Well, accidents happen, Mitchell. Try to be more careful the next time." A chameleon, all right.

4

TWO WEEKS LATER, I STOOD ON THE PORCH SINGING,
"Rain, rain, go away, come back another day." And,
"Sun at seven, rain at eleven." And also, "Rain from
the hills, more water for the mills." It was raining.

But weren't the preparations inside a little late? My
mind still has the picture of Uncle, Mother and Julius
sitting this time, not eating, at the dining room's cloth-
less table. This time their brown fingers hustling, scrib-
bling on the tabletop. This time they were stone serious, and they were intense and silent, as if the full
importance of the coming event had pressed their lips
shut. Sure, the other radio, the big mahogany Emerson
(with the radio dial that had often been my airplane
speedometer) was playing, but even from my seat on
the rug in front of it I could barely hear the speaker.

Dig: they were doing wedding announcements appropriately designed and produced by the great stylist and
soon-to-be groom, Julius Clark. I'll be damned if I can
say where he came from. All I know is that I hadn't
seen big, corny-footed Larson since my foot put something on his hat that night. Julius just pops up, and the
next thing I know, he's going to do that thing, going to
get married to my mother.

So, Mister Julius S. Clark, huh? Step forward so that
you can be checked out: medium-brown, about my
complexion and a very natty dresser. His rags, I'm

sure, had labels from Harlem's best shops—the best pawnshops. So, Mister Clark in tan slacks the color of Jeff's hide; sharp cheekbones; alligator shoes of dark green; long, polished fingernails on all fingers, two of which had rings (one of these shone from his little finger like a streetlight). So, Julius—a process even. Beautifully combed with a part separating the side from the top, and waves, as I used to say in grade school, that made you seasick. Yet, even wearing that chemical counterfeit of white men's hair, he was still a black man, still had the wide nose and the big lips. But a pretty black man, he'd probably say.

At a later time—not too long after the wedding— Uncle told me that Mother had bought the ring for Julius. I can believe that.

Now, when they finished their correspondence, Uncle, the principal amanuensis, stacked up the dozen or so three-by-five index cards, and shuffling them, clearing his throat, pulling one over the other and clearing his throat again, read the names out loud. They were all relatives—some of whom I knew only by name. He ended with "Cousin Ranida."

Wow! I knew Cousin Ranida, all right. Obese, woolly-headed, puff-ankled, jewelry-wearing Cousin Ranida from Boston. I knew her. She could stare you down to dwarf's size if you were lying to her. She could tell you to go to hell at five, and call you sweetie at five after five. She could get the spirit (they said) before the preacher even began, and could bang sin out of a piano. And she could—well, she also has enough information to write a book, but she's no hero as I am. Wow! Cousin Ranida coming to the wedding. Whoowee.

Okay, so Uncle stuffed the invitation index cards into long business envelopes (already addressed), got up and headed toward the door.

"Come on, boy," he said, "gone to the post office to mail these invitations." And we were off, running through the rain. The soon-to-be newlyweds sat staring.

We bumped along the sloshy back road, which still isn't paved, toward the post office.

"Your mother's gettin' married, boy, two days from now—Saturday. You know that?"

No answer from me.

"Damn, I wrote so many invitations for them, the names are fixed in my mind," he said, head almost bumping against the black-cardboard car roof. "You are welcome to the wedding on September twelfth of Mister Julius Clark and Pearl Mibbs at one in the afternoon at her house."

This answer: "Why is she getting married, Uncle?"

"For security—and love, boy. So Julius can help her get started as a singer in the big time. For love," he said again, opening the door and bopping into the P.O. And he repeated the words when we returned to the house and stepped down from the Ford's runningboard.

Morning of the September wedding: finally, everything all together, uptight and groovy. The Oriental rug rubbed over with a damp mop; curtains dusted and washed white with a bleach-soaked wet rag; wallpaper brushed with a feather duster; and all the goodies on the dining-room table. They had the potato chips, pretzels and peanuts; the sardines, crackers and cheese spread, mints, and a big vanilla cake with chocolate icing, two candles stuck in the middle.

Mother dressing in the front bedroom and Julius in the rear one near Uncle's, and Uncle racing back and forth between the two rooms. I on the couch in a blue vine, face shiny from petroleum jelly, hair parted in the middle.

And I almost forgot the bottles of scotch, bourbon, blended whiskey, and the four gallon jars of wine mashed from the grapes in the back yard's arbor. Resting, all of these, on the floor in the far corner of the dining room.

I was standing on the porch, was leaning against one of the posts, my legs crossed and my lips pursed for whistling, when I saw the low, fogged headlights bouncing up the road. Low rumble and popping of an engine. Windshield wipers fanning. Big Larson coming back to get his ten-gallon? But no, my heart slowed down to a normal beat when I saw that the short was black; even was a sports car. And the only invited guests who accepted the invitation for the macabre wedding pulled themselves out of the four-wheeled animal.

"Hey," she said, panting, struggling up the steps as fast as any hippopotamus could. Those poor steps creaking.

"Hi, Mitchell," said Cousin Samuel, slamming his Jaguar's door, push-buttoning his umbrella out and sprinting up the steps, stopping momentarily to assist Ranida by pulling her arm, next pushing her girdled and wide carcass, but giving up after one one-armed push got her only a step higher and almost propelled Samuel sprawling backward. "Phew," I heard him say under his breath, "good God, she's all woman," and then, louder, "I'm in a hurry, Nida, see you inside," he said, up to the porch.

"So your mom's going to do that thing, huh, Mitch? Ain't nothing wrong with it. Nothing at all." In through the door. Next, Ranida, turning sideways.

"Where's the bride and groom? Where's the preacher? Where's the other guests?" Samuel asked Uncle.

"They'll be here—you're three hours early, you know. Hi, Ranida. Don't think you gonna get more liquor than anybody else, either, Samuel. Have a seat."

"I'll have a drink. Uncle, who's this guy, Julius, anyway?" asked Samuel.

"Why you not dressed like Ranida?" asked Uncle.

"Because I don't go in for dresses." Samuel laughed. "That's why," he said, pulling his sweater over his pot belly, tapping his sneaks on the rug. Always a jokester.

"Julius is from the Apple," said Uncle, "New York."

"What's he do?"

"Bartending—professional," said Uncle, dressed to kill. Uncle, I have to admit, was sort of a killer-diller when it came to getting vined up. Like that day—he wore the hell out of his four-button teardrop suit. Plus a chest-warming tie.

"I'm taking off my shoes for a while until this show gets on the road," said Ranida.

I had to get off that rug or suffocate. Those toes, those fat dirty toes at the end of the ashy, puffy ankles, were more than my nasal sensibilities could handle.

For a while, idle talk. Ranida had been going to the doctor's every week. It had been a long ride up from Boston. When would we come down to visit her again? For Samuel, the difference between J&B and Cutty Sark was important. Also, how the auto-repair business was going and how many suits he had at home. After Samuel had mentioned that, Uncle again asked Samuel why he wore sneaks and a sweater to a wedding.

"Too much rain to get dressed," he said.

At around noon or a little after, the bowler-topped, black-coated Baptist minister, Hutchins, arrived (drenched).

"Okay, let's get this show on the road," he said. "Where are the guests?" he asked. "Where are the groom and bride? Are you the father? No. And these two the witnesses? Very well, bring them out," pulling off his coat and throwing it on the couch, leaving his brim—a derby—on his head, smoothing his gray moustache, fingering through a small, red Bible, rocking on his heels at attention. He was a short man, had long, fat fingers and wrinkled hands.

Uncle, in a whirlwind of confusion, turned in a circle—this way, that way; to go here or to go there? To do this or to do that? He was making me perplexed.

Ranida said, "Turn on the music," and Uncle

33

turned, went to the box, placed an organ march on the spindle.

"Knock on the door, tell Pearl to come out," he said, going to the back. And finally, the two, Mother and Julius, standing in the center of the living room, the both of them standing and holding hands in a room darker than a movie theater. He, Julius, shorter than she; he sporting a makeshift borrowed tux with tails that Uncle must have worn at some strutter's ball a time ago. A top hat, bell-bottomed trousers, bubble gum in the mouth, wavy-haired head raised up in dignity.

"We're all set," said the groom, chewing vigorously, taking Mother around the waist as she wavered in her very high heels, so that her toes pointed inward. Mother rocked to the side and belched loudly, so loudly in fact that it startled her groom.

How would Van Eyck have painted the scene? Probably with no candle flickering on the coffee table, shoes obtrusive and shined, and a dirty, finger-marked mirror on the wall. Van Eyck's brush would have put them in their places.

Of the two, Mother was definitely most boss. Her makeup—really tough enough this time, almost making me look twice and asking, "Mother, that you?" My eyes pinned the black stockings with the runs around both knees; also, the black, dirty velvet dress that had been ironed a dozen or so times, now shiny and fitting her tightly—which was her style; seeming to choke her in the waist, where the red-plastic, wide-buckled belt was wrapped. Her hair? Her hair was just there— no style, no direction, no pattern except for the unruliness of the strands falling over her eyes.

Oh, if I could only say the bride wore white. If I could say she wore a gown of ivory peau de soie trimmed with alençon lace and seed pearls. But no such arrangements here. No bow holding her tulle veil, she

34

was carrying no cascade of white roses or gypsophilas or miniature chrysanthemums.

The preacher asked who was giving away the bride.

"Me," said Uncle, taking his place beside the two. And the preacher began that outlandish ceremony, a ceremony for a circus church. Julius placed a tarnished ring on her long fingers, kissed her, looked like a bewildered, stray calf.

After it was over—the long kiss between the newly marrieds, the congratulations and then dark silence as eyes coasted over each other's faces—we went back to the dining room for the reception.

Another series of congratulations, and unharmonic singing by the makeshift, two-man choir of "Here Comes the Bride," and a restless sighing and clearing of the throat by the preacher. No, he said that he wanted no grape-arbor wine. No, he wanted no peanuts or potato salad or cake. He would be going. Looking expectantly at Julius, the preacher said he would be going.

Bridegroom Julius Clark, who didn't even have a paranymph, said that he would walk preacher to the door. They stopped in the front bedroom, and I, only I, saw the condescending, fat-fingered bowler-wearer come out shuffling his feet. But obsequious now. Coming out with a fawning smile and sycophantic holding of the bowler brim in his hand.

This moustached carpet knight began, "Bless you, son. Bless you and yours. Bless your wife, and may the splendiferous grandeur and majesty of this most sacramental moment in your lives be ever manifested in your coterminous dealings in a misguided and immoral time." Raising his black sky to his head. "May the Almighty's presence, may His grace and wisdom be a ubiquitous force in your lives." One hand bulging in the right pocket, head high, voice addressing the ceiling: "I beseech You, good Lord, to look upon them with the

35

same endearing spirit that You gave to Eve. For, oh, we are sinners, we are . . ."

"Cut that shit out!"

Uncle dropped his glass. I pretended not to hear. Cousin Ranida, wallowing, shoeless, pointing a long, long finger toward Mister Pious.

"We don't need you now, my man. The marriage is over. Didn't want to be bothered at first. Now you got your little bonus, you're our savior. I saw you go in there. You got your tip, now get out before I go upside your head."

Advancing backward toward the door, he stuttered. "But . . . but . . . but . . . ma'am . . . I . . . please, have respect for the cloth."

"Get out. Into the rain. Out, you rat."

Out the door. But the rain had stopped.

Everybody looking at Ranida.

"Okay, back to the reception," she said, clapping her hands.

The needle on the record had reached the end of the hymn, and briefly nobody moved or seemingly even thought; indeed, as if existence had been in abeyance, the needle's scratching grated against our ears, grated and scratched, softly popped, clicked, clicked and crackled. And no other sound but breathing.

"Fix the record," said Mother in a not-so-soft voice. "Put on a jump tune and turn it up loud, because I want to have fun. This is my wedding day, and I want to have fun!" Her voice was shaky, almost had no tenor, didn't sound half-believable. The mug of whiskey tilted to her lips. A trembling hand. Julius went next to her.

Cousin Samuel to the rescue. He popped on a new side—Earl Bostic—slapped his hands together and grabbed Ranida. "Let's go. Let's liven up this wedding, chick. I came here for a good time. Watch this,

Mitchell. Watch your cousin work out. Watch this fancy footwork, kid."

"You old, crazy fool," said Ranida, laughing, with her head back, glad to be in a man's arms again. How long had it been, Ranida—months, years, decades? I know how you felt, you poor, fat, suffering victim of circumstance. Think we had little in common because of an age and weight gap?

"Here, look out, Ranida, let me show you how," said Mother, nearly falling as she advanced. "Hold my drink, Jul." She commanded without looking at him, with her back to Jul, and probably wasn't even sure that the hand which took it belonged to him. He gave it to Uncle, who placed it on the table.

"Let's go, Ranida. Come on, let a real slickster sock it to you. I'll teach you the Hundred Twenty-fifth Street shuffle, show you how we do it in the Apple."

Uncle came over to me, and we both sat by on the couch.

Four dancers going through their paces: all shoes kicked off and pushed under the dining table. No pattern of movement other than spontaneousness. Hands flailing in the air, hips gyrating, breath coming forced and louder. The rug being pounded and thumped.

And Uncle and I—who were we? Mere pinners of the action, he holding a glass of wine and a few chips, I a dish of potato salad and a glass of Kool-Aid? Hautboys out of our time? Audience allies? Grateful Colosseum watchers of an amateur Dionysian exercise? Or just plain unfortunate fools?

"Sit down, Jul, you aren't doing anything." Mother rubbed her nose and undid the wide plastic belt, seemed to loosen herself from a conventional harness, a discretionary reminder. "You can never do anything right anyway, Jul. Why don't you sit down?" Another belch.

A great chuckle came from Cousin Samuel.

"Whatcha say to that, Jul? Whatcha gonna do, huh? You gonna show us some stuff? You gonna get down, or what, my man? What's your style like, jack?"

Slick Julius's hair was tousled, was loose and stringy, and strands stuck to his perspiring forehead, making him look like a black Napoleon. He was stumbling now in the fury of his efforts, for his legs kicked up with less gusto, the thin-moustached smile was gone, he was a tired flagman at the airport waving in a plane for landing.

"It's none of your damn business what I'm gonna do, understand what I'm saying?" Julius's reply was barely intelligible, his words were heavy, seemed to falter and get in each other's way, just as he himself was suddenly in Ranida's way.

"He can't do anything," said Mother. Now the four of them standing face-to-face: Mother to Samuel. Ranida to Julius. All out of breath, dancing no more.

"Don't look like he can," said Samuel. The music stopped.

"No need to put on more records, Melvin," said Mother, her short nose twitching with pleasure, "Julius is all pooped out. He poops out early, gets tired very quickly. Can't work no style at all." Mother, in her dark but shiny bridal outfit, swayed on her tall frame with half-closed eyes and spoke with a slur.

Samuel, sweater-clad, piped out, "I bet he can't do nothing."

Julius made it known right away where he was from. "I bet you one thing," he said, sticking his index finger into the very center of Samuel's belly, "I bet you this— I can put your lights out—and in a hurry."

"He can't," said Mother. "He can't beat you or anybody in our family. Don't believe him."

"Suppose we take this outside," Samuel said, content with Mother's evaluation.

"He's scared," said Mother. "He can't fight."

38

Uncle and I still watching, watching, listening.

Then Samuel grabbed Julius by the collar and lifted him up—only for a few seconds—long enough for Ranida to faint, causing the sofa legs to groan as they dug into the rug.

"Let's take this outside."

In the new mud, the rain having recently stopped and the air fresh with the smell of rinsed trees and ozone, orioles and kingbirds in a mad chase over our heads. Julius and Samuel fought in that new mud.

"Now, don't fight, boys," said Uncle, standing far enough away from them. And I was leaning (again) against this same old Ford. And Ranida was still out on the couch inside. And Mother was on the porch, she was a mademoiselle waving the flag, spurring on the knightly suitors. She should have had a box seat and a courtly red handkerchief.

The combatants squared off, or circled off, in the newly made mud. Both barefooted.

"You're messing with the wrong man," explained Julius. He accepted a wild jab in his right eye. Cousin Samuel was smiling, dukes up to his eyes, his feet dancing and jumping him around. He smacked Julius again with another jab—to the forehead.

"You're in a world of trouble, getting me angry," said the new groom.

"Ezzard Charles," shouted Samuel, looking back to Mother, "here's how he does it," demonstrating with another wild jab. "Now, watch this—watch out for the right—wow!"

Mother, her hands on the porch railing, threw back her head, laughed at her groom, laughed with her cousin, laughed at old family against new family. And Uncle again, this time closer to me than before, saying, "You boys ought to stop that mess." Then a step forward, quickly withdrawn after, "Come on, I'm gonna walk right between you two and break this up."

While I leaned against the safety of the black Ford's wooden tan door.

Julius, breathing hard, so hard that his jacket's tail rose and fell, rose and fell on his back, licked some blood dripping from his eye and said, still a sham, still shucking, "You done did the wrong thing now, you're in for it." He took a hopeless chance, a hopeless gesture of a punch, not a real punch, but a wish (he had his eyes closed) for a punch. It was Julius's haymaker. And big-time, party-time, lover-man Julius spun around with his eyes closed, his right arm completely horizontal. His right fist with the very big, very bad ring whizzed over Samuel's head. Who was set. Samuel, keeping his cool, turned his head to the side. Perfectly set. Stance: left foot in front, right foot in rear; flat-footed; right arm high with elbow away from body; eyes watching Julius's eyes (closed); left foot sliding forward; weight shifting onto left; right foot too sliding forward about a foot, and Samuel had a waltzlike rhythm going for him, as if he were counting feet—one, two, three, four; one, two, three, four: as footloose keeping his footing as an eighteenth-century footman serving tables in an inn; as grim-looking as foot soldiers in a swamp; and paradoxically, as colorful as an actor stage front, greedily collecting the glare of the foot-lights; so, right fist moving as fast as a shotgun hammer and nailing Julius on the side of the chin, near the brain, with foot-pounds of power. Julius, losing his footing, fell to his knees after his eyes opened—opened big and blue for an instant. His fat lower lip dropped, and he blinked like a child discovering Christmas gifts.

"Joe Louis," said Samuel, footling, dancing on his skinny toes, and placing his arms up in a vertical victory sign. "The champ," he announced, adding a footnote.

Mother clapped, jumped up on the side of the porch, smiled as if she had strewn winner's flowers.

Julius—what a mess. On two knees and two hands trying to get his makeshift tux and body out of the mud. And he couldn't rise. Looking footy as a doped boxer, Julius was on four limbs scrambling around in the Maine mud on his wedding day. A puppy unable yet to walk; nevertheless, trying to put his best foot forward now that he had put the other in his mouth. "I could have killed him. He don't know how lucky he was, boy. One good punch from me and he would have had his lights put out, I'm telling you."

By now Samuel was on the porch with Mother. Uncle, walking toward the porch, was passing by the stricken groom. I followed Uncle.

"You boys shouldn't fiight," said Uncle, and kept on getting up toward the porch. As I was passing Julius, he fell back, sat down with his legs spread. Extending a hand upward toward me. Eyes puffed.

"Help me up, Mitchell, please."

But before I could even think, he waved me away, picked up a clump of mud and threw it over his shoulder. Julius's shoulders heaved—heaved even more than mine did in Larson's car with Uncle that night. Even the crying was worse. Louder, and almost more mournful in the middle of the muddy road in front of the station wagon on his marriage day. I haven't heard a man cry like that since.

5

UNCLE, FILLING HIS PIPE WITH TOBACCO BOUGHT FROM
Tony's, stood over and said, "Today's the day, Mitchell."

Hot diggity. Sakes and shakes, pow-wow coon box
and lickety rickety split for hearts and dales hooray.
Today's the day, Mitchell. Those words ran through my
body, tickled my toes, dizzied my head. Today. Today.
Today.

How long had I waited? And all of a sudden, it just
pops up on you. Times does travel, I swear, jim.

I stopped pumping water from the back-yard pump,
turned my head to look through the apple-tree branches
at the barely visible sun, sniffed the grassy, early-
morning air—took it all in with my nostrils fully
opened—and sighed loudly. Then my eyes pinned Uncle. He had the Winchester twelve-gauge cut in two and
was looking down one barrel with something of the
artist in him. He knew what he was doing, Uncle did,
searching for the tiniest, picayune detail that could mar
his shooting. And how he kept his cool without cracking a smile. I am certain Uncle knew I was trembling
with anticipation. He knew my eyes were on him in
awe. I dropped my bucket of water and for an instant,
didn't even feel the sting of that morning frost.

"Hunting?" That's all I dared to say, for fear that it
would be a false alarm.

"Yep, you old enough, you're ten," he said, clicking shut the black, steel double barrel against the shoulder stock, plucking the triggers, looking down the sights, soon weighing the whole gun in his hands, feeling for the touch. The artist again: feet perfectly spread for the aim. Deep intake of breath, then a slow, agonizing and turtle-slow squeezing of the trigger, until—click. And then again, on the next barrel, the same maneuvering, until—click. Uncle, the artist, made that beautiful sound of precision and destruction, of patience and judgment.

Nothing new to me. I had seen three of those double-barreled beauties lined up in the attic (when I sneaked up there). I had looked down their sights and killed many a running deer up there in the dusty, junk-cluttered attic. But only vicariously. Boy, that attic is something. On one thousand separate occasions I have discovered some twine-bound airmail letters, stacks of dirt-plated records, loose planks of flooring, pots, pans, two-gallon jars with cork tops in them.

So now: the real thing. Getting right down to the nitty gritty. So, Uncle was taking me out. He thought I had reached the age. I waited for more instructions.

"Come on, Mitchell, let's get prepared," he said, and started toward the back of the yard.

They loved him back there. The chickens, clucking, short-stepping along and flapping their wings, tottering, standing on one leg, cocking their beaks to the side, snapping up a bit of dirt. They knew who Uncle was, and the procession started behind him as Uncle strode and strutted in that back yard with an undeniable majesty.

We got to the kennel, and Uncle might have played Caesar bringing home a conquest, for the racket the dogs made. But he quieted them with just this: a hand held high over his head. No more barking. But still, their claws clung to the wire fences, they whined, licked their tongues, scratched the ground, carefully skipped around their waste, shoved and pushed to get to the front to see pipe-smoking Uncle, the master. I saw Blue, Tojo, Major, Plato, Nellie and Rough. Then, one at a time, he called out to them.

"Hey, Blue, come here, boy." A big ecstatic yelp, paws on the fence, a nose through a square opening. Uncle patted Blue, tall and thin, black-and-white-spotted Blue. Uncle patted Blue on his nose. I came closer to give my regards (the chickens had retreated), but Uncle stayed me. "No," he said, "you'll spoil them if you play too much. Don't baby them, treat them rough."

Next, the shed in the back yard where Uncle kept most of his hunting gear. He got a couple of boxes of shells, boots, jacket, two blaze-orange hunting caps, a flashlight, his plastic-coated license, gave half of it to me, and locked the door. We dropped everything in the side yard by the pear tree.

"Let's go eat breakfast, and we'll talk about what to do," said Uncle, his breath smoking in the cold, dewy morning.

Mother and Julius had not yet awakened that Saturday morning, so Uncle (and a very good cook he is) fried up the eggs and grits and bacon.

While soaking his bread in egg yolk, he began, "I'll give you a few pointers on shooting; you don't need too many, because I've done this before with your BB gun. Then we'll let you practice, next a haircut, after that, sleep."

"What time do we leave, Uncle?"

"About three in the morning," he said. "Won't nobody be awake."

I asked him what we'd be shooting for.

"For rabbits, deer and muskrats," he said. "We're after all of them. We'll have a good dinner tomorrow night, if you can stay awake."

Uncle put the dishes into the sink and started toward the front door.

"Come on outside, Mitchell."

In the side yard, Uncle pointed out everything to me as if I hadn't seen it all before, as if I hadn't watched him prepare a million times when he went out by himself or with Tony or Jake or Herman.

"You'll need boots; try these on for size." Throwing the boots at me. "Here, heavy wool socks." He gave me the gray, thick socks that had red and green stripes around the tops. More like basketball socks. "Corduroy pants, army jacket to hold your ammunition and food, an orange cap so's nobody won't blow your head off, a whistle for the dogs, pair of binoculars, and a shotgun. And here, try this thermal hunter's shirt —don't want you catching no cold," he said.

How was I going to carry all of this stuff? Surely I wouldn't be able to walk with so many clothes weighing me down. Surely I would stumble and fall, shoot myself in the leg or fall into a mud patch.

"Now, I'll show you how to shoot a gun so's you never miss. Remember, every time you miss, you lose money—it's a shell wasted." Uncle took up one of the Winchesters lying on the brown grass and held it up to his face. "Now, what's rule number one, Mitchell?"

"Never point a gun at anyone."

"Okay, I see a squirrel standing on a rock or something. I take aim and pull the trigger as fast as I can, right?"

"No, you squeeze the trigger real slow as if you are afraid of hurting it. You squeeze it until the shot goes off. That way, you don't jerk the barrel, and your aim is steady."

"Good; now, what if the squirrel's moving?"

"You aim a little in front of him, it depends on how fast he's going, and you keep swinging the rifle even after you've shot it."

"Good. You know your stuff, Mitchell. You'll make a good hunter."

But that was nothing new to me. I've always made it a habit of knowing my stuff—whether it be flying a kite or skating a figure eight. If I'm not exceptionally boss in whatever I do, I don't.

So we left all the apparatus in the yard and rolled down the dirt road, the dirt road I'm looking at now with its ragged grass middle, with its plethora of soda caps, candy wrappers and dried-up prophylactics left by weekend lovers.

Uncle and I arrived so early, we opened the barbershop for Morris.

"God, you early. Can't wait?" he asked, shuffling along through the old door that needed no lock. But of course not: what can you steal from a barbershop—a chair? "Dee really calling you, huh? Had to come in early in the morning." He pulled the switch in the middle of the shop, and my eyes checked out the curled-up hair, unswept on the tile floor (or floor that had been tiled once), my nose pulled in the odor of hair oil and electric motors, my ears detected the sound of a rat scurrying through the wallboards.

"Dee who?" asked Uncle, always a gopher—a man who would always go for anything.

"Dee barber, that's who." Morris laughed. A lot of jokesters in this report of mine.

And why should Morris's shop be unlike the others? Except for the kerosene stove in the far corner, he had the usual two chairs, one of which was used only for waiting customers to sit in; the comb (black) stuck in antiseptic water in a peanut-butter jar on the counter; the year-old calendar with a smiling, busomy white chick; out-of-date girlie magazines, out-of-date crime magazines; mirrors here, mirrors there, mirrors everywhere, and a cat slumped on a twill rug in front of the unproductive stove. I say, no different from the others, except for the stove.

"Let the kid go first," volunteered Uncle. "I've been cutting his hair at home all these years, but this is a special occasion." Then into the leather chair, so high that my feet couldn't reach the steel footrest. Morris shook out, then pulled the white striped cotton blanket over my body, tightened it around my neck. I looked at the chart of hair styles and chose number seven.

"Number eight?" asked Morris. What a cluck. Morris can't see for looking, I thought.

"Number seven," I said, "close on the sides and medium off the top, a little hair oil, and make sure you get the hair out of my ears when you finish—please."

"Do good, we're goin' huntin'," said Uncle, filling his pipe, clearing his throat.

"Where?" asked Morris, looking less and less, now that I recall, like a barber; no thin moustache, no bald head, no fat, overlapping tummy. And to me: "Number eight it'll be, Mitchell," adding, before I could answer him, "I can't do number seven yet. Come in next week and get number seven. Today it's number eight."

"We'll take the north woods." Uncle sat back in one of the rickety, wooden, creaky chairs with thin-as-a-pin legs, then tilted his back against the wall.

"I hear there's not much out there this time of year, Melvin. You ought to know that." Buzzing of the electric razor over my head, hair tumbling into my lap.

"Sure," said Uncle. "I know those woods like the palm of my hand. They'll be there waiting for me to shoot. What shall I bring back to you, Morris—coon, rabbit, venison?"

A ringing of the bell over the door, and three black men stepped inside, bringing the cold with them. They gave out boisterous greetings to Morris, threw off their coats and scarves and hung them on the hooks to the side of Uncle.

"Melvin, you old son-of-a-gun," they all seemed to say at the same time. Just three men, no individuality worth speaking of, almost dressed the same, and the same height, weight and complexion. "We saw your car outside, figured it was you, Melvin. You did drive down here, didn't you?" Rough laughter, slapping of thighs, heads rolling back. Through the mirror, I could see even Morris cracking a smile. I felt uneasy. These men were not Uncle's type, not his style. They didn't have the artistry or precision that Uncle had just exhibited with his guns. Rough men, unshaved, with red eyes and coarse, ashy skin covering their hands. Men who had probably seen hard times and had relished them. Men who had, in the main, never been outside the state of Maine. Narrowminded. Sacrilegious. Disrespectful. Violent?

"I wonder where you wind it up at," said one. More laughter.

"No, what happens is, the kid pushes for a block and Melvin drives, then Melvin pushes for a block and the kid steers."

"Naw, naw—you cats got it all wrong," said the third one. "It's an electric car—they've got it plugged into a socket back home, and a cord is running from the living room."

"That car can run. She can run most of these modern heaps into the ground," said Uncle, clearing his throat, coughing.

"Well, I'll tell you, if I were a modern heap and saw this old contraption coming, I'd hide into the ground."

The three laughed, choked, coughed while standing in the doorway. Guffaws, snorts, snoozles.

They shuffled in front of Uncle. "If you didn't look as weak as that old contraption, I'd challenge you one," said the first rascal.

Uncle stood up, stood up because it was his nature and because he was part of a family who taught you

48

never to back down from a man, and he said, drawing in and exhaling in as cool as he wanted to be, "We'll see how weak I am. Come on, let's go."

And so the two hustled in the back room (separated from the front by a hanging curtain), brought out two chairs and the chess and checkers table. Uncle pulled up his sleeves, knocked out his pipe, stomped his feet.

"I'm ready," he said.

Two were standing, one was sitting opposite Uncle, and this one was rolling up his sleeves too, exposing the scar on his forearm, smiling with gold teeth on the side of his mouth. When he clapped his hard hands together, it sounded like light thunder. His two cheerleaders stood in back of him, hands in their pockets. Morris was changing my blanket, sharpening his steel blade on the leather strip, and getting ready for the razor trim-up around my neck.

The two contestants put their arms up on the table, clasped their hands together and exhibited prodigious frowns and grimaces. The breathing became rough; gritting of the teeth was audible and eerie. Uncle's arm was pushed down to three inches from the top of the table, but he summoned up a tremendous reserve of energy from—from who knows, maybe pride, maybe from his ancestors, maybe from his blood of wine. He pulled himself together and strained his arm back to the middle of the table until both arms were vertical and equal again, and now—and now he was gaining once more, moving to his left one, two, then three inches until the arms were at a forty-five-degree angle and I was afraid to get out of the chair, even though Morris had finished.

"You've got him, Uncle," I shouted, "you've got him, you're still the champ of the world." But before I could finish that one simple encomium, before I could revel in victory that we so badly wanted, Uncle's opponent had rallied, equaled the arms to an upright position again, pushed it farther down, then suddenly slammed down Uncle's hand on the table. . . . Suddenly, a two-man chorus of hoorays and cheers. For me, terrible sense of loneliness and defeat. I got out of the chair, and Morris said, "Next, who's next? It's you, isn't it, Melvin . . . come on, let's go, man."

But Uncle stood, slid a sore right hand into his pocket, and paid for my haircut, saying, "I'll come back another time, Morris."

"Hope your stagecoach has a little more strength than you," said one of them.

"It's too early in the morning, that's why come he lost, he don't get his strength until after noon time."

Their laughter hurried us out of the door. We were a silent couple of hunters-to-be riding back to the house. Uncle had pitted his hunter's spirit, his artist's sense of precision and rightness against their brunt and boister, and he came out vanquished. Portent of things to come?

"Used to be a time when I could lick anybody in Chatsworth, Maine," he said. He was staring straight ahead, almost hypnotically, favoring his right hand as he steered. "But I guess there comes a time when you can't win always, remember that, Mitchell. You can't win always, and sometimes the best don't win—life is funny that way."

Mother and Julius had left the house. I sensed that just as soon as we tackled the road from the highway and the old castle was visible, sitting there high on our right just as aloof and stately as she had ever looked. Somehow, someway, she appeared a bit more peaceful, seemed a little more innocent, so I surmised that Mother had gone to the Living End.

And she had, we two hunters discovered, as we stalked up to the front gate.

"We'll eat lunch and later dinner, fix up our food, and take a nap until tomorrow morning," said Uncle.

50

Well, it was the shortest nap I've ever taken. (I had begun to sleep with Uncle since Mother's marriage.) He woke me up by pulling me out of the bed so that my legs were on the floor and my chest and arms were on the bed.

"Time to go," he whispered, and standing now, on the cold linoleum floor in my woolen underwear, feeling as if my head were loaded with lead, my mouth with Uncle's socks and my eyes with eyewash. I thought, I don't want to go. It's too cold, too dark, and I might get shot and I haven't copped enough Z's. Later for this stuff. Uncle, you're my main man, you're my ace boon coon and all that, but we can't be road partners tonight. No good.

"What's the matter?" asked Uncle, noticing me hold my head.

"I think I've got the virus, pneumonia and the flu," I said.

"I'll give you something to take for it," he said, leaving for the bathroom on his tiptoes as if Mother and Julius were there, then returning, and since the light was out, I could see only his ghostlike, tall silhouette in the doorway and—and then something raising up, falling upon me and knocking me unconscious for a split second. I was chilled to my toes. Uncle had awakened me abruptly and cured all my ills with a bucket of cold water in the face.

It was an easy task getting ready, for we had prepared beforehand just as all great hunters do. On the floor in our bedroom was more of our equipment: the knapsack, wax-paper-covered chicken sandwiches, first-aid kit, silver flashlight, compass, knives, red-topped thermos of cocoa. We eased into our army combat boots (Uncle wore size twelve), buttoned our hunting jackets, picked up the box of shells and the shotguns from off the floor. Uncle reached for his clothesline on the back of the door—for the dogs. Hunters two—intent, brave and determined, we marched to the front.

What's that? You want to hear about the pull of the dogs on the clothesline leash, the stinging cold smarting our eyes, the marching through ponds and mud, the sighting of a bounding hare? No such luck for you nor for me nor for Uncle. You see, when we marched out to the back yard, there was a strange quiet. And rightly so. Mother, so we discovered later, was the culprit. In a drunken frenzy, she had released the dogs. All of them. Every single one. Even Blue.

I had had a feeling that Mother had been responsible. As I watched Uncle finger the rusty latch on the fence door and my head burned with disappointment, I thought to myself, Mother has something to do with this mess. But why on my first hunting trip? Why not the second or the third? We needed this togetherness, I thought, as I watched Uncle jingle the door latch. In his hunting gear, he stood playing with the fence as if he were hypnotized.

"They'll come back," he said, tightening his jaw muscles.

Sure, but not that night. Not the night I had looked forward to for so long.

"I've got something in my eye," I stuttered, turning away; then, "Damn," not even caring about the profanity. And when I was near the steps, I said, looking at Uncle's figure, "Goddamn."

6

COLDEST NIGHT OF THE YEAR IN CHATSWORTH. THAT afternoon, I had gone on a hike with Boy Scout troop 13. We had to call it quits after an hour: the cold against our faces, the hard ground freezing our feet, was more than we scouts could bear.

Coldest night of the year in this Maine town, and the four of us in the living room, a couple of couples, our stomachs filled with cornbread and greens and ham, sitting bunched up within ourselves, listening to the boxing match on the Emerson. Julius and Mother on the couch sharing a heavy, plaid wool blanket. Uncle and I in chairs facing the couch. We were facing them.

"He'll nail Walcott in the next," said Julius, and I saw his hand under the blanket slide down Mother's leg. "He's stunned him with that left hook."

"No good," said Uncle. "Walcott's still in good shape."

"He's old, over the hill, Melvin. No way in the world he can beat this young boy. Should have quit a long time ago."

Mother's long index finger ran around the inside of her glass, tickled two ice cubes, clinked them together inside her drink (the Canadian whiskey bottle sat on the table), then she placed the glass back on the table, on the wet ring of condensation.

Listen: the Hawk was out. The Hawk was roaring

like the exhaust from a jet plane. Like a Grecian chorus, it whistled at all the windows in the house. The Hawk was talking that evening, and I was not willing to hear more than I had to; there was no way in the world you could have got me outside to get blown against a tree trunk. We all had an ear cocked out for the Hawk, were listening more attentively to him than to the boxing match. The windowpanes rattled. Uncle had put two good army blankets at the bottom of the front door to cover the crack, yet occasionally a stream of air shot through to us. The Hawk. Even the walls of the sturdy old house cracked. From the Hawk.

"AND WALCOTT TAKES ANOTHER LEFT TO THE JAW, AND ANOTHER. HE'S WOBBLING, FOLKS, HIS KNEES ARE SHAKING . . . MY GOD . . . NOW HE'S ON HIS BACK. WAL-COTT'S EYES ARE GLASSY. AND IT'S SEVEN . . . EIGHT . . . NINE . . . TEN . . . HE'S OUT. WALCOTT HAS BEEN KNOCKED OUT, LADIES AND GENTLEMEN."

"See, I told you, Uncle. That old man was on his way out in the last round. Once you're over the hill, it's all through . . . you might as well hang it up."

"Damn," said Uncle, hitting a fist into his palm, standing up, bent for the kitchen. "Damn," he said again. "I remember when he was a greased-lightning heavy. Now this—knocked out."

Julius, shouting out toward Uncle's exiting figure: "Well, you can't stay young forever, Uncle. You know that. When you get old and decrepit, you should forget it, sit down, and wait for the hearse."

Uncle came back with his glass of red wine.

"Well, I got years ahead of me," he said. "I ain't that old. I got plenty years ahead of me." Clearing his throat.

"What!" Julius stood up, his blanket fell from his waist like a dead animal. "You're in your sixties, old man. You don't have nothing, you ain't going to get nothing. What's left for you to do? You don't even

54

exist anymore, hardly. All you do is play with those mutts out there, get a haircut, shoot off those rusty rifles, stumble along in an antique car, pick up your social security and pension checks. Your life is finished, Uncle. Ain't nothing else for you to do. When you die, nobody will even notice it."

Uncle stood too, as if he were Walcott rising from the canvas, and he said, looking with bright eyes at me, his heavy voice trembling: "I've got plenty of things to do, don't you worry. When I die, people will say I did things, they'll remember."

"Oh yeah? What? Now, just what makes you so different from people who just come on this earth and die and nobody even notices? Me, I'm gonna be a great musical producer, and Pearl's gonna make it as a singer. But you—what?"

"I took care of Pearl all these years, and I'm taking care of Mitchell most of the time now. You been here for three years and ain't helped with nothin' hardly!"

"Julius works hard," said Mother, adjusting herself on the couch and sipping again.

"I work hard too," said Uncle, and I wished he wouldn't get so excited. "I have to pay all the bills and do most of the cleaning, and I do a lot of shopping in the stores. I go to all the PTA meetings. You never go, Pearl."

"I'm too busy to be going to some PTA meeting," Mother answered. "Mitchell's doing okay in school, aren't you, Mitchell?"

I nodded.

"Well, you ought to have more concern," said Uncle.

"You got some nerve," said Mother, placing her glass on the table, "talking about concern. You didn't have so much concern about Maybelle."

"Maybelle—who's Maybelle?" Julius pounced on the issue like Jeff on a bone.

"Didn't Uncle tell you about his wife, Maybelle?"

55

"No. What'd she do, where is she?"

Mother: "He never told you about what happened to Maybelle? Well, I'll be."

"Never mind about that," said Uncle, Adam's apple rising. "What's important is that I take care of Mitchell. I'm gonna see that he makes something out of himself."

"Go ahead then," said Mother, and she was flushed in the face now, her lips were poked out and her eyes were half opened. "I did it all these years. Changing dirty diapers, picking up food off the floor, hearing all that screaming at night. Crying, crying, crying. Nothing but mess and trouble, that's what children are. And when they grow up, they don't even care about you anymore. No wonder Danny left. I don't blame him. I'm going to bed."

She picked up the bottle and her glass and maneuvered sideways between the table and the couch.

"You takin' the bottle with you?" It was Julius.

"Uh huh."

"What about Maybelle, you gonna tell me about Maybelle?"

"Some other time," she said, her back disappearing into the darkness of the bedroom entrance.

"See, you got her mad," said Julius, standing, smoothing his moustache, unsure of his next move.

And the Hawk still roared, the living-room lights blinked, the news was going off the radio. We sat, listening to the Hawk, and tense from the exchange.

"I'd be singing at the Boston Garden now if I didn't have . . ." Mother's voice came ringing out of her bedroom. Uncle and Julius looked at me.

7

"YOU'LL REALLY GO FOR THIS SHOW, MITCHELL. IT RE-
minds me of the Apollo Theater in the Apple," said
Julius.

Two of us were on each railing: Mother and Uncle on
one, Julius and I on the other. And we had to ease
down the steps carefully, one slow foot after another, as
if we were astronauts walking the moon. Because the
Hawk was out again in greater force than the previous
night. We had to place one boot at a time on each
snow-covered step, had to go down sideways, holding
the railing with both gloved hands. Snow was blowing
in my eyelashes, getting up my nose. So, we were
tipping down the front-porch steps like that with the
full moon out and the fresh snow clothing everything:
the fence, the hammock, everything.

When we reached the snow-wrapped vehicle, all of
us kicked and scraped and brushed until the white
coating cracked and fell off and the Ford's familiar tan
siding was visible again, and the rear, side and front
windows were clear. I remember Uncle, standing with a
hand on the front door, in his double-breasted greatcoat
with fur collar and belt around the waist. He flapped his
big mittens together, looked like a Russian cossack,
stomped his knee-high boots, straightened his cap with
the earmuffs, and said, his scarf flapping around his
mouth, the Hawk whistling, "Okay, let's go, people.

Everybody in." And barely able to walk because of our heavy wraps, we fell toward the Ford's doors.

"I've got shotgun," announced Julius, pushing me to the side after Mother had tumbled in. He jumped in the front next to her, so I had to sit alone in the back seat where Jeff rests now. Nothing new to me.

For a while, four freezing explorers clapping our hands together, blowing cold smoke rings, stamping our feet on the floorboards while the Ford's engine choked, sputtered, coughed, did everything but start. But we knew it would. And it did.

Uncle eased her down the road, yet still the heat was not circulating, and we kept ourselves balled up, kept our arms folded around our chests.

"Yeah, Mitchell," said Julius, "this show is going to be tops—only the best. Right, sweetie?"

And Mother turned—only halfway, because she was so squeezed up in the middle of the front seat between the coats—turned so that her face was actually toward Julius and I could see only her cheekbones and part of her mouth not covered by the scarf and turned-up wool collar. She said, "You'll like it because Mommy is going to sing, honey." Then, turning forward, looking through the windshield, which still had some snow on its edges, she said, "Mommy's sorry about last night, Mitch, honey. You know I wouldn't hurt you for the world."

"Yes, Mommy," I answered, barely hearing, hardly even listening to her and certainly not looking in the direction of that black wool coat in the middle of Uncle's car. I really didn't care. It was too cold. And had it been the middle of the summer, I wouldn't have cared. Too late then.

"So, you're going to prove to me that you've still got something going for yourself, huh, Uncle Melvin?"

"Sure am." Uncle's fur-covered mittens holding the wheel, and his jaw was straight, face shaved. "I'll show

58

you I've still got my stuff—the same stuff I had twenty years ago. I'm glad you invited me, Julius. I'll probably take the show."

Julius, riding shotgun, looked at Mother, and they both smiled. Uh huh.

On our way to Boston. We slid on the thruway more than once, Uncle lifting his elbows high and grasping the steering wheel and moving into the skid. Not another car did we see for the entire ninety-minute drive. Banks of snow lined the highway—banks of snow that glistened silver. The heater was blasting, so we dared open our coats. Mother sang along with the radio, Julius snuggled his head against her shoulder.

We parked two blocks from the theater in a street that was wet and slippery. Black tire marks along the curb. Holding on to each other, we sloshed and crunched, the four of us, our way around the corner, crunched and sloshed through snow that could be treacherous if you didn't watch your step.

RIALTO in red neon, with holes in the A and L. On the marquee, BIG LOCAL TALENT SHOW FEATURING LOCAL TALENT OF ACCLAIMED. SATURDAY ONLY, FEBRUARY 10. CONTENTIOUS ENTERTAINMENT. In through the main entrance and standing in the lobby. Julius, leading us, stopped by a flight of stairs on the side and said, not looking at us but along the walls checkered with photos of cinema stars and local guitar singers, "Mitchell, you and Melvin go along up in the balcony. I'll take Pearl to her dressing room and meet you both upstairs." And they left us in the lobby to watch the spectators enter.

My eyes too, swept over those walls that had zigzag cracks from ceiling to floor, and I thought that the pictures must be covering more cracks. Or maybe a hole? Photographs of stars, some with moustaches crayoned in, some with crayoned beards, even some with crayoned eyeglasses. All head shots, all smiling—some facing left, some facing right. In one photo, a starlet held a finger to her chin; in another, a star smiled with folded arms; and also one with a hat falling over his eyes.

"They still look young, boy. I remember them from the days when I used to come to the Rialto as a thirteen-year-older like you. They look—look at Bessie, Billie, Prez—good as new."

Sitting now in this four-wheeled limousine, organ of my own continuous entertainment, I smile as I think back to our reaching the upper balcony and finding our seats. Their first segment of continuous entertainment was this: a Tarzan movie. So Uncle and I began to take off our heavy wraps, and I turned around as I swung my coat off, and I saw that the balcony was fairly crowded. Next, the seats squeaked, I stepped on some popcorn kernels, and—was it a roach? Tickling me, crawling up my shinbone for comfort? I slapped my pants and felt the bug fall through the hair on my legs, so immediately I guessed from its size that it wasn't a roach—no, even bigger—waterbug. In my seat, my hand jerking away from the melted chocolate bar on the armrest, I glanced at Uncle, whose knees were cramped against the back of the seat in front of him. So then I turned and looked straight down at the screen. Sitting in a collapsible chair, digging the flick while the frank-furters and popcorn cooked behind us and my foot stuck now into chewing gum and people in back of me talking as if they were at a ballgame and kicking the back of my seat, I watched Tarzan swing through the trees.

Not for long, however. Lights out, torn curtain fall-ing down and covering the screen, no more movie. A band from nowhere—their sound all around us—in back, ahead, above, blasting away. The audience—the invisible audience, for I saw no one, only heard—yelled and cackled. All I saw were shapes of heads in front, shapes to the side, shapes behind me. All this noise from them? Next, handclapping, foot stomping, and these shouts: "Let's go, let's go, let's go." In this din, Julius arrived. I checked him out. Almost-frozen trench coat over the arm, he was bent over, looking down our row. Uncle whistled out to him, and Julius waved, bumped his knees against five or so persons, brushed his coat over my head, took his seat next to mine.

"Show's starting," he said. Thanks for telling us, Julius.

Maine-line Martin on the stage now: a three-hundred-pound master of ceremonies sporting a green, shiny vine, a process that rivaled Julius's, and doing the jitter-bug.

"Hey, cool mamas and slick daddies!"

And an uproarious, "Hey, Maine-line!" from all around me, including Julius.

"I'm Maine-line Martin, your Martian maniac, your main man from Maine with the most in music, here in Boston. Yes sir, senoritas and senors, here we swing. It takes some schoolin' to beat my foolin', but when I'm serious, the beat's mysterious. Say, look"—holding the microphone and patting his white shoes in time with the band, unpressed pants shaking—"without further ado, I want to introduce to you some of New England's finest acts, and here are the facts: Cousin Dynamite Calvin playing the electric guitar!" A roar of assent. "And Duke Gibson doing his tap-dance routine." Murmers and grumbling. "Miss Pearl Mibbs, guest-appearing from Chatsworth, Maine's, Living End Club." Shouts and woohoos. "Oscar Moore and the Swinging Four do-ing their new one that may get them a record contract. And—listen to this—a surprise guest appearance from my home state of Maine." Then, about two thousand black stentors exercised their lungs, brought their palms together, stamped their feet. "Now, on with the show—ho! And if I'm lyin', I'm flyin'."

A second curtain in the stage rear opened, exposed a

dozen band members in orange suits. The drummer was in the center, higher than the other musicians. Having done his thing, Maine-line was dancing off the stage on the tip of one shoe. My ears were inundated with trumpets, the bass, clarinets and trombones. But the drummer, crisscrossing his arms like a drowning swimmer, caught my eye. Keeping in time beautifully with his partner, the bassist, he was still his own man, his own personality commenting. With his left hand accenting, embellishing the beat, he was a traveler in a hurry with his right hand, swishing over the skins, tip-tapping. Even when he hesitated, slowed down, he was a paradox, for the tempo was somehow still rapid and the band was moving ahead. And this virtuoso with sticks was a bird too, flying between the melody, pecking at new seeds of expression, diving into an unknown. A two-handed whirlwind of creative energy.

The show went on. I watched Duke Gibson tap-dance with a mouthful of teeth flashing, and Dynamite Calvin swing his guitar with so much rhythm, he almost propelled himself off stage.

When Mother finally walked her walk onto the stage, whistles sailed toward her. Because of her dress? It was a shiny, silver gown that had a a slit down the side exposing her right thigh, and a wide, low V-neck opening in front.

She stood in the white circle of light, Mother did, and went about her business like a professional. Only a single stage light hit her, and Boston was no place for her, was not large enough a city, she seemed to be telling us through her singing mastery. Soon the audience was so hushed (Uncle was leaning forward, chin between his hands), I heard the microphone wire slide across the stage floor as Mother pulled the mike in front of her. Even from my high vantage point, way, way up in the upper balcony, I heard the mike wire slide. Mother's head was lowered, she was chirping a provocatively soft ballad, her hand slid down and over her hip and thigh and, leaning over, she showed the top part of her breasts to everybody high enough to look down upon them. Even me. So, Mother performed. She switched her hips, made designs in the air with her arms, threw back her head, turned in circles, licked her lips with that long tongue, rolled her eyes. All this while singing:

> *I had all kinds of luck.*
> *But it's all been bad.*
> *Nothing's left for me to do,*
> *And I'm feeling so sad.*

That soft voice again, working on a crowd this time. And because of the tenderness of her voice, I remember feeling very, very lonesome, feeling very sad myself, in the dark balcony of the Rialto, feeling compassion for this poor singer who had had so much misfortune. Yes, her soft, hypnotic voice could have had that audience picking blueberries for Mother.

And when it was over, there was a split-second silence as Mother put the mike back on its stand (it clicked) and started to stride off with her tan and beautiful, her supple and long legs. A split second it was of wishing—wishing that she hadn't finished but was only preparing for the next tune, but then we all knew it was over and that the only remaining ritual was to applaud her. And we did. There were whistles, shouts of "More," "Sing another, baby," "Come on back," but Mother was too skilled in histrionics to return. Partially hidden by the curtains, she waved from a corner of the stage instead. Let them want more; they wouldn't get it that night.

"Beautiful," said Julius. "Uptight, beautiful. We're on our way to the top." Talking to himself, biting his nails and ignoring Uncle and me.

I don't even remember the two acts following Mother's. I looked down but didn't see, heard but didn't comprehend the figures dancing around on that dusty wooden stage. I just remember seeing Mother's act, hearing her voice. Until Maine-line, now in a purple formal, including tails, slid back into the spotlight.

"And now, cats and kitties, the moment you've been waiting for. Yes siree, the big event." Then a quick look backstage. "Is my man arrived yet?"

Suddenly Julius leaned in front of me again and said to Uncle: "Come on, old man, you gonna do it or not? I ain't gonna ask you no more. You're the one who said you wanted to." Uncle's hand clenched the armrest, and he stared through Julius, gave his answer via his cold eyes.

"I don't know what's happening," said Martin. "He's around somewhere. I wonder if he got lost in the curtains."

Without warning, Julius, like a sailor discovering land, jumped up on his seat, yelled out in his loudest voice, his rings sparkling on his raised hand, one finger pointing at Uncle: "Here he is. Here he is, Maine-line."

And every face in the balcony turned toward us. Even people downstairs were bending their necks.

"Hey, now, that's what I call being tricky," said the emcee, "but we don't want this to get sticky. Come on down." The band started a marching tune. "Come on down here. Ladies and gentlemen, without further ado, I bring to you Mister Melvin Pip. Now, ain't that a blip. Okay, let's hear it!" More marching music.

Julius again, this time standing on the side of Uncle's chair, his hand up high over his head, standing on tiptoes, forefinger pointing down vertically at Uncle's graying hair, he yelled, "He says he ain't gonna perform, and he don't care how much you paid for your tickets."

Before I knew it, I was watching Uncle being carried

on the shoulders of four huskies toward the "Exit" sign, in a corner of the balcony. Minutes later, I caught his head below on the main floor, bobbing down the aisle, bent for the stage.

Uncle in front of a microphone on a Saturday night in Boston, Massachusetts, U.S.A., before thousands of curious and demanding faces. Uncle standing, shaking Maine-line's hand as the emcee gave the performer his best wishes and eased off—but not before whispering over the mike: "He's a comedian." Uncle on stage. The band stopped playing. The audience was silent. Julius sat on the edge of his felt-and-wool seat. We all watched Uncle pull out his pipe and begin.

Poor Uncle. His first joke must have been the saddest story ever told in New England. Such a frightening adumbration of his later stories. Most of the audience sat dumbfounded. In the balcony, I looked around, hoping no one would connect Uncle with me. Some were scratching their heads, others were leaning toward another, conferring, trying to understand the punch line, trying to agree on a meaning or an evaluation of Uncle's performance. Murmurs spread throughout the theater. Meanwhile, Uncle, still wrapped in earmuffs, a greatcoat and furcovered gloves, stood, saying:

"You see, the punch line is when the guy says, 'But I already have a dog.' Get it?" He was holding out his arms in explanation when the tomato splattered against his perspiring forehead. Then a chuckle, expanding to tittering throughout the loge; outright, boisterous laughter in the mezzanine; spreading to that and catcalls too in the balcony around Julius and me (I trembling and Julius smirking, bent over with giggling), until the entire Rialto was rocking—with laughter.

And another tomato—splat! Later, an egg, snowballs, paper cups, water bombs, even a hotdog bounced up and slid along the stage floor. Uncle was standing, peeping out from behind the microphone, which he held up as a tree of protection, and the missiles whizzed by him. The band played one of those fast burlesque tunes, the projection man switched the spotlight on and off, and I?—I considered the odds, concluded that I would be no help, tried to convey telepathically to Uncle that he should run off the stage. Julius was falling over from laughter.

"Your mother sure comes up with good ideas." He laughed.

Everybody was laughing and booing. The noise was getting louder. The walls, the red "Exit" signs, the profiled faces—they all spun around and around, until I fainted.

8

THREE COLD DAYS LATER, AFTER THE SNOW HAD melted, Uncle and I were walking down Atlantic Avenue toward the Harmony Shop.

"Don't make no sense to me," said Uncle. It was after school, and I had rushed home and hurried Uncle to the car. "Whatcha wanna get drumsticks for, and no drums to hit on? And don't think I'm gonna buy you no drums later, if that's what you thinkin'."

On the narrow sidewalks of downtown Chatsworth—just Uncle and I walking in step below a dove-gray sky. My eyes were watering and my nose dripping from the cold. Uncle, head held high, swung his arms, swung the arms of that great-coat, and stomped ahead. His face knifed through Chatsworth's cold like a cutter through ice. Uncle, the mighty, without blinking or squinting an eye, pushed his face through the four P.M. cold. And we saw people: Uncle lifting his smoke-throwing pipe out of his mouth, Uncle tipping his hat, Uncle stopping to shake a hand, Uncle smiling.

"This here it?"—pointing one rough finger from the right hand toward the sign reading HARMONY SHOP— MUSICAL INSTRUMENTS FOR SALE OR RENT. ESTABLISHED 1910. With that one finger pointing and the other hand on his hip, then touching his cap, taking it off, scratching the gray kinks of hair above the ears. That left hand back on his hip, Uncle said, "This must be it, got all those musical whatnots in the window, Mitchell."

"Yes, sir," said the salesman behind the counter in a white shirt and armbands. We walked through the door and stumbled—first I, then Uncle—because we hadn't noticed the sign reading WATCH YOUR STEP. "You better watch your step, there, gentlemen," he said.

"We want drumsticks—for the boy, here," said Uncle. He smacked together his mittens.

"That all?" said the salesman, not looking at me, but bending over as if he were bowling; sliding the glass door of the display case to one side (his eyes squinted behind his hornrimmed glasses), reaching in, two, three fingers grasping, making contact, edging around a long, thin cardboard box; then, pulling the box out carefully, so he wouldn't knock over the harmonica standing lengthwise or the trumpet mouthpiece, and placing the box on the counter.

His face, now completely inside the display case, reminded me of clothes in a washing machine. And his face was swirling around in a sudsy maze of reeds, recorders, clarinets, keys, notes, bars.

"They come in boxes?" asked Uncle.

I separated my lips, must have shown my teeth, but the "yes" didn't come out; it was buried by the weight of my excitement somewhere below my heart, which was fluttering like a mad-brained, runaway metronome. I nodded my head up and down. The salesman held the box an arm's length away and blew off the dust. And I pressed my toes against my shoe bottoms to keep my knees from knocking.

There was a strange unreal timbre filling the store. I heard noise of a kind but wasn't sure I really heard anything. The room filled my ears with its peculiar sound that was really nonexistent. There was a clanging that was not jarring; chimes unlike the sounds of bells; indistinguishable strains and medleys, canticles and chants swirling around the store, but yet—I heard and did not hear, felt but didn't really feel.

"Do you hear that?" I asked Uncle.

"What?" he said.

"Never mind."

Finally the two sticks being taken out of the box; held by the clerk's white fingers; two wooden, tapered, light-tan drumsticks. Drumsticks. And then the hand waved them back and forth, creating a persistence of vision—a blur. The salesman held them out to Uncle.

"Wanna try them out?" asked the seller, his voice not quite serious, pointing the two sticks—fat ends in his palms—at Uncle.

"Here, Mitchell, try them out," said Uncle.

"You'll need a practice pad—can't bang on my glass display case," said the salesman.

"More money?" asked Uncle.

"A few dollars. But you don't have to buy drums. See?" He slid the rubber-centered, wooden practice pad in front of Uncle. Uncle handed me the pad and the two sticks, and the bundle of three objects clicked, made sounds of hollow wood, because I was fumbling everything, trying to get a good grip on them. I placed the pad on the counter's top and stood there with each hand holding a drumstick. I was just about to start a roll when the salesman grabbed the pad.

"Shall I wrap it all up, sir?" He was turned away from me, was looking at Uncle, yet holding his palm out in my direction on the counter for the sticks. I placed them in his hand, which closed around the sticks. Uncle had them wrapped up, paid, and I took one last glance at the dark store. My eyes cruised over the dusty steel sheet-music holders holding dusty sheets of music. I looked at the guitars (two), ukulele, banjo and tambourine on the shelves behind the counter before I realized that the place didn't even have a drum set for sale.

"Might as well stop by Tony's."

I knew that. Might as well. See the fellows. Talk that talk. Drink wine and carry on while people going north to Bangor or Portland blew and blew their horns outside, waiting for gasoline. "Might as well," I said.

"He'll probably want to see your drumsticks," said Uncle. Sure.

Tony had company. Three of his and Uncle's friends were sitting on turned-sideways boxes placed in front of Tony's pot belly furnace. When we entered and they greeted Uncle, we caught them with their arms outstretched in front of the furnace—warming their hands, looking like Indians at a pow-wow.

"What's in the boy's bag?" asked Tony, pulling out a half-filled bottle of wine from under his chair (the only one in the room), and the others suddenly doing similarly: a steel cup from inside a jacket; a glass from between the knees; a cup concealed inside a hat sitting on a lap. Uncle got himself a glass and a box from the corner. I sat on a crate in the corner.

"Drumsticks," said Uncle, pouring the liquor, standing now in the middle of the circle, four sets of eyes glued to his hand that throttled the good juice.

"Drumsticks! You don't eat meat on Friday, Melvin!" He laughed from deep within his throat, stomped on the floor, stood and grabbed the bottle from Uncle.

"These are *playing* drumsticks. You play on drums with them. Musical. Boogie woogie, Charleston, bebop." Uncle snapped his fingers, hummed a little ditty, as a flash of furnace light illuminated his wet lips for an instant.

"Ain't he a little young?" asked another. This time it was his turn to reach for the bottle.

"Mitchell," said Uncle, throwing off his greatcoat, warming up to the moment and the fire, "come over here and show them how smart you are. They think jus' because you don't say much you don't think much.

70

Or maybe"—I could tell from his deep intake of breath that it was going to be a hummer— "maybe you think he's *got* to be dumb 'cause he's colored."

Falling over chairs and boxes, foot scraping, coughing, slapping of a thigh. All standing.

"Now, see here, Melvin Pip, don't come around here causing no trouble. You know we ain't like that."

"That's right, Pip. Some of the smartest Negroes— some of the smartest *people* in this state are colored."

"You're just trying to get us fidgety, Pip. We drink out the same bottle, and all of a sudden you call us down for no reason. For no reason at all."

"No sir! Not a reason in the world."

"Well, I only know how it sounds," said Uncle, putting his arm around my shoulders.

"But you been here long enough to know what kind of people we got in Chatsworth, Melvin. When you moved here, how many Negroes lived here?" said Tony, fat, sitting now, looking like a white Buddha.

"I been here since I can remember," said Uncle. He pulled out his pipe, bent over, and started knocking it on the heel of his boot. That look of afar came to Uncle's eyes. He began scratching his hair, clearing his throat, and I went back to my seat. Uncle was about to tell a story, I knew. "My parents were born and lived in the same house I'm staying in now."

A voice from the far corner: "Didn't your wife stay with you for a while after your folks passed away, Melvin?" And the others threw quick glances of disapproval at the voice.

"Yeah, she stayed with me for a time," answered Uncle, circularly walking now, knowing he was the center of attraction and perhaps glad and yet not so glad. "Right after high school I went up to Augusta and got a job in the lumberyard with my father. Then Pearl came along"—pointing at me—"his mother—they had her late, and I took care of the whole family after my

71

dad retired. We had to use the pump in the back yard for our water, the eggs we sold for extra income, and the steps didn't creak. Only about two or three colored families in the whole city then, and they all lived where most do now"—pointing at some wall. "You ever start wondering about yourself, Tony? How you got here? Why your parents moved here, or how they came anyway? What you made of your life? Don't you get confused, Tony? Jake? Herman?"

"Now, see here, Melvin," said Jake, taking from a dark corner a drink wrapped up in a navy parka. "There's no sense in regretting. We lived good lives—brought up families, held good jobs, had a little fun. What else do you want?" And the others, nodding their necks like horses, concurred.

"I wish I could—I wish I could have had more education, so I could carry on good conversations," said Uncle. "Now, watch what I mean. Come here, Mitchell. Tell us some things you learn in school, son. This kid's smart as a whip. Smarter than any of us here. Mitchell, what about some of those facts you were telling me of Maine."

So I stood on the linoleum floor, and under the bare twenty-five-watt bulb of a spotlight, I told them that Maine is known as the Pine Tree State, that the first naval fight during the Revolution was at Machias Bay, and I talked about Sebastian Cabot, Leif Ericson, Benedict Arnold, Daniel Webster, and soon I was like a doll unwound, like a pendulum that had fallen from potential to energy of motion, and I was gone—gone in a frenzy of verbal locomotion. I cleared my voice and eventually achieved a resonance that was—well, just a little louder than necessary. I gesticulated with my drumsticks toward the walls, toward the one window over the potbelly furnace, toward the blur of faces (Uncle had sat down). From the corner of an eye, I dug the opening and passing around of another bottle. The

72

lessons in the history of Maine fixed in my memory, were filtering through my mouth like programs from a computer. The lessons, the facts, the pictures from textbooks—they were clogging my brain, knocking against my mind, and I had to keep my mouth going. And I went on and on even after feeling drops of perspiration from my underarms ease down my side. Recited until I began stuttering and searching for more facts, and my tempo was slower, and the muscles in my legs were flinching, my mouth was dry, and my fingers trembling.

"And so that's it," I said, ending on, "Baxter State Park has 201,018 acres." Looking for approval; listening for ejaculations of admiration and awe, perhaps applause, searching for wide-eyed looks of surprise. Were they looking for ants? Were the tips of their shoes dirty? Could they have been praying—for my continued intellectual growth? "Well, that's it," I said again, this time laughing the words out and shuffling my feet, clicking together my sticks, swinging my arms.

"Hey, he's finished," yelled Uncle, coming to his feet.

And the nodding heads jerked up, the eyes blinked. One wiped his mouth; another yawned.

They all had been asleep.

"You see how smart he is?" Uncle was putting on his mittens.

"Yep," they said in unison.

"Um hum."

"Plenty smart," said Jake, tilting the bottle back to his head as Uncle and I headed for the door.

"We taught them a thing or two," said Uncle as we got into the Ford and drove fast toward home. There, Julius, wearing an ascot, opened the door for us, and the rush of comforting, warm air against my face made me glad to be in the big old home again.

"Whatcha got there?" he asked, policeman-like,

snatching my bag away, shooting a hand into the bag, pulling out a stick, another stick, and the pad. "Oh, yeah? Gonna be a little drummer, huh? I used to play with these too, before I went into the talent-scouting profession. Here, let me show you." Inside, he sat down (Uncle went to the kitchen) on the couch and started tapping his left foot in three-four time, humming, and beating on the pad placed on the table. "Here, you try it"—but before I could reach for them—"Wait, I want to see if I can still roll, yeah. Oh, hell yeah, Julius, you still as good as you always were." He placed the sticks down on the table. "Don't touch, kid, I'll be right back"—sliding in his slippers toward the record player, rejecting a record, coming back to the sofa, pushing a plant and an ashtray to the end of the table, clearing a space on the table and tapping along with the music of Duke Ellington. There, on the sofa that big, corn-footed Larson had sat—or sprawled—was Julius, drumming with my sticks in the dark living room of Uncle's house, and I was standing with my hands behind my back, my coat and hat still on, my hands fidgeting, my lips wanting to form the question: "May I play with my sticks now, Julius?" Strange recurrence: there I was again, standing by the door, unable to move, not knowing what to say, and a little bewildered to realize that this was happening again. Or was it? The same couch, scene? Had I suddenly fallen back in time, like some backwards Icarus, to the rehearsal of that denigrating moment with Mother and Larson? I had chills as the suggestion swept over me.

"Stop!" I yelled, almost scaring myself. Mother, robed, came in from the kitchen, and I could see Uncle's head behind her. Julius had stopped, looked up at me, and was drumming again.

"What's the matter, Mitchell?" Mother, with her wide eyes, an earnest look of concern, a dish towel over

74

her arm, and Uncle, clearing his throat, coughing, looking over her right, then her left shoulder.

"I'm showing him how to play the drums," Julius said. "You know, I used to do this before I went into the talent-scouting business, Pearl. You're glad of that, aren't you?"

"Yes," my mother answered, softly, of course, rubbing her hands in the dish towel, cocking her head to the side, smiling.

"If it wasn't for me, you wouldn't have won that talent show in Boston, right? And we're going places, honey. Soon as I get my connections together in the city, we're going to leave this hole. No more singing on the weekends in the Living End. The big time. You and me"—another bang. "Put on another record," he said, and she did, and as the big bad blues blared out, Julius jumped up, caught my mother around the waist, elbowed Uncle in the waist, just missed stepping on his shoes, turned Mother around, threw his head full of shiny black hair back, and sang, "We're going to leave this place, right?"

"Right." Mother laughed.

"We met at the Living End, and we're going to the top together."

"You said it, Julius." Mother laughed.

And they laughed, and circled around in their own dance, and Uncle pulled out his pipe, began tapping it, and I reached for the sticks and pad that Julius had laid on the table, and I headed for the door. When I turned with my hand on the door, the two entertainers had stopped, were standing, holding each other around the waist, breathing hard, smiling as if posing for a portrait. Uncle was standing next to them like an aggressive waiter. I rushed out the door before Julius could ask for my sticks. Yes, rushed out to the good, old, trusty Ford, and drummed until it was time for dinner.

And after eating, I went right to bed. Later, with a cracked left eye, I watched Uncle pull off his clothes, felt the side of the bed give as he knelt to say his prayers. I smelled his strong, warm, outdoor smell as he jumped in the bed with thermal underwear. And I waited, waited until Mother's and Julius's bedroom laughter stopped; waited for the slam of their door and the click of the light switch. I listened to Uncle's snoring, punched him in the chest (in my sleep) to make sure he wasn't awake, then got out of bed, assembled my clothes, dressed, got my drumsticks and practice pad, and stole toward the front door. Passing Mother's room, I heard her whispered words pierce the air in disgust: "Christ, Julius, what kind of a man are you? Poop out, that's all you can do." Then, on the porch, wrapped uptight and ready to take care of business, looking at the half moon between the trees across the road, I stomped down the steps in Maine's coldest night air, undid the fence, made for the car. My feet crunched on the frozen ground, my ears ached, but I went on those few steps, looking so much like an Arctic explorer, I'm sure. Finally, I got in, placed my pad on the back seat, took off my gloves, and began practicing.

The music was in my mind, had been pent up there for a lifetime, I guess, and now, in the moonlight, in the cold night, in nobody's sight, it was spilling out, and I was playing along with the fat cats: Bix, Gene, Coleman, Duke, the Count. I could see them just ahead of me on the bandstand in the woods, and I was moving them along, pushing the trumpets, complementing the bassist, inspiring the pianist. I. Me. I was into my very own personal thing in Uncle's short. Drumming as if my life depended upon it. Soon, after I had finished, after I had worked up a sweat from my wild, ecstatic playing and had dropped my sticks, fallen back in the seat of Uncle's car with a beautiful sense of exhausted fulfillment, I just sat and watched the stars, listened to the crickets. My feet rested on the top of the front seat. The applause from the audience was so staggering, I had to make a short address: "Ahem. Ladies and gentlemen, it was most kind of you to come up here to the first annual Chatsworth Jazz Festival. This was our first concert, and I must say, uh, the response has been overwhelming. Never have we had so much appreciation. You really make us feel wanted. You really make us feel very wanted." But the lie of that statement tripped my emotional progess, and a sudden wave of depression hit me; everything was suddenly dispiriting— the trees, the moon, my sitting in Uncle's car. I was choking from something that wasn't even in my throat, and something was draining my insides. I felt closed in, sinking, losing my balance, and suddenly I was falling through the sky, was tumbling head over feet. Not wanting to cry—and I felt myself moving to tears—I jumped out and ran to the house steps. Even when I reached the front door of the great old castle, my shoulders were heaving. So I waited until I had settled down. Then looked over my shoulder at the trees, went inside. That was my first night with my drumsticks.

9

WE HAVE HAD OUR MOMENTS OF—HOW SHALL I SAY—
of mother-and-sonness. On a couple of occasions, I have
been the recipient of Mother's restricted form of maternal love, a love so evanescent, one had to be constantly
on his toes to spot its short-lived nature. Hers was a
maternal love that could slip through your fingers if
you hesitated in recognizing it or in grabbing at it with
a smile or soft word. So I'd better write of the times
when Mother was—well, was a mother, before they slip
my mind.

Pin this one. Catching the bus at the circle near the
other side of the highway, Mother and I found seats by
the window, and as the bus, its gears screaming,
lurched its way to the center of the road, we fanned
ourselves with our open hands. Nobody else was on the
bus.

"Why are we leaving so early, Mommy?" I asked,
remembering how she had awakened me at six, remembering how she had whispered that we were going
sailing, hurry up, get dressed quietly so you don't wake
up Uncle or Julius.

"We've got a long day. First, we go to Portsmouth."

"New Hampshire?"

"Yes, and from there we sail to the Isle of Shoals,
walk around for a while, then sail back. It's going to be
a long day." She patted my head, smiled her smile that

had more ambiguity than Mona Lisa's, crossed her long legs covered with white slacks, folded her sweater in her lap, rubbed her nose.

I said, feeling childish even at age eleven for shivering in the middle of summer: "Why didn't we bring Julius and Uncle with us?" We were sitting so my legs touched hers, but we had to shout as we bounced up and down on our seats, as the bus tore through the town, swerved, braked too quickly, blew its horn, and stopped at a railroad crossing and opened its doors.

"It's a surprise," she said.

And what a surprise! When we walked down the gangplank at Pete's Marina in Portsmouth, New Hampshire, I had no idea that the lovely, single-masted *Wayfarer II* would be our destination. Not the *Wayfarer*, longest vessel in the marina; stately, white, thirty-five-foot sloop that can run with the wind as Jeff can with a bone. Not the *Wayfarer*, sleek craft which swallows distance like a greyhound at sea. Not the *Wayfarer* itself, slick sea sled that slides over the blue. But oh, yes, the boss *Wayfarer*.

"I'm looking for *Wayfarer II*," said Mother to someone.

We reached the slip where she was moored, found Carl, white-haired and white-skinned, sporting short pants and bony knees, tanned and peeling around the neck. He stood on the trunk cabin. He was fixing the sails.

"Hi."

"Hello," said Mother, her bright eyes flashing, reaching for his hand, laughing at nothing, climbing aboard, then reaching for me. "This is Mitchell. This is Carl." We spoke. "This is a big boat"—sitting down, running her eyes over *Wayfarer*—"did you build it?"

"Oh, no, Pearl," he answered. Then bashfully, looking at his watch and speaking almost too soft: "I'm glad you came." And Mother didn't answer; did smile, though.

The sun was pushing through the clouds now, shining on Carl's forehead as he stood still, hands resting on stays above his head. He was looking down at Mother, seated, and for a moment the three of us glanced at each other, rocked a little with the boat, smiled at each other, listened to the water lap. I breathed the healthy salt air, closed my eyes, and pointed my face toward the sun.

Soon Carl started the motor, and we moved away from the pier and beyond the lobster traps. The outboards zipped past us.

"The current's making a stand," he said, pointing to a buoy, one hand on the stern. "That's good for moving out to sea." Out, farther out past the Coast Guard station, past the fishermen on the wharves, past the regal, bay-windowed homes. "Take the horn and blow it four times. They have to open up the bridge," he said when we neared it. Mother blew, the bells rang, a man ran out to stop the bridge traffic, blockades closed on the bridge, and it opened up for us. I waved at the cars, the bridge attendant waved at me. We were under and past the bridge. And on, gentle *Wayfarer*, on; past now the navy yard where Uncle once worked, past the naval prison, past this, past that; on, on out to sea.

It was too much for me. I eased my way up the steps to the deck, waved at dozens of boats, until I could hold it back no longer, and I almost frightened them both with a loud, "Ahoy, you blustering fub-dubbers, ahoy. Man the stays, prepare to make way and hold on to course. Up with the spinnakers, lay her into the wind. Now, prepare to come about, and don't get her in the irons. Okay, now gather way, ply the oar and steer the leeway sternly. Ahoy, you roustabouts, scrub the decks." Maybe I was drunk. Maybe the excitement of being alone with Mother, the salt air fanning my face, the rocking motion, the other sailboats dotting the sea farther out, was too much for me. Mother was beside herself with laughter. Never since or before have I heard her crack up so gleefully, so freely. She was throwing her head back, pointing at me, laughing uncontrollably, laughing loudly, laughing with her hair all over her face; laughing and slapping her thighs, pulling a tissue from her bag and dabbing her eyes, blowing her nose. Mother, laughing and having fun, reminded me of the amazing laughing fat woman at the circus.

When she caught her voice again, she said: "Mitchell, my God, where did you learn all of those words? Carl, did you hear him? Wasn't it something? Oh, Jesus, I can't stop laughing. Mitchell, you're a killer-diller, honey, I swear."

I just grinned, Carl just grinned. I soaked up the sun, although I needed a tan like the *Wayfarer* needed another sail, and I soaked up Mother's praise, basked in it.

After he had taken her to deep water ("It's one hundred and thirty feet out here—would you believe it?"), Carl put Mother at the helm ("I'll crash, I know it"), got me to undo the stays, throw this rope off, make that one fast, and he was hustling about the deck, hoisting the sails, cursing at something, running one way, then another, until the sails were up and we were moving. The inclinometer showed fifteen degrees, and I thought I was standing sideways. Carl took the helm, and I, able-bodied seaman already, took my trusty sea legs up again to the trunk cabin, peered through the binoculars as I leaned against the mast with my legs crossed. We burst ahead on the Atlantic. We burst ahead, see-sawing, hovering, billowing, hitch-hiking the wind, skiing on melted ice. I went up to the foredeck, eased my way down the foreward hatch, inspected the inside; saw two bunks, and thought, sleeps four; saw a gas range and thought, can cook food here; saw, farther up, a refrigerator and thought, must have soda; and farther up saw the two sternside bunks, saw the head, came up the steps to the cockpit and found Mother sitting and Carl at the helm. The portable was on FM, Mother was smiling with her eyes closed and I sat down opposite her.

"Are Julius and Uncle fine?" he asked, turning his head to prevent his words from being carried out to sea.

"Yes, they were asleep when we left," Mother answered; and next, "Having fun, Mitchell?" I nodded, smiled, swung my feet. "I'm glad, too," she said. "Are you hungry, son?"

"Fix us a cocktail first," Carl said.

I said I was hungry, and Mother went below, became a blur of white blouse and slacks as she moved from refrigerator to sink—bending, slicing, pushing, pulling, arranging.

"Would you like to go to a private school, Mitchell? Just visit your mother on the weekends?" Carl was licking his lips, frowning, staring ahead over the helm. But before I could answer, Mother came up with a sandwich. "You got the drinks, sweetie?"

Mother put her hand on my head, rubbed the back of it, then faced the helmsman. "My son comes first," she said, holding on for balance when Carl turned from the tiller to look. And he lost his course, almost making a semicircle. Jaws tight, no doubt; sucking his teeth probably.

But the highballs came eventually, and Mother really relaxed, her voice came slower and softer, her eyes brightened.

I went down to the head, almost asked Carl if it was for kids only, the seat was so small.

"Holy Jesus," he shouted to Mother, "did your kid go to the head? Oh, Christ, he'll sink the boat. Don't try to flush the toilet, kid. Did you hear me, *Do not flush the toilet*. Take over the helm, Pearl." I heard him tumble down to the door. He snatched it open, stood over me with legs spread, face contorted. He smacked his palm over his nose and said, "Ooh, phew, worse than rotten eggs," pushed the door closed, and shouted from outside the door, "Look, when you get off, unloosen the valve counterclockwise. Then turn the little lever, then pump the handle. Phew, you *really* had to go."

Soon I was back on the afterdeck. Carl at the helm. Mother's long, smooth legs were scissored together, she was leaning back on her elbows, perfect pose of experienced sunbathers.

"Pearl, have you been thinking about—"

"Yes, Carl, I've been thinking about it. Please don't rush me, will you?" interrupted Mother, and I busied myself on the life rail, appearing not to hear a thing but straining to hear all.

And we chopped along, the three of us, sailing for Shoals on a Saturday afternoon. As free from care as a gull in flight. We lapped along, the sea washed up against our boat top, we inclined another five degrees, we were really skimming. I, self-appointed second-in-command, took my stand on the foredeck, leaned insouciantly against the mast. Without a skipper's cap, cigarette or kerchief, I was slightly deficient in material but made up for it in attitude. When a cabin cruiser skimmed by us on the port side, I yawned with the unconcern of a young millionaire as we exchanged waves on the waves.

I watched their wake widen, and the cruiser struck out farther and farther, it was getting smaller and smaller. Suddenly our sloop started rocking, pitching. I looked astern: Mother was at the helm, and she was holding it with one hand, was bending over starboard trying to pour herself another drink. Carl was advancing toward her. I turned to the bow so I could go below deck through the forward hatch, but was jerked portside, fell to my knees, grabbed onto the wire rigging, burned my hands, yet felt safe even lying on my stomach. Until I looked down. When I looked at the water splashing inches from my face, it was bad enough. But then that nasty-tasting saltwater flew up my nostrils, and I knew I was in a world of trouble.

Some gigantic rotating disk had been placed under my feet, and it was spinning me around so that everything was a blur. The cruiser—the cruiser I had just waved at—was disappearing on the port, then at the bow, next at the starboard side, later astern, and it came back around to the port side again, then disappeared. The sea was splashing, coming at me from all sides, yet I tried to get up on my knees, strained with an exploding stomach full of lead to lift my legs to a kneeling position, grabbed the rigging tighter, hoping it would apply the brakes to this runaway disk. When I got to my knees, I dared to look up, saw the clouds hurtling around, coming together, falling toward me, separating and forming again, and I couldn't stomach it, brought my eyes down, but now the horizon itself was turning upside down. Everything was in reverse, upside down, going wrong. I, dethroned but determined second skipper, kept my eyes on my sneakers as I pulled myself up from my knees, and out of courage and fear, tottering like a table minus two legs, strove to look astern. And there were Mother and Carl at the helm. Their mouths were wide, forming admonitions and advice. Their arms and fingers were gesturing, waving, and I felt like a violinist following conflicting directions from two conductors. Allegro? Andante? Felt like a runner far away on second base receiving signals from two of my Little League coaches on first. Steal? Hit and run? Sacrifice? The smell—that awful nastiness of a sea skunk inundated my nostrils. The taste—that brackish, briny and sour urination from the skies splashed on my tongue, lips, and in my eyes. Like a TKO'd boxer, I held on to the ropes—the rigging—must have been glassy-eyed, stepped like a toddler on a tightrope toward the bow. Then, feeling it surging forward, feeling the load from my stomach push its way toward my mouth, I leaned over the grab rail, and my mouth became a passageway for the regurgitated cargo from my stomach. Blowing lunch. Again I tried, placed and lifted my feet as if walking were a new experience—tried for the forward hatch. I got within a few feet of the hatch and just fell toward it, crawled down the ladder and flopped on the bunk. From my porthole I could see that the horizon had moved back to its normal horizontal position. My dizziness had stopped, and I was off that demented, spinning disk.

"Mitchell!" I heard Mother's call, heard her unsteady progress from aft, and lying on my back, I could see her, shoulder bent low as her hair missed the overhead by inches, moving toward me. She put her hand on my stomach. "Are you all right? You got seasick, didn't you baby?" I just groaned, tossed my head back and forth, lifted up my knees. "Mommy's sorry, Mitchell, she lost control of the boat for a while." Next, the soft, long fingers on my forehead. "Feel better, honey? Can you last the rest of the day?" I nodded, knowing we couldn't turn back then and trying to spur my courage to hold me for the day.

She finally coaxed me off the bunk and through the boat. She held, led me with one hand as the two of us stumbled going aft over the unsteady floorboards toward the cockpit. Carl was grinning at the helm. "Seasick, huh? What kind of sea legs were you walking on, huh, kid? We haven't even rocked much yet. When I was your age"—lifting off his cap with a free hand, throwing back his hair—"I could sail all by myself—no help!"

"Mitchell's smart," said Mother, losing her balance from either the inclination or the highballs, so much like an amateur soft-shoe dancer as she regained her footing. "He can do all sorts of numbers tricks, he knows the capitals of all the states, and he's the smartest in his grade! He's plenty smart," she shouted, pulling me toward her with an arm around my shoulder. The two of us facing Carl's nautical back. Mother rubbed the back of my head, rubbed the nape of my neck as we watched the isle move closer to us, and my stomach felt like an empty gully. We were still leaning starboard, almost standing diagonally because of the ship's incline, and the *Wayfarer* pitched through the Atlantic at a good eight knots.

"Just like when you were a baby, Mitchell," Mother said in her softest voice. "You used to get sick on your stomach every day after the first week from the hospital. And Daddy used to get upset, especially that time when you threw up all over his new suit." We had taken seats in the cockpit, and I was huddled against her, who, even in the salt air, smelled perfumy and clean; her arms were around me, my forehead touched the side of her breast; the sun had gone in, so she had stopped squinting, wrinkling her brow. "God, you used to cry so much when you were a baby, Mitchell. But I sang lullabies to you, and you drifted off. You had the tiniest eyes and feet." She squeezed me tighter.

"Pearl?" Interrupting us with a quarter-turn of his head, showing us his profile, Carl spoke: "Have you been thinking about our conversation, dear? Have you said anything to Julius?"

Mother loosed me from her embrace, bent down and picked up her glass from the deck, sipped, looked at Carl's back, and decided: "It won't work, honey. Too many complications." And for the remainder of the day they just exchanged courteous words about the boat, weather and the sea. I was glad. Mother spent most of her time with me.

Just like the train ride to Boston.

"TRACK SEVEN FOR PORTLAND AND BRUNSWICK. TRACK SIX FOR BOSTON, PROVIDENCE, NEW HAVEN, ALL ABOARD, PLEASE. ALLLLLLLLL ABOOOARD. WATCH YOUR STEP PLEASE.

"Let's go, Mitchell." Mother, carrying her new white Samsonite, pulled my hand. I had Uncle's suitcase—a brown tweed-patterned case with two strings around it to keep it from exposing the inside. "We can't miss this train, because Aunt Ranida will be waiting for us at South Station. And she won't wait long." We rushed through the tunnel toward gate six, climbed the stairs. Mother said, "Aren't you excited? This is your first trip on a train. That's pretty good for an eight-year-old to go on a train trip—for a weekend." But that third step from the top of the platform was something else. My bag banged against it, throwing me off balance. I clutched on to Mother's skirt to keep from falling backward, felt the bag's metal handle slip out of my perspiring palm, heard distinctly the snap-snap of the strings around the suitcase as they broke, and standing with one hand on the railing, the other on Mother's white skirt, watched the suitcase (having left a trail of two underpants, a water gun and a McIntosh apple) tumble down to the bottom of the steps and open flat with a loud *clack*.

"Oh, my goodness, Mitchell," whispered Mother, and she turned her back in a gesture of disaffiliation, and I expected her to leave me there on the steps.

But hands were at work for us. Some were covering snickering mouths. A pair picked up my briefs, tried to beat off the dirt from them; a pair saved my plastic water gun from a plummeting heel; a pair—no, several pairs—were retrieving the broken string; other hands were pushing the two sides of the suitcase together, trying to close it. Hands were waving, directing stair-way traffic around our accident. And then hands were handing the bag back to me, hands were wiping brows, dusting off pants legs, hitching up trousers and smooth-ing out skirts. Finally, a pair—I could just see the fingertips under the case—was handing my suitcase back to me chest-high.

"You dropped this?"

"Oh, yes," said Mother, descending the stairs in high spirits like a real stepper, even throwing back her head and smiling apologetically with all her teeth. "My son—well, take the bag, Mitchell, don't leave the nice gentle-man standing there with the suitcase. My son travels with me all the time, and he likes this old bag for sentimental reasons. Say thanks to the man, Mitchell. I guess now you'll bring your new bag with you. This has never happened before." Faces were craning forward as he gave me the suitcase and I thanked him.

"And thank you all, too," said Mother, waving her hand to the faces. And they waved back, nodded, shook their heads, pooh-poohed that it was nothing, wished us luck, went up the stairs.

The train came around the bend from nowhere. The sun, hitting this silver-and-orange beauty, made starlike glints along the aluminum sides. Newspapers, chewing-gum wrappers, ticket stubs and pigeons flew out of her path as she tore down the track, shaking the platform, sending men's hands reaching for their hats and wom-en's fingers holding down their dresses; making us squint and breathe through our mouths and turn our faces away from this berserk giantess of the rails. But what a difference after we passengers boarded and were seated in the two cars. Sailors were sprawled in various seats; some took up two chairs; some had their feet on the seat tops; the windows were cracked, cigarette holes dotted the blue cotton chairs and the aisles were dirty, filled with soda tops, candy wrappers, cellophane.

As we roared southward, Mother, sitting by the window, began with how the railroad trains had gone down. I asked how they were in the old days.

"Your father and I used to ride them all the time on the weekends," she said, that nostalgic lowering of her voice coming on the last several words. She looked out the dusty, cracked window. "Uncle used to baby-sit for us. Oh, those seats were brand new then. They smelled good, and the windows were always clean, and the sandwiches weren't so high."

"Where did you meet my father?" I asked, feeling the moment was pregnant for this question, yet knowing the answer so well.

She rubbed her nose, uncrossed her legs, and said, "In Philadelphia. I was working for the city, coming home on the trolley one day, and he said, 'Hey, little girl, where are you going?' "

"How did he look?" I had seen the photo of him in army dress, had looked at it many times, searching for the semblance of expression, of features, of anything. She kept it hidden in the bottom of her drawer under her sweaters.

"He was handsome, just like you," she said, rubbing my head. "I've got a picture of him when he was in the army. I'll show it to you someday." The conductor punched our tickets, told us the cars would be completely renovated soon and to have a safe trip.

"Where is he now, Mommy?"

"I don't know."

"Did he leave because of me? Didn't he like me?"

And she pulled me toward her, placed her arms around my shoulders, hugged me, kissed me on my forehead and said that of course he loved me as much as she did, but that Mommy and Daddy couldn't get along without fighting all the time, so he decided to leave. But all parents loved their children so much, so very, very much. Having a baby is the happiest event in a couple's life. Babies bring love and tenderness to households. They bring cheer and happiness, merriment and glee. They bring pride to the parents. Babies, children, high-schoolers, collegiates, sons and daughters —continual gladdening of the heart, until death do them part. These were her words, honest.

"Mommy's glad you're her little boy, and she loves you very much, Mitchell. She wouldn't trade you for any kid in the world. She wouldn't hurt you to save her life. You're"—squeezing me tighter—"Mommy's little angel."

Uh huh, yeah. Sure, okay, angel.

10

EXCUSE ME WHILE I DIGRESS A LITTLE. AS I TURN THE pages to my chronicle's halfway mark and note the drying driplets of rain on the cracked front windshield, I like what I read. I should be able to wrap up the proofreading on my rap sometime late tonight by flashlight, if Jeff gets himself together. Jeff, strong, sturdy canine that he is, could start his own brand of boxer rebellion on the basis of his nocturnal wind-breaking. In the small, closed-up, limited air interior of a broken-down station wagon in these woodlands, Jeff could make it nasally unbearable for me to continue reading. Just the other night, when the moon was bright orange and I was penciling in some manuscript corrections, Jeff, whose head was hanging on my chest, suddenly turned and put his white-haired hind up against the seat top near my head, looked out the rear window as if he were eyeing a following auto—did all this moving—and then broke wind. Without a sound. I gasped, held my nose, let the windows down and the cold in, but it was worth it.

"Jeff, you should be ashamed," I scolded him, hitting him lightly on his buttocks. But I love him just the same, and even told him that as I patted him while he licked my face. "You're still my main man, boy; good boy."

But I like what I have read. And I haven't got to the meat yet; haven't got to the—well, we'll see.

After I wrap it up, then what? What kind of game will I be putting down? What will the manuscript's reception be? Where shall I leave this miniature tome? More evidence of my master intellect: that I should have considered and solved these queries days—no, weeks—ago.

Old lady Dixby, my landlord in town, thinks I come out here to mourn the death of Uncle and to search for some clue to where Mother may be. Poor nostalgic white woman in her long gray dresses, her tan, opaque stockings and her black, thick-heeled shoes; I lead her along.

"Mitchell," she says, stabbing my room carpet with a dust mop, bending over like a drunkard watering a garden, "you shouldn't go on fretting like you do, boy. Get your mind at ease—take a trip." How well I have pondered her advice. A trip to the West, land of opportunity, freedom, sun (I could tan the bottoms of my feet and my palms, but would the bottoms of my ankles mold?), nudist camps. What a perfect test trip for the old station wagon if I got her fixed up and ready to travel again. But no, I like her as she is: a museum piece of peaceful shabbiness, beautiful in her weatherbeaten, stale and frayed way. And of course this too: her cankered existence is just a reminder to me of how tough things can be. Nay. To rejuvenate the Ford would be no good. Rejuvenating the station wagon would be like forgiving and starting all over again. And there is no time for either now. The deed is done. I've done my thing.

I almost welcomed the sight of her crashed-up body when I first saw the wagon after the accident. Coming back from Brown for a weekend during my freshman year, I craned my neck out of the taxi bringing me up the road from the bus circle. I checked out the crashed-in headlamps. After I paid the cabdriver, I looked at the Ford leaning on one side, and I wanted to cry and laugh. She was out of it, yet she was saying something. She was down but she looked somehow like the champ. I dropped my bag by the fence, went over to the old girl, checked her out and said, "You look like you're in a junkyard, old girl, old Ford, but you're beautiful, still." And I took a deep breath to hold back the choking in my throat, pulled out my handkerchief and wiped off some dirt from the door handle.

Uncle came crashing down the steps. "Mitchell," he shouted, hobbling, sounding his boots down the steps, waving his hand, then balling it up and putting his fist against his mouth, coughing. We embraced, my chin resting on his shoulder for an instant. "How's school, Mitchell? Julius borrowed the car one night, got drunk, had a complete wreck, ran into a telephone pole, and then the car turned over, and look at her, Mitchell. She had to be hauled back here. They were going to have the wrecking truck cart her to the junkyard, but I made them bring it back here." He was like a little boy beaten up and running to his older brother.

"I'm sorry, Uncle Melvin," I said, looking down. "But I'm glad you brought her back here—to rest. Can we fix her up?"

"Maybe"—he was looking into the pines in back of me and pulling on his suspenders—"but it'll be tough, Mitch. They really don't care about us, do they, son?"

"No, Uncle, they don't give a damn. We don't even exist. They just run all over us, Uncle."

"Let's go down to the cellar. I've got a bottle of Fancy Passion there. We can talk there, Mitchell. I took care of your mother since she was a baby. I just don't understand. How's school, son?" Coughing.

So the station wagon must stay here with me as part of the plan and part of the past. Won't lady Dixby be surprised when she gets the note! I'll leave it on the bed tomorrow morning, slide over here and lay. Something like, "Mrs. Dixby, I have an important document explaining the circumstances of my mother's death. Yes, she has been murdered. You might call it a necessary case of matricide. The book is in the back seat of Uncle Melvin's auto. Will you please bring the sheriff and all interested citizens and pick up the manuscript this morning? Jeff and I shall be waiting for you."

I'll be waiting, all right. I'll have on my shades and boots, bell bottoms and turtle neck. When they arrive— I expect half the townspeople—I'll just be in the front seat cooling it with Jeff. Maybe I'll beat out a little solo on the dashboard for them with my drumsticks. Scooby dooby dooby. Ooh bob she bop. I'm also planning a press release: A young black genius, sitting comfortably in an abandoned auto on the outskirts of town, announced today that he has killed his mother for the best of all concerned. His testimony is a novel, profound manuscript of some eighty thousand words, listing various and sundry acts alleged to have prompted the macabre slaying. The acts have been arranged in narrative form, and the manuscript has been cited by leading literary authorities as extremely accomplished.

Oh, the attention, the attention. Television crews shining lights in Jeff's face and holding meters near my chest. Radio announcers sticking fat, round mikes up to my lips, reporters scratching notes on their pads. Crowds being roped off by the twelve-man Chatsworth police force. People pointing at, whispering, staring, pushing forward. "Is that him? There he is, there. With the dog. He's playing drumsticks. Look—just a youngster of eighteen or nineteen. I know him—seemed like such a quiet boy, too."

I might get out of the sheen and read a short defense statement, which I have not completely reread yet, but which will probably go like this: May it please the court, defendant argues against punishment on grounds of youth and particularly entrapment—entrapment through inordinately cogent influence of Mother's nefariousness *inter alia.* Defendant pleads that court will sympathize with *moliter manus,* that court recognize it is cheaper to kill than to injure, and further, that court accept motion of nonsuit on ground of parental negligence of deceased contributing to fatal act. Under circumstances outlined, may it be accepted that defendant acted out of compatibility with a reasonable regard for his own emotional sustenance. Defendant recalls that suggested excessive altruism would be an equally deleterious departure from our standard morality, just as excessive enmity and selfishness is. Indeed, a question arises as to whether the omission of defendant's act could be termed morally praiseworthy if the omission would not succor him from additional psychological burdens. And finally, defendant argues that negligence would befall him if there is probability of sufficient damage and harm to his sensibilities so serious that ordinary men would take precaution to avoid and/or subdue this damage. Your honor, may accused approach the bench? Your honor, defendant calls upon an examination of history both nonce and lang syne. Defendant brings as evidence the disturbing events of today that permeate our front pages. Politicians, statesmen, students, innocent bystanders, returning and arriving tourists, teachers, bankers, bums, philatelists, amanuenses, libertines and paranymphs—all walks of life have had their lives taken by the self-styled gods of our day. Murder and crime are rampant, omnipresent and omnipotent; murder and crime are pervasive, ubiquitous and moored at the shoreline of our civilization. How can we subjugate the urge for violence when it's all around us—buzzing around our haircuts like bees, stuffing itself in the pockets of our minds, embracing our consciousness like humid air? Violence beckons us, and only the deaf are immune to its Circe-like call.

Further, *in re Maine v. Mibbs,* may I call your attention, your honor, to the authority of the violent past. Forget not that Cain, getting his brother into the field, slew Abel; that Orestes killed his mother, Clytemnestra; that Danton ordered ten thousand people massacred in Paris prisons; that it goes on and on, incessant and continual. May it please the court, defense argues for amnesty on these grounds also.

Furthermore, defendant makes a case for his contribution to a societal ritual. Have I not done what so many of us wish secretly, what so many of us enjoy vicariously, to deplore, ruminate, discuss? Does not society want these barbarous acts to identify with, to wonder at? Doesn't it envy the man brave enough to act on his own, to do what we all have furtively entertained? Defendant urges court to consider his donation to society's craving for the unrestrained, the abnormal.

The genius again, spilling out like a titan among dwarfs. From a cursory reading of legal decisions and history, I have formed my defense. And a carefree defense it is, for I have little regard for freedom, amnesty or exculpation. There is nowhere for me to go, nothing to do, no one to meet. This book, this report, remains the last remaining act of my life's drama. Can I do more? Jeff and I have seen our fun. Like old marrieds, we must wonder if there's yet a modicum of adventure left in our lives. We've played hide-and-seek until it's become run-and-follow. We've chased cats and rabbits, snuggled up in the back seat during a thundering night. I've taught him to do the boogaloo, the mashed potato, the slop, the Watusi, the monkey and the mambo. We've watched the moon and the North Star. And myself— I've practiced my drumming until Jeff has howled out. So this long memorandum on matricide should be the final act indeed. In a too short list of artistic incentives and activities that have kept me going, this narrative ranks as the only thing that's left. Uncle, with his craftsmanship of the rifle and the way he went about his uncomplicated life—Uncle and his art are gone. Jeff, proud-stepping, bent but strong-legged Jeff, good-doing, stub-tailed Jeff—he will not be a canine Tithonus, no immortality for him either. These drumsticks, wooden tokens of my musical bent—even they will rot. And I—although a genius, sufferer, boss dresser, last of all artist—even I don't profess immortality. Only the manuscript will live on to tell it like it was, to rap in an uptight way, to put my game in the street. Only this journal of the soul lists the participants of the fray for all time.

Even the venerable, time-honored and decaying abode we should have called Pipsmith or Pippersley— to put it on a level with the summer estates along the shore—will be gone. Soon—Mrs. Dixby says next week—the wrecking crew will be here to begin cleaning out this area for construction of a paper plant. This home held scenes of love and death and even birth (my grandparents), of marital sacrament and sexual sacrilege, of frustration; also of dimly lighted fun scenes with Uncle. This imposing gray bungalow, cathedral, castle—call it what you wish—will cascade to the earth soon. I even had a thing about the house. And I still do, as the gray, peeling paint stirs the imagination to conceive of her royalty when she was off-white. The railings on the steps (barely) lean to form a V shape. There is no whitewash on the pear tree on the side, and the hammock over there is spotted with holes and bird droppings. The fencing surrounding the property is leaning forward. It is a house gone old from inattention. And inside—well, we don't dare go inside to meet the dust, cobwebs—and that carrion smell from the attic.

Max and Tom were my two main road partners in the fourth grade. We were the only black faces in the

97

school. When they find out about what I've done, they'll probably take a very pragmatic stance, say something like, "We always knew Mitch was crazy." If they were as hip as I am, they'd say, "Go on with your bad self, Mitchell, go on with your very bad self, your very, very, bad self indeed. You did your stuff and it was tough—tough enough. Go on, Mitch, and work out some more." But no good. None of that talk from those squares.

They did, though, offer me the encouragement and reassurance which were so vital to my grade-school capers. I remember one day after classes in the spring, we were hanging around the playground outside the school when the idea just came to me. "I'm going to break the seesaw record," I said, giving Tom my lunchbox. "Hold this."

"But there ain't no school record for seesawing, Mitch," said Max, running behind Tom and me as we broke for the play area.

Max sat on the other end, and we got our hats. We started out at a moderate speed, and it wasn't until we had been going for a good half-hour before we started drawing a crowd.

"What's Mitchell doing on that seesaw? Why don't he give somebody else a chance? They say he's been up there for hours. Just seesawing," said Murphy Jones, the baddest cat in the school.

Max: "He's setting a school record."

"For what?" asked Murphy. I could see the big bully calculating how much more attention I might get than he.

"Because Mitchell is that way. He's a champ, that's all," answered Max, looking down his shoulder, which had just risen six feet in the air.

"Mitchell does things like that," volunteered Tom. I saw people dropping their bats on the mound on the other side of the field where the diamond was and thundering in our direction; saw bony-legged girls stop hopscotching and trickle over to the gravel seesaw pit; saw freckle-faced, red-haired, short-pants-wearing marble-shooters leave their rings to come watch. And I saw a few fifth-graders abandon the basketball court to come dribbling over, saw girls jump out of their swings and propel their bow legs and shining patent-leather shoes toward the seesaw pit. I watched the crowd gathering in a circle around Max and me.

"What gives?" A voice in back of me as my sneaks touched the ground.

"Seesaw record. They're going to seesaw all night." A voice below me now as Max lifted me up so high I could see the tops of their heads. That was it! All night. We could seesaw all night—it came to me as I was going down.

"Why don't you get down from there and let somebody else on the seesaw," said Murphy, spitting at the gravel.

"Let him break the record, let him break the record, let him break the record," came the chant, drowning out Murphy's voice at four in the afternoon.

"Is that all you gonna do, is just sit there and rock all night?" Murphy sucked his teeth, pointed a finger at my face.

So I pulled up my knees as I went down, hunched my back and placed my toes unsteadily on the shellacked wood of the seesaw. Then, holding onto the iron handle and feeling my balance, I drew in my breath (head pounding), let go of the handle, slowly unbent my shaking knees, until—until I was standing up with my arms outstretched as if I were walking a tightrope. I stood there for an instant like that, and the onlookers encouraged me with whisperings between themselves; some expressed their admiration through outbursts and shouts, and I became a lone elevator passenger slowly

99

moving up to the next floor. When we were perfectly horizontal, I teetered a little for dramatic effect.

Then up I went, up with my hands now on my hips, up smiling, up looking down at Max, up and drunk with power. They clapped politely, whistled, yelled hoorays, and I dug a few leaning over to drop their lunch baskets in front of them. We were going great guns.

An hour later, Max said, "Mitchell, let's stop. We must have broken the record by now, huh? I'm getting hungry." But I couldn't. He was the runner panting behind me as I led during the last lap of a mile race, and I couldn't give in to him.

"Let somebody take your place, if you're tired," I said, feeling the callouses forming on my hands. "This is for a record, Max. I may be here for days—just seesawing."

Tom put down my red Hopalong Cassidy lunchbox, and he jumped on the seat from which Max crawled, almost stumbled, and I could see Tom's underwear at the cracks of his short pants, it never occurring to me that one day in junior high school I would have one of the worst fights in my life with this cat. Rocking up and down on a seesaw whose yellow paint was peeling, we saw this as the best of times shared by the best of friends. And I even mentioned this moment to Tom when we stood in the teachers' parking lot on the side of this same school here four years later when snow was on the ground.

It was so cold that day, we had to walk around in a circle and beat our hands against our hips. Some of the crowd around us stomped their feet and rubbed tears from their cheeks.

"I don't want to hafta hurt you, Mitchell, 'cause we've been friends for a long while."

"I don't want to fight you, Tom," I said, lifting my feet out of one snow pile, placing them back in another sideways. "We sat on that seesaw over there breaking a record for hours when we were in the fourth grade, remember? I wouldn't lie to you about nothing."

"You pushed my girl down the steps, man, I'm gonna kick your butt. Nobody messes with my girl, white or black, especially black."

Keeping my footing, I turned to look for Carolyn, but she was not in the crowd. No sun in the sky. All the teachers had gone, and my face was getting hot. I thought of hot carrots from Mother's lamb stew burning my tongue. I thought of rushing in the front door and pushing my face against the wall of hot air from the oil stove. Thinking warm thoughts and freezing in the school parking lot.

"If Carolyn were here, she would explain, Tom," I said.

"She went home crying."

"Well, let's wait until tomorrow when she can tell you the truth about what happened. I didn't push her down the steps."

"Why'd you do it, man?" Tom was moving forward, closer to me. His lips were tight, and he began very businesslike to take off his wool gloves, and I could hear the crunch of many boots behind me moving closer, narrowing the ring. If he didn't look like a black Bob Steele wearing elevator shoes, I quit. A thin smile was crawling on his lips; his eyes were balls of fire burning through my pupils. Tom, my old friend of the seesaw record, who was bold enough to go with a white chick—a rich white girl, at that—then began to place his wool gloves in his coat pocket (without looking downward). Tom was boldacious enough even to strut around school with Carolyn Meters—only child of lawyer Meters—holding hands too.

"I'll take off my gloves too, then," I said, attempting to be conciliatory, yet thinking that if he was brave enough to do all that with Carolyn, what would he do with me, and I'm black. But then beau Tom, who looked strangely grown-up and who would look awfully ludicrous at that age wearing short pants with his underwear showing, reached into his other pocket and pulled out another pair of gloves—black leather.

"Carolyn gave me these," he said, slipping them on with effort, sucking his teeth, and his ears were red. "I'm gonna really do a job on you, Mitchell, I'm gonna cream you," smacking one fist into an open palm.

"Aw, stuff," came a voice in back of me.

And another: "Look out, now."

And this one: "Holy cow."

My heart had shifted into a rapid, unstoppable gear, my knees were talking to each other and I was just about able to get my gloves on in time for Tom's advance of two black leather fists with huge knuckles held high in front of his face. He came in high but went for the stomach, still with too little force to penetrate my heavy underwear, wool shirt, cardigan sweater and wool overcoat. I grabbed his hand, and we went down into the hard bank of snow. We tossed and grunted and swung wildly, and grabbing handfuls of snow, aimed for each other's faces. Soon I was on my back swallowing snow, and then I was on top trying to push snow into Tom's face, and we both tried to get up but slipped and landed on our backs. Our clothes were getting soaked, my socks were wet and freezing my feet. When we both finally got to our feet, I was hit with the strange idea that this could turn into another seesaw record, that we could slip and turn in this snow all night—maybe until we caught pneumonia. But gaining our footing, we went at it again. My fear had been assuaged through the heat of battle, and my heart was beating calmly. But neither of us gained the advantage. Tom and I fought until most of the crowd had left for dinner, saying that wasn't nothing and neither of us was doing anything. And when Tom and I looked at each other, saw that we were drenched in snow, had buttons missing from the front of our parkas, and were staggering to stay on our feet, to keep our balance, we just stood there. Until puffing, he said, "Don't put your hands on my girl again," so slowly it sounded as if he were measuring the decibel level of each word. Tom waved his hand at me and walked away.

I started to run after him, but was stopped by the difficulty of explaining my story to Tom. I couldn't tell him, one of my main boys, that Carolyn and I were testing the front steps at the same time, she on the right banister and I on the left.

"Mitchell, can I hold your hand? I'm afraid I might fall," she said.

She, Carolyn Meters, moon-faced, round hips moving inside her winter coat, smiling, was standing on the other side of the steps. She had one boot on the higher step, and she was holding out her arms toward me. I thought she must have been joking, so I smiled and took another step down.

"Mitchell, will you help me?" She came over to my side of the steps with two brave, huge steps. Was looking right into my eye. Put her white hand out. Touched mine. Was looking good. So I gave her my hand and led her down the steps as if we were playing ring-around-the-rosy. Reaching the sidewalk coated with ice, I turned to say good-bye just as she slipped on her heel and grabbed me around the waist and pushed her blond hair into my face. I pushed Carolyn—her eyes widened as if she were flying on a backward roller-coaster—pushed her away and saw her stumble, grab at the sky, and fall on the ice, legs going up to show black panties.

"Mitchell?"

I started walking backward, my eyes on her. Carolyn's eyes were glassy, and she scrambled around in the snow on her knees, and I turned and ran. Now, how could I tell Tom that I did not feel equal to touch such snow-white beauty? It would be asking too much to expect him to understand. Tom, your girl's touch sent the kind of chills through me that one feels in the presence of regality. And who was I to pretend worthiness? Can you dig that with your boldacious self? Can you see how, in my confusion, I had to get my hat? Oh, I know race relations in Chatsworth were good. But I still didn't feel capable of her touch.

If that was the worst of our many times, surely the great seesaw venture was the best.

"Hey, Tom," I said after he had been on for a while. "She saw seesaws at the seashore."

The gang laughed as Tom tongue-twisted over the words.

After we were sawing for a time, a few of the spectators explained their leaving due to circumstances beyond their control. Others had to leave for dinner, but all would return. Up, down, up, down. The seesaw was starting to squeak in the middle, so we sent someone for oil. My hands were puffing up as fat as pig's feet. My knees felt glued to a ninety-degree angle, my arms ached as if I had ambidextrously hurled a doubleheader. And was I seeing correctly? Was Tom's thumb Tom's thumb or was it his arm? Somebody brought back an alarm clock. Murphy kept wolfing, kept jumping bad about our being scared, until I balanced myself on my head while holding on to the rungs. Tom got tired and had to be replaced. Somebody brought a portable radio.

It got dark. My remarkably ingenious schoolmates lined up flashlights along the operating path of the seesaw. They cheered us on, clapped us on, stomped their feet on the gravel. It was all and everything for Mitchell Mibbs, the great seesaw record-maker.

The food started coming about eight-thirty. They brought matzo balls, meatballs, baked potatoes, collard

Elect your
Local 79
Executive

Dubas, Anne — President
Casey, Denis — 1st Vice-President
Dembinski, Ann — 2nd Vice-President*
Draxl, Rudy — Recording Secretary
O'Keefe, Brian — Treasurer
Collins, Muriel — Membership
Secretary*

Kenney, Steve — City Unit Officer*
Holder, Livy — Metro Unit Officer
— Metro Licensing Unit
Officer
Boodhoo, Thelma — Riverdale Service Unit
Officer*
Jovellanos, Anastacio — Riverdale Professional
Unit Officer*
Lagacé, Lina — Metro Part-Time
Unit Officer*
Acclaimed

Executive Board

Blair, Vivolyn
Bower, Maureen
Capati, Mila
Goodfellow, Russ
Hamilton, Kim
Johnston, Wendy
Jones, Doug

Kaur, Sarjeet
Kelpin, Wolfgang
Kuusela, Irene
Marcelline, Peter
Taylor, Fred
Umengan, Josie

A STRONG TEAM FOR TOUGH TIMES AHEAD

 108

25/04/58

1993

S M T W T F S	S M T W T F S	S M T W T F S	S M T W T F S
JANUARY	**FEBRUARY**	**MARCH**	**APRIL**
. . . . . 1 2	1 2 3 4 5 6	1 2 3 4 5 6	. . . . 1 2 3
3 4 5 6 7 8 9	7 8 9 10 11 12 13	7 8 9 10 11 12 13	4 5 6 7 8 9 10
10 11 12 13 14 15 16	14 15 16 17 18 19 20	14 15 16 17 18 19 20	11 12 13 14 15 16 17
17 18 19 20 21 22 23	21 22 23 24 25 26 27	21 22 23 24 25 26 27	18 19 20 21 22 23 24
24 25 26 27 28 29 30	28	28 29 30 31	25 26 27 28 29 30
31			

S M T W T F S	S M T W T F S	S M T W T F S	S M T W T F S
MAY	**JUNE**	**JULY**	**AUGUST**
. 1	. . 1 2 3 4 5	. . . . 1 2 3	1 2 3 4 5 6 7
2 3 4 5 6 7 8	6 7 8 9 10 11 12	4 5 6 7 8 9 10	8 9 10 11 12 13 14
9 10 11 12 13 14 15	13 14 15 16 17 18 19	11 12 13 14 15 16 17	15 16 17 18 19 20 21
16 17 18 19 20 21 22	20 21 22 23 24 25 26	18 19 20 21 22 23 24	22 23 24 25 26 27 28
23 24 25 26 27 28 29	27 28 29 30	25 26 27 28 29 30 31	29 30 31
30 31			

S M T W T F S	S M T W T F S	S M T W T F S	S M T W T F S
SEPTEMBER	**OCTOBER**	**NOVEMBER**	**DECEMBER**
. . . . 1 2 3 4	. . . . . 1 2	1 2 3 4 5 6	. . . . 1 2 3 4
5 6 7 8 9 10 11	3 4 5 6 7 8 9	7 8 9 10 11 12 13	5 6 7 8 9 10 11
12 13 14 15 16 17 18	10 11 12 13 14 15 16	14 15 16 17 18 19 20	12 13 14 15 16 17 18
19 20 21 22 23 24 25	17 18 19 20 21 22 23	21 22 23 24 25 26 27	19 20 21 22 23 24 25
26 27 28 29 30	24 25 26 27 28 29 30	28 29 30	26 27 28 29 30 31
	31		

1994

S M T W T F S	S M T W T F S	S M T W T F S	S M T W T F S
JANUARY	**FEBRUARY**	**MARCH**	**APRIL**
. 1	. . 1 2 3 4 5	. . 1 2 3 4 5	. . . . . 1 2
2 3 4 5 6 7 8	6 7 8 9 10 11 12	6 7 8 9 10 11 12	3 4 5 6 7 8 9
9 10 11 12 13 14 15	13 14 15 16 17 18 19	13 14 15 16 17 18 19	10 11 12 13 14 15 16
16 17 18 19 20 21 22	20 21 22 23 24 25 26	20 21 22 23 24 25 26	17 18 19 20 21 22 23
23 24 25 26 27 28 29	27 28	27 28 29 30 31	24 25 26 27 28 29 30
30 31			

S M T W T F S	S M T W T F S	S M T W T F S	S M T W T F S
MAY	**JUNE**	**JULY**	**AUGUST**
1 2 3 4 5 6 7	. . . 1 2 3 4	. . . . . 1 2	. 1 2 3 4 5 6
8 9 10 11 12 13 14	5 6 7 8 9 10 11	3 4 5 6 7 8 9	7 8 9 10 11 12 13
15 16 17 18 19 20 21	12 13 14 15 16 17 18	10 11 12 13 14 15 16	14 15 16 17 18 19 20
22 23 24 25 26 27 28	19 20 21 22 23 24 25	17 18 19 20 21 22 23	21 22 23 24 25 26 27
29 30 31	26 27 28 29 30	24 25 26 27 28 29 30	28 29 30 31
		31	

S M T W T F S	S M T W T F S	S M T W T F S	S M T W T F S
SEPTEMBER	**OCTOBER**	**NOVEMBER**	**DECEMBER**
. . . . 1 2 3	 1	. . 1 2 3 4 5	. . . . 1 2 3
4 5 6 7 8 9 10	2 3 4 5 6 7 8	6 7 8 9 10 11 12	4 5 6 7 8 9 10
11 12 13 14 15 16 17	9 10 11 12 13 14 15	13 14 15 16 17 18 19	11 12 13 14 15 16 17
18 19 20 21 22 23 24	16 17 18 19 20 21 22	20 21 22 23 24 25 26	18 19 20 21 22 23 24
25 26 27 28 29 30	23 24 25 26 27 28 29	27 28 29 30	25 26 27 28 29 30 31
	30 31		

Published by the Campaign for the Executive Team

08.02.91

19.11.59

04.10.58

19.05.81

04.02.8?

greens, cold rolls—and it all tasted good. Dogs were running and barking over the schoolyard. A parent came over, shook her head and left with her son (who was a punk anyway). Pennants were brought, and I waved one in the air while supporting myself with one foot on the seesaw.

Soon there was a line of substitutes by the other end of the seesaw that must have reached across the street. "My turn, my turn," they yelled. "Let me get on." Not until I noticed a familiar-looking girl did I realize what they were putting down: some were getting back into the line again. I jumped (or fell) off the seesaw, looked at my watch, announced that I had just set the record at ten-thirty, and was going. Yawning, they gave me spirited applause, picked up their blankets, flashlights, pizza boxes, slippers, dog chains, stopwatches, binoculars, cookies, radios and other notabilia.

"You're the champ, Mitchell," announced a half-dozen, dragging their equipment. Murphy was silent, was easing away, hands in his pockets. I was exhausted. I touched but couldn't feel, inhaled but couldn't smell, ached all over. But as I wobbled toward home and at last struggled up the steps, I kept hearing them proclaim me the champ. As I collapsed on the rug in the living room, the crowd's yelling was still in my ears.

Now, if they think I was bad then, if they think I was something of a hero at age thirteen, wait until they hear about this. Tom, Max, Murphy—they'll all blow their minds when they pin the champ's recent escapade.

But now, on! Enough of this digression. On to the nitty gritty. Old men, tighten up on your hearing aids. Old ladies, adjust your rockers and wipe clean your spectacles. We're shifting some well-oiled gears now, we're ready to motor, jim. Ready to hear about Jeff?

11

THE WHOLE STREET SMELLED LIKE PUMPKIN PIE, AND
the Chatsworth people were acting as if they had snakes
in their boots. Pumpkins, some weighing 278¼ pounds,
were piled up on the sidewalks, on buck wagons, in the
middle of Atlantic Avenue, lined up and piled everywhere. The pennants and signs were streaming from the
telephone wires, flyers were tacked on the telephone
poles, notices were propped up in the windows of the
Rexall drugstore, the Kresge five and dime, Sarah's
soda-pop store, even Pep Boys' hardware store. The
biggest pennant, made from someone's torn bedsheet,
was strung from a telephone pole to a light pole; it
spanned the whole street, reading 15TH ANNUAL CHATS-
WORTH PUMPKIN FESTIVAL, and kept turning over from
the wind. And there were red, white and blue streamers
stuck on the pumpkins.

Uncle and I stopped in front of Sadie Lawson's
streetside stand.

"Melvin, you better come over here, chile, and get
some of these concoctions before I run out," she said,
apron already spotted and splotched with pumpkin so
early in the morning. "You know the white folks love
my cooking, and they'll buy me out before our people
can get their pocketbooks together. Where you been
keeping yourself, anyway? Don't never come over

across the tracks anymore, staying cooped up in the woods."

"What do you have, Sadie?" asked Uncle, shaved and face smooth from being smacked with alcohol. He spread out his legs, pulled on the straps of his blue-denim coveralls.

"Melvin, you know better than to ask"—laughing, the barrettes in her silver hair glinting in the sunlight, fat sides shaking under her apron; this old Negro woman cook was laughing and bending down, looking under her stand now, reaching down. "I've got so much, it all can't go on the table. Here—try this—pumpkin fudge."

"Pumpkin fudge?"

"You ain't seen nothing yet"—reaching again—"how about pumpkin marmalade or pumpkin preserves?" Then throwing off the white table covering and exposing everything, "I've got—if you want something hot —pumpkin burgers, pumpkin soup, pumpkin stew and pumpkin hash. Over on the edge of the table here I got cold things: pumpkin ice cream, pumpkin custard, pumpkin pudding, pumpkin Jell-O."

"I don't see nothing I like yet, really," said Uncle, scratching for a beard that wasn't there.

"Well, how about some pumpkin cake? See here? Or maybe you'll like pumpkin cookies, pumpkin dough-nuts or pumpkin bread."

"Do you have any pumpkin pie, Sadie? I think I'd like a pie."

Uncle took the pie, and we moved farther up the street. The high school marching band, dressed in gray and blue, was parading down the street as if they had been scattered apart by a cannon. Because of the pumpkins everywhere. The drum major was leading a sinuous course around, between, over and across the pumpkins lying in his path. They were all out of tune, stepping on pumpkins and losing their balance, the tuba player almost falling and taking that loss of footing as a warning to walk ever so slowly, falling way behind the rest of the band—so far that his blowing was like a faraway owl's hooting. The trumpets were on one side of the street, on the sidewalk; the drummer was trying to keep his footing on the other, his rolls more like scattered beats. But they, the people of Chatsworth, didn't care. They, bitten by some pumpkinitis bug, acting mad as pink spiders, waved their streamers in the air, yelled, clapped for the dispersed Chatsworth High School marching band.

"That's some band, huh, Melvin? Listen to that music. What is it, 'Stars and Stripes Forever'?" It was a neighbor we hadn't seen since the last festival. "How you been, anyway? Getting ready for the deer season?"

Uncle: "Yeah, I guess I'll do some shooting. How you been makin' out, Will?" We had started up again, were taking a side street, and Will stayed with us.

"Not bad. You seen my Sally's pumpkin pie yet? It won the prize, you know. Come on, I'll show you," pushing Uncle around another corner.

It was sitting atop a twelve-foot wooden judge's stand with a red ribbon hanging from a wire pin, another pin holding a sign, "First Prize." Uncle and I had to bend back our necks, then we had to step back one, two paces in order to get a full view.

"It's two hundred and ninety pounds, and it took six and a half hours for her to bake, Melvin. She used one hundred and twenty pounds of milk and water and thirty-six pounds, five ounces of pie dough. How do you like it? Big, huh? Say, are you going to be in the pie-eating contest?"

Silence. Uncle jingling change in his coveralls, licking, and then sticking up a forefinger to test the wind. Popguns, noisemakers and horns were going off in the background on Atlantic Avenue, and the gigantic yellow pumpkin smelled like a squash farm, and Will was leaning over toward Uncle, he was looking my uncle straight in the eyes and kicking dust up while some strains from a fiddle broke the silence and we knew the square-dancing had started—all this hesitating while I, holding the tin pie pan in one hand, pinched my nostrils for fear of suffocating from the odor of so much pumpkin. Uncle drew in a deep breath.

"Melvin, are you going to be in the pie-eating contest? I am. I didn't eat dinner last night and haven't had breakfast."

I knew Uncle was considering the prospects for failure, was considering the uncountably preposterous contingencies that only someone with his outlandish penchant for the unexpected would fear; I knew his imagination brought up these eventualities: having his nose pushed into the middle of a pie; eating a pie that had turned rotten; choking on the pieces; and countless kinds of weird phenomena that would stand in the way of victory.

"No, I think Mitchell and I will mosey on over to the auction. I don't feel like eating too much today. Stomach acting up."

So we passed more piles of pumpkins; passed a group gathered around men in the pumpkin-lifting contest, struggling to raise up a pumpkin that had the number 235 painted on it. We marched down the side street, passing the baton-twirlers' contest, and started into an open field, beyond which you could see almost to the mountains in New Hampshire. It was mud now, and our feet sank into it as if we were trudging through soft clay. We saw the barker standing on the tent stage, Chatsworth residents, restless, shifting their positions in the high weeds. We moved into the thick of the crowd. Uncle nodded, waved at acquaintances, I still had the pie.

"Now, what we have here, folks, is a rooster wagon. Who'll start off with a bid of two bucks? Come on, who?

Do I hear two bucks? Who'll start off with a deuce?" He sold it for six dollars.

"Now, who'll give me an honest bid for an eighteen-ninety raisin seeder—in amazing shape. Who, huh? Do I hear seven . . . will somebody give me seven . . . start at seven . . . anybody?" Sold to the woman with the pumpkin-colored dress and shawl for thirteen dollars.

"Now, here I have a crimper for ruffles and things, and I'll start out with just asking for three bucks. How about you, Mel Horner, don't you need a crimper?" Laughter. Slushing of shoes in mud. "Who'll beat Mel out. Who'll start the bidding at three before Mel takes this crimper home with him, humm? Come on, get off some of that pumpkin money, move those mouths. Do I hear three bucks? Do I do I ahear three um bucks uh do I do I ahear ahear a three a three bucks uh wanna hear a three a three a three uh who's got the three th three th three bucksa bucksa three bucksa bucksa comma comma ma gimme gimme gimme a three a three . . ." Sold for four bucks.

Megaphone high in the air, the caller said, while I watched a baton fly high over the rooftop of a building near Atlantic Avenue: "Now, what I have here is the buy of a lifetime. A pure thoroughbred, pedigreed boxer dog of eight months. Somebody left him in front of the dog pound with his papers," waving papers above his head, "and I've got them right here to prove it. Now, who wants a good watchdog or companion? Look at his white stockings. Look at the beautiful white mark on his chest, look at those ears, look at the limbs. Who'll start with fifty? Do I hear a hear a fifty to start it off?"

"Fifty dollars bid!" The voice was so high-pitched, so piercing, and so unexpectedly thrust over the heads of the audience, it took everybody by surprise. A little girl? Voice that was so similar in pitch to a crow's caw. Then a few full-throated laughs filtering from the back of the crowd. Voice that surprised even me, and Uncle looking down at me, all kinds of wind-swept Maine faces turned in my direction, some grinning with teeth missing, one pointing—all this before I realized that the words had come from my mouth.

"What ails you, boy? You don't have no fifty dollars, do you?"

"Okay, we gotta gotta fifty from Melvin Pip's boy over there. Melvin's got more dogs than enough, but he knows a buy when he sees one . . . do I hear a hear a sixty?"

"Can we get him, Uncle? Can we get him just for me?"

"Whatch you gonna do with a dog? Don't we have enough?"

So Uncle won the bid at one-fifty, and I ran through the mud to the top of the stand, grabbed Jeff, who took to me as if we were old friends. He jumped up on me and licked my face, didn't he?

It was time to go, then.

"You don't even know that much about dogs to take care of a pup!" The pie was in the back seat, and Uncle was starting the motor, clearing his throat, tugging at his coverall straps.

"Listen, Uncle," I started, "do you know why dogs circle around a spot before they lie down? Because it goes back to their ancestors who lived in high grass."

"That right?"

"That's right. And I know plenty about dogs. I've been watching you all these years handle Tojo, Major and Plato. I can take care of him. Do you know why dogs have cold noses?" I was sitting on my knees now and leaning my head out the window.

"No."

"I'll tell you someday," pulling my head in and looking back at Jeff, whose head was on the edge of the seat, whose paws were on either side of his head, whose body was lying in a semicircle. We turned into the road that brings you past the side yard where the pear tree and hammock are. And the dogs started barking like whooping Indians. Like pumpkin-festival goers at the beauty contest. Like hounds on the rabbit's tail. Jeff sat up, was rolled up against the door as Uncle turned the Ford to the front of the house, regained his balance, sat up on his haunches. I imagined the hounds charging over the fence, galloping through the back yard, breaking that yard's gate down, stampeding through the side yard, leaping over the front fence, and rushing toward the Ford to get at Jeff.

"They smell him," said Uncle, clearing his throat and clearing it again, more insistently and louder the second time. "That's why they're barking, making all that noise. They won't like him so much; better keep him away." He turned off the motor. The four of us, the first time that we were together as a family, were a portrait photographer's find. I could have stood on the roof (would it have held me?), Jeff could be looking out the back window, and Uncle could be standing by the door with his foot on the runningboard. Because of the way we were sitting there wondering what to do and how to do it and when to do it—it would have made a good entry in our family album. The motor, now turned off, was still ticking, and Uncle was staring ahead through the front windshield with his pipe held steadfast and his jaws tense. Thinking. I suppose his mind was digesting alternatives, weighing options, determining methods, drafting a mental blueprint. He looked over to me and said, "I can't think of anything. What are you going to name him, anyway?" Pushing down on the doorknob, swinging his long legs from under the steering wheel and out to the ground.

"Jeff," I said, for no reason at all except that the name came to my lips just as automatically as a tapped knee jerks. As easily as I would say hi or good-bye, I named Jeff, Jeff. For no special reason. I got out, and we led Jeff—new-found, new-named confidant and sympathizer among our ranks—up the steps to the porch, to the welcome mat, to the doorknob.

"What's this? What the hell are you two bringing here?" Looking down at Uncle, Julius was standing high on the doorstep, hands folded, blocking the doorway. "Pearl"—turning his head to the living room—"they're bringing another dog in here." Listening to her voice, then, "Where did you get it from?"

"I bought it for Mitchell at the pumpkin festival," said Uncle. We stood abreast, facing Julius. Jeff sniffed Julius's toes.

Again leaning inside: "They got it at that silly pumpkin festival. Uncle bought it for Mitchell, he says." Listening again. "What kind of dog is it, and where will it stay?"

"Can't you see it's a boxer? We plan to keep it inside with us. He's a family-companion dog."

Julius again: "They plan to keep it inside as a family companion, Pearl. Can't hear you . . . what? How tame . . . oh, house-trained." Addressing us now: "Is the dog house-trained?"

Uncle: "I think so; we'll see."

Julius: "They think so, Pearl." Then, moving back a step, pushing the screen door all the way back so it yawned, he said, "Okay, she says bring him inside, but don't let him get on the furniture."

We tramped back to the kitchen, where Mother was bending over the oven. I held Jeff's metal collar.

"This is Jeff," I said. "Uncle just bought him for me as a pet."

Mother, aproned, turned from her stew pot, looked at us while holding a long cooking fork. Looked down at Jeff, frowned. Looked at Julius, compressed her lips, and rubbed her nose with her left hand.

"This is Mitchell's new pet," I heard Uncle say,

kneeling down, rubbing Jeff's forehead, smoothing the short hair of my boxer's back. "We've got his papers and everything. Mitchell's going to keep him in the house for a pet."

Mother, next to the oven, was swaying back and forth on her sandals, and the long fork collected the light from the window and beamed in her hands, shone in my eyes. Her eyelids were dropping and opening, and Mother's head seemed to be attached to a rubber neck which couldn't hold the weight. Perhaps a sleepwalker. Perhaps a wave-drenched swimmer stumbling out of the surf. Perhaps a deep-sea diver walking on the bottom of the ocean. Maybe even a blind woman.

"Oh, Christ, Melvin! Another pain in the neck? He'll be crapping all over the rugs, jumping on the furniture and leaving hair, smelling up the place with dog odor!" She leaned on the sink with her elbow, and the sunlight caught half of her face for an instant, turned her face yellow-tan, but she moved her head back into the shadow of the kitchen light. "I have enough trouble as it is keeping this place clean—dusting, mopping, scrubbing, now a dog."

I was kneeling down and patting Jeff too. Both Uncle and I were down. My eyes were level with Mother's knees, and I was suddenly appreciating the fatness of her thigh, the fullness and symmetry of her finely tapered lower leg. Her legs had a fuzz of hair covering them, and they looked strong anyway, but stronger when the muscles worked as she pivoted, turned, lifted on her toes to reach the cupboard. Her legs were promises that only a painter could accept.

Mother said, reaching for cups, "Why didn't you ride your bike to school yesterday, Mitchell? I paid good money for that thing. You begged and begged me for it, and I finally got it for you, and now you just keep it in the cellar. You don't appreciate anything. You beg for something, and then you don't use it." And then, turning, opening her eyes wide, struck by a thought, she said, "Just like you, Julius. You beg and beg and then poop out." Raising her voice. "You're just like a kid, can't handle what you ask for, right?"

Julius crossed his legs, leaned against the glass window of the china closet, blew sighs and tsk tsks, shook his head left to right.

Jeff thumped his paws against the worn squares of tile, got up on fours and looked around at us, raised his left rear limb beside the kitchen table leg and shot out a hot, yellow, liquid line of urine under the table. The line splattered against the wall, arced down to the floor and trickled under the chair, and soon Jeff's own rivulet was crawling across the floor. And wasn't it fortunate that Jeff had no tail to tuck between his legs, for he would have had to do some tucking. Instead, he resorted to ducking—ducking his head right out of the kitchen and into the living room.

So Julius became a roaring asshole, a cyclone of laughter. He was pressing his back against the closet. His mouth was opened wide like a puppet's, his head was thrown back—his hair smeared the cabinet glass—and his knees started to give, bend, and so he was half-kneeling, sliding his back down the closet, pointing at the urine that was inching toward the middle of the kitchen. Howling, wheezing, snorting, coughing. Then losing his breath and just holding his stomach with his gold fillings flashing and his eyes stuck upward as if he had been stabbed or shot, the rings on his fingers gleaming. Gasping and catching his breath, he choked out, "Did you see that? Did you see that four-legged bastard cock his leg and piss all over the kitchen?" Clapping his hands together, next pointing at Mother. "Ah haw, ah haw, look at Pearl, she don't know what to do. Look at the look on her face, will you? Ooh hoo hoo ooo whee." Cheeks sucking in. "Get the mop, Melvin!"

I jumped up from the floor. Uncle hustled to the back corner, got the mop, dabbed and patted and swished it over the floor.

And Mother? She had been wavering, still with the cups in her hand, had been watching Julius fall into a paralysis of laughter. But now she was bitten by the same bug and grunted. Then coughed. Then shook her head up and down while grinning with closed eyes, started snickering, then laughed outright. She put down the cups, Julius came over to her, and they leaned their backs against the sink, held hands, and directed their laughter at Uncle, who was mopping as if his life depended on it.

"Don't forget that little spot over there, Uncle," laughed Julius, patting my mother on her thigh, and she sniggered. "Phew, how can you stand it, that smell," said Julius, squeezing his wide nostrils and exaggerating his breathing. "Ain't that smell something, Pearl?"

"Oh, let's get out of here. The dinner's almost done anyway. Damned pain-in-the-neck dog." Walking out, leaving Uncle and me in the kitchen.

Nor was the dinner such an auspicious occasion for Jeff's first appearance in Uncle's grand old house. We had collards and pig tails, and Uncle and I were dropping bones under the table for Jeff. He was cracking and pawing the bones, playing with them, placing his face sideways on the floor to get a good tooth grip. Suddenly Jeff got up, trotted over to the sink and hunched down his hips as if he were sliding under a fence.

"Jesus Christ, he's going to shit!" Julius jumped up, grabbed Jeff by the tail, and dragged him to the back door, flung him out. "Not in here you won't."

"You didn't hurt him, did you, Julius? He's only a puppy," I said.

"Hell, I can't eat my dinner now. Damned dog.

Crappin' at mealtime. Why don't you house-train that mutt? No, I didn't hurt him, but I should have kicked him up his ass."

Yes, Jeff, old fellow, there were rough beginning days for you in the house, but you eventually came through beautifully, holding your own. Even when you broke wind in the living room—remember, big fellow? It was after dinner that same Friday. You had been allowed back inside to listen to *Mr. and Mrs. North, Johnny Dollar, The Shadow,* and *Amos 'n' Andy* with us. We were in our customary seating arrangements, Uncle and I facing them, but now you in the middle on the rug. Uncle, drinking wine mixed with beer (calling it a certain kind of champagne). Mother, sipping from a whiskey-sour glass. Julius, slurping beer. I had my drumsticks tapping on the rug.

It was when the insurance investigator was ending up with his expense accounting and signing off as "Yours truly, Johnny Dollar." There was the buzz of the radio, the silence before station identification, then an odor diffusing throughout the living room. Mother's eyes opened, she formed wrinkles in her forehead. She looked at Julius. He frowned, looked at her, then Uncle, then me. Another gaseous release from Jeff, this one obeying all laws of physics, rising as all light gases must, piling on top of the previous discharge, joining with it, encircling the four of us, mixing with Uncle's tobacco fumes. Uncle cleared his throat. Mother rubbed her nose and kept her fingers near her nostrils seconds longer than usual, and Julius patted his hair, sucked his teeth. Whom to blame? She and he squirmed on the couch, moved away from each other toward the edge. Uncle stood up, brushed the front of his wide-bottom denim trousers. Naturally Julius, with that broad, smashed-in nose of his, was the one to pinpoint Jeff.

Standing up so fast that he dripped shot-glass amounts of beer on his cord pants (this hurt him),

Julius pointed a long-nailed finger at Jeff just as the next program was beginning and shouted, "It's the mutt. That nasty-assed dog has been farting here all night. He's trying to gas us—get him out of here." Waving his hands in front of his face, letting out a few phews. "Phew, it stinks," he said. "A dog—a nasty little puppy dog making all that stink." He turned off the radio, and the two of them went into their bedroom with their glasses and beer cans.

Like a theater audience waiting for the screen to be illuminated, we three, Uncle, Jeff and I, sat in the half-dark room looking at the bedroom door that had been slammed in our faces. From the crack of light under the door we could see shadows moving. And the voices, muffled, seeped through: "I'll get you out of this crap, Pearl, baby, don't worry. We'll hear from New York soon. I've got a lot of irons in the fire there, lots of my main men are working their backs off to get you that one break. Just one break is all you need, honey."

"I'm over thirty now, Julius," we heard her say, squeaking the mattress as she climbed into bed and the light went out. "I don't have much time to make it."

"You'll make it—somehow. Say, did you talk to Melvin yet about the house—about making sure he leaves it to you?"

"No, not yet."

Uncle and I tiptoed to the dining room. We formed a triangle with Jeff—sitting on the rug. Uncle turned the radio on very low. We listened to *Amos 'n' Andy* in the dark on the floor. We patted Jeff on his head and back and shoulders, and I tapped on his back lightly with my sticks, and Jeff kept the bottom of his mouth on the floor. He was facing both of us. His pupils were wide, and the whites were bright and he seemed contented. We didn't get some of the jokes because the radio was so low, but we were happy, the three of us, and we sat as closely as we could.

12

"JULIUS CLARK, JULIUS CLARK, PLEASE. TELEGRAM FOR Julius S. Clark." Hard banging against the front door. I climbed over Uncle, who lay on his back in gray-flannel pajamas. He was jerking one side of his snoring, unshaved face to the other. I climbed and got a whiff of his underarms and liked his hardy huntsman's smell, jumped out of the bed and ran to the door. "Telegram for Julius Clark, please. Sign here. Thank you, Mr. Clark," turning from me, machine-gunning his feet down the steps, jumping on his bicycle and making it.

"Hey," I said, my hand reaching out to him. The first visitor we'd had in months, and gone already. Even Jeff, then a one-year veteran of our abode, stuck his nose out to watch the bicycle streak down the road, the shadow of wheels and churning feet telescoping against the trees.

"What's it? Somebody called for me?" Julius's bare feet paddled against the hardwood of the front bedroom. He was scratching his pajamas at the stomach, had his hair tied up in a scarf, smelled—not virile and husky as Uncle, but musty, rancid—reminding me of a foul-odored vassal from my readings of *Ivanhoe*. "What's that—a telegram—for me? Gimme!" He snatched the message from my hands, tore through the glassine, halted, leaned against the wall to bend his leg and pick and flick dead skin from between his toes.

And his big toe looked like a walnut. He read the telegram. "Hot the mighty mo! My prayers are answered. Oh, Jesus, you have come to save us. Pearl, Pearl, come here. Get out that bed, gal, I've got good news."

I could hear Uncle rustling with his dreams and groaning in the back room, could hear the mattress squeak in Mother's room, heard the grandfather clock ticking in the dining room and the chickens clucking from the back yard, even heard a trailer truck from the highway, it was that early and quiet. Mother, lifting her robe over her body as if it were a cape, leaned from the doorway.

"What?" Picking sleep from the edges of her eyes.

"Pearl." Julius swung around, feet missing Jeff's paws, caught Mother around the waist, danced her past me. "Listen: 'Come to audition tonight.' That's what it says. This telegram just came. We got an audition, baby. 'Signed, Oscar Cooke.' *The* Oscar Cooke. Handles all those name stars at the Blue Fender. Baby, we've got it made. We dump this place for the Apple. No more Living End or Rialto for us. The big time. THE BIG TIME. Cadillacs, furs, diamonds, champagne, you name it. I knew my boys, I knew my contacts in the city would come through okay."

"Let me see."

"Oh, no you don't!" Julius laughed, uncircling his arm from Mother's waist, hopping on the couch, and waving the yellow, rectangular message over his head, a gold-toothed mountebank.

"Let me see, Julius," said Mother, the softness of her voice wavering in anticipation, a smile of cool but yet of expectation and maybe imminent delirium. A smile about to explode into ecstatic laughter. One of the softest, girlish, most tender smiles I have ever seen Mother wear. I think I even smiled. "Come on, silly, let me see, let me read it for myself," holding out a palm toward him.

Julius was gone again, leaping over the table and out to the dining room, shaking the walls with his hard-skinned heels. Shortly, stepping his little legs upon the seats of the diningroom chair; soon, on the table—*standing* on the table itself; in the middle of the table with his arms outstretched, forming a Y and waving the yellow message. When Mother put a knee on the chair's seat to balance her ascent, a tan breast fell out from her robe and swung, startled me, made Jeff whimper and squat. Soon she too was on the table. They both were on the table. High-stepping around on Uncle's table in the dining room. Screaming and giggling through an improvised war dance. And Jeff whimpering and snorting and shaking his head. I still in my pajamas. Mother snatched the telegram from Julius, read it to herself, I saw her eyes bulge, then she shouted, threw the telegram in the air as if it were one big piece of confetti, grabbed Julius, her husband, around the neck, and they danced in a circle singing until Uncle finally woke up and came to the doorway with both hands scratching his eighth-of-an-inch growth of hair.

They were even laughing when Uncle asked, "What's all this noise for?" They said something about how he looks like a ghost standing there by the door and started tittering. They, holding hands, jumped off the table, and dancing in front of Uncle, ricocheted their voices off his forehead.

"We're leaving this place." They said it together. Then, startled that they should have said the same words at the same time and rejoicing at that discovery.

"Pearl has an audition I got for her in New York to-night. We're going to the Apple today—by bus. We may never come back to this old place, Uncle, once we hit our stride. You'll be sitting here listening to Pearl on the radio, on the record player, stuff like that." Turning

121

around, looking at Jeff and me, who were standing—we must have looked awkward, must have had no cool at all, standing and staring like penguins. Julius pointed to us, nudged Mother. They both cracked up, split their sides, rolled. They were through, done for with laughter. "They're just staring at us, Pearl, look, honey. Oooh hoo hoo whee hoo." He clapped together his hands. "Ah hawk ah hawk ah ha ha ha ha." Uncle was still scratching his head. "The Apple, baby, you and me. Birdland, Red Rooster, Count's, Minton's, we are going to ball. Brooooooom Ball. Whoooo Wheee. Go get your things packed."

But did they have to take all morning packing? Was it necessary to whoop and bawl, nearly step on Jeff's toes, elbow me out of the way as they tracked back and forth all morning from their bedroom to the attic?

Julius, for instance: "I'm taking my best underwear with me. If I get hit by a car and sent to the hospital, I don't want them to find my BVD's with holes in them."

And Mother, bringing out long white, musty, lacy, velvet gowns: "Julius, do you think I should wear this one or this one, honey?" Carrying dust-layered hat-boxes from the middle bedroom and parading through also with shoe boxes on top of shoe boxes. She transferred black straw hats too, with crushed imitation roses on top and large stick pins as well. All of these things smelled like mothballs.

"I'll never go back to Georgia, I'll never go back, oh no," sang Julius after he had filled his stomach with breakfast. Later it was "I'll take Manhattan, the Bronx, and Staten Island, too," as he pushed his hand and wrist through a sock and found a hole at the end.

When Mother came through one time with a long, wrinkled, pink slip, I was sitting on the couch. I was tapping my drumsticks on the table, while Jeff lay at my feet. Uncle was slouched in the corner chair, his knees looming up, hiding his face. She came through humming, gliding between Uncle and me, when Uncle rose to intercept her. Mother was humming, "Oh when the saints go marching by," and Uncle interrupted her on "marching."

"That's Maybelle's slip, and what are you doing with it?" Uncle stood tall, gestured with his pipe toward the slip on Mother's arm. The other hand trembling by his knee.

"This thing ain't no good, Uncle. I may use it for a dustrag. Why do you keep all those things in the attic and in that bedroom, anyway?" She brought the slip to her nose: "It stinks like mothballs." And rubbing her hand over an area: "It's rough as nails."

My Uncle Melvin Pip raised the back of his hand to his mouth and cleared his throat, then pulled at his wide, canvascloth army belt, then patted out tobacco from his pipe into his palm. "Maybelle's things don't leave here until I leave."

"I'm just taking a few things for my act," snapped Mother, turning into her bedroom.

"What are you taking, Pearl? You've been in and out of that attic all morning. Trying to clean out Maybelle's trunk?" He walked into the doorway of the bedroom. Jeff and I followed. Julius was straightening his stringbean-thin tie in the mirror, and Mother was standing by the bed, her hands on her hips, looking down at her wares on the still-unmade bed. I saw old black hats shaped like knights' visors. I saw white hats with fruit gardens on top. I saw cardboard belts and opaque brown stockings similar to those lady Dixby wears. I saw shoes that had heels as thick as cigars and scarred tips. I saw dark-brown, funky-smelling leg bands, and besides all of these items from Maybelle's past strewn all over the bed, I saw also two leather handbags that had green mold on the sides, scarves with frayed edges and moth holes in the middle, a cable-knit sweater with elbow pads, and a pair of glassless eyeglasses. "Put Maybelle's things back."

"What are you saving them for?" asked Julius, tugging on, pulling on, jerking on his tie. He looked at Uncle through the mirror.

"You forgot, Jul, we don't use her name around here," darting an eye sideways at Uncle and raising her voice. "Why can't you remember, Julius?" said Mother. "Maybelle is real special to Uncle, still."

"Is?" said Julius, raising his eyebrows. "What do you mean, is? I thought she was dead. I thought she had some kind of disease that couldn't be cured and just kicked the bucket."

"I wish you would put those things back, Pearl. You shouldn't bother with her clothes like that. I had them all packed away in the attic and in the room nicely."

Ignoring Uncle, Mother spoke: "She left him, don't you remember I told you, Julius? A thousand times I must have told you about Uncle and his Miss Maybelle. Don't you remember? All these old clothes, these things Uncle keeps in the attic, are memories. He sneaks up there in the middle of the night and plays with this stuff. He's got pictures of their marriage ceremony, and even pictures of her"—glancing at me—"of her with no clothes on."

"What? Melvin?"

"Sure."

"Why?"

"Must be a glutton for punishment. He wants to remember, I guess. She didn't even love him."

And then Mother went on, while Uncle, Jeff and I stood in the doorway watching them pack, watching them pull socks and panties from the drawer and throw them in the suitcases on the floor. She told how Uncle had met Maybelle at a dance when both could jitterbug their shoes off. They fell in love and got married, Uncle convincing his new bride that they should live with his parents. ("That was stupid.") But Uncle was a man of the outdoors, would gather his dogs, guns and traps on the weekends, kiss his wife good-bye, and head for the middle lakes country.

So one evening Uncle brought home a friend for dinner from the lumber mill. The three of them had dinner by candlelight. "Right in that living room out there," she said, pointing. The friend came to visit a few more times. The three of them became very tight. Sometimes on the weekends, they—all three—would drive to the hunting area, Uncle would get out, and the friend would take Maybelle back to the house. Sometimes he would borrow Uncle's car to take Maybelle for roadside tours. "Uncle didn't have the slightest idea of what was going on." Then one day Uncle, on his way to shovel snow off the front steps, was met by a Western Union messenger. He hadn't even noticed yet that the car was missing. But the message said, "WIFE AND DRIVER KILLED IN CRASH IN OHIO." Uncle tried to pretend that they were just out cruising. He refused to believe, even when told of the two suitcases in the trunk and the Pullman tickets to Reno, that Maybelle hadn't planned to come back. "One of his best friends stole his wife and his car. Can you beat that?" Mother threw balled-up socks in the suitcase.

"You let some cat take your woman, Melvin? Damn," said Julius. "You dumber than I thought you was. Well, you don't have to worry about us, we're taking a cab to the circle and then a bus from there to Portsmouth, and then a bus to the Apple. We may never come back to this place, even if you sell it."

"Maybe we'll send for Mitchell in the summer, Julius?" asked Mother, already kowtowing to her manager, suddenly part of the retinue and not the principal.

"Maybe. But Uncle will have to stay here for—for his health. Can you see him in the Apple, on Forty-second Street? They'd run him down." Julius threw back his head and snickered through his nose, smoothed his thin moustache.

So they packed; we watched. And after we had eaten lunch, I remember standing on my shadow in front of the house at noon time and looking at the trunks and bags sitting on the road like pirates' captured goods. The early-spring wind was cutting and whistling through the pines and blowing Uncle's blue kerchief in his nose, and we had to shout to hear each other. The Hawk was whipping Uncle's wide pants around his legs. Mother wore her hat cocked down, over the side of her face, and Julius was twirling his gold-plated keychain. They were looking down the road, they were standing in front of us. Jeff kept blinking his eyes, kept pointing his face down and away from the wind, licking his paws. Now, after having packed music books and underwear; Maybelle's old, long coats and dresses and slips and hats; bright silk ties and Continental suits— after packing bags and trunks all morning, they were ready to say good-bye.

"Do you think I'll make it?" Mother had made a complete about-face, was looking right at me. "Do you think I'm really good enough?" Her lips, pursed, were trembling, and she had her hands together like some reverend mother.

"I think so," I shouted. And she took one small step forward, grinned without separating her lips.

Cupping her hands, she shouted, "I wasn't talking to you, Mitchell." My mistake.

"You got it made," said Julius, patting his hair. "Damned wind puttin' somethin' on my hair."

"What did you say?"

"I said," Julius began, placing his face nearer Mother's, raising his voice in her ear, "that you've got it made, baby."

"Julius, I'm thirty-six years old, you know. I'm no young chippy."

"Don't worry," he said, closer to her ear. "Julius has got things uptight."

Uncle gave Julius a hand lifting the baggage into the cab. Julius rode shotgun. Mother, after the cab had turned around and was ready to go down the road, looked out from the window, and said, "Take care, Mitchell; Mommy will write you." Soon she was a blur of waving hands going in the distance, one of two passengers seen through the cab's back window. The tires spit dust, which was whipped in our faces by the wind. And Uncle coughed, cleared his throat. Jeff was standing forward on all fours as if he were about to bound. So the cab twisted down the road, got smaller and smaller until it faded out.

"They're gone, Mitchell." The three of us were standing facing each other, forming a triangle, when Uncle said that. He didn't even have to shout, although the wind was still high and loud, because we were so close together. "There they go," he said, looking down at me, pulling on his hunter's cap. Then he dabbed at his eye with his kerchief, turned abruptly and went toward the house. Jeff, playful attacker, nipped at the heels of Uncle's boots and he and I followed the owner of this stately old house up the front steps.

We followed him up the steps of the attic too, after we had gone inside, and Jeff's legs thumped and slipped against those steps that started in the middle bedroom.

Careful that we kept our feet only on the support boards so that we didn't step and fall through the floor and end up on the dining-room table, Jeff and I marched behind Uncle. It was a mess of an antique fair, that attic. Julius and Mother had gone through it like scavengers. The letters and faded newspapers were scattered everywhere; records had been cracked, cardboard storage boxes had been rifled. Uncle bent down and picked up a round picture frame. "This is Maybelle,"

he said. "I'm glad they didn't break the frame, Mitchell."

"Did she run away, Uncle?" Slip of the tongue. I was
sorry as soon as I asked, for I knew the question must
have stung him, must have made him doubt my alle-
giance.

Sitting now, Uncle held the picture of his wife in
front of him. "Yes," he whispered, and I was willing to
let it go at that, but he cleared his throat and added,
"but I forgive her. I paid too much attention to my own
life. I guess she just got tired of waiting, so it was my
fault."

"Oh, don't say that, Uncle." I spoke the only words I
could, not being the sentimental type, and knowing he
wasn't either. I couldn't go over to Uncle and pat him
on the back. It's always been difficult for me to express
myself sincerely without feeling as awkward as a man
out of his century. On a dozen occasions I have wanted
to say to—and only to—Uncle, "I love you." But each
time I have weighed the words in my throat, tossed
them around, examined the implications, and looking
over my shoulder for help, abandoned the thought of
such hypersensitive expression. With Jeff I could be
verbose as I wanted. I could rap with Jeff for days on
end, because he couldn't talk back to me. Nevertheless,
I know Uncle was always hip to my feelings for him.
I'm sure by the way we stuck with each other, by the
way we went down together, he knew the set of my
mind toward him. Therefore, although it wasn't the
most strategic comment, it was all I could offer. "Come
on, I'll help you gather up her things," I said, bending
over to grab a clothes hanger.

After I had put the last dusty, ribboned pack of
airmail letters down in a cardboard box, we went
downstairs, Uncle taking some old records with him.
And you'd better believe we had a ball. He put on a
Louis Armstrong, took off his boots, rolled up his

sleeves, threw his cap on top of something—a chair, a table, I can't remember—and said, "Watch me do some steps." Armstrong was blowing and singing some fast song about mama had better do right. I drummed on my practice pad in the middle of the floor, Jeff's nose was by my leg, Uncle—I had never seen him so free— did steps that were out of sight. In his gray hunting socks with the green and red rings near the elastic, he turned in a circle, snapped his fingers, twisted his hips from side to side. "This is called the hucklebuck. May-belle and I used to do it all the time." And he dropped his knees to the floor, eased his back to the rug, and reminded me of a male belly dancer. Jeff whined, sneezed, shook his head as if he couldn't believe it. And all the while Uncle was cutting his rug, laughing and singing, it came to me that I had never in my life seen his teeth show so much. "Listen to this song I used to sing all the time, when I was your age, Mitchell:

> Rainbow at night,
> Sailor's delight.
> Rainbow at noon,
> Rain very soon.

Well, he threw back his head and vibrated the walls with his laughter. "Ain't that something?" he asked, wide eyes bright. "Ain't that just something," stamping his feet. "Hey, Mitchell"—he looked to the side as if someone were listening, then taking the record off, whispering—"how about some wine?" So, on the first of many days where just the three of us romped in that Chatsworth dwelling—on this first day we spent considerable time in the chilly cellar drinking vino of un-known and uncared-for vintage. The hell with 1952 Beaujolais. We went to destruction in the cellar. We blew our minds away, we drank so much cool, red Fancy Passion down there in the dark dampness. And we came out—I staggering and blinded by the spring sunlight. We fell up against the back yard's grape arbor, sat on white lumps of chicken droppings and laughed. And laughed. Jeff bounded after the chickens, who cackled with beaks forward and flapped their wings hard enough to lift their chicken feet one inch off the ground. Jeff fell too, as his hand legs failed to equal the pace of his forelegs. He rolled over on his back, stuck out his tongue, was trying to regain his footing. Oh yes—we had given Jeff some wine too.

"Mitchell, I want you to take care of this house after I die, son," said Uncle, when his elbow bones cracked while getting up from under the arbor. "I have it made out to Pearl now, but I'll change it. Don't let them get it and sell it. You can sell it if you want, but I want you to decide." That was the first time Uncle had ever mentioned the old gray castle's future to me.

We got no letter from Julius and Mother for months, but we didn't mind at first. We could hear anything we wanted to on the radio, and Uncle brought down all of his tough sides on the Mercury label. There is one called "Straighten up and Fly Right" that we played all the time, every night. I got to practice with my drumsticks more, I booked longer and seriously, spending time on material which was not assigned. And wasn't that when my genius began to blossom? After I'd finished my schoolwork, I'd stay up late into the night, reading philosophy, religion, fiction—getting all kinds of smarts.

One night I picked up some lines that almost put a whipping on my mind, they were so clearly meant for me. I read and reread the poem, turned the page upside down, smelled the paper, examined the type face. It was about two in the morning, and I wanted to wake up Uncle and read the poem to him, wanted to share it with someone, anyone. But I knew he wouldn't understand. I started laughing to myself and closing my eyes in the faint light of the living room. I took the book into the kitchen—I was tiptoeing—and read it there to Jeff, who lay and wagged his tail and watched me standing, rocking with the poem's rhythm, gesturing with my arms at points of emphasis. And in my pajamas, the kitchen floor chilling my feet, the poem taking my mind for a ride on words, I shouted out to Jeff:

I saw the best minds of my generation destroyed by madness, starving hysterical naked.

13

WE WERE MAKING IT DOWN THE BRUCKNER EXPRESS-
way, and I had shotgun. In the middle of July. In the
night. We were driving a steady forty, so cars were
sheening, shooting past us so fast, I thought I knew what
it would be like at Indianapolis.

"How're we making out, Mitchell?" asked Uncle,
decked out in his summer finery of white-on-white
shirt, patent-leather shoes, Panama straw hat, wide-
legged pants. I? I was chewing on a peanut-butter-and-
jelly sandwich and trying to navigate us to the Theresa
Hotel in Harlem. I had the map on my lap—wearing
short pants—and my sweatshirt was sweaty. We weren't
making good time at all—had left at noon, here it was
close to ten.

"Everything okay if we get on to the Cross-Bronx
Expressway," I shouted, searching the highway for a
sign, any sign that made sense. "Say, Uncle, do you
think Tony will take care of Jeff and the other dogs?
Do you really think Jeff will be okay?"

"Oh, yeah," looking ahead, biting on his pipe, "Jeff's
in good hands. He'll probably even gain a few
pounds."

So there we were. Finally pushing for the city. Uncle
had gone to the post office that morning, had returned,
had lain in the hammock, had jumped up and announced, "We're going to New York City, Mitchell.

We'd better see what's going on, why your mother hasn't written a word." I thought I knew why she hadn't written, but I kept quiet.

"Hey, there's the Cross-Bronx, turn here, Uncle," I shouted, and we took the exit almost on two wheels. "Now," I said, catching my breath and swallowing down my heart, "all we need is the Harlem River Drive, and we're all set."

But Uncle must have been afraid to awaken me when I fell asleep, must have been swelled with a new sense of confidence, for the next thing I knew, a white face was spitting and bellowing in my ear, frightening me to consciousness. White gloves clenching the door. Bright silver star sparkling on a dark-blue chest.

"What the hell are you doing, bub?"

I was beginning to get myself together. Car horns were screaming like alarums. Headlights were blinding us up ahead. Passersby, surrounding the car, were peeping in at us from the back, from Uncle's side window, as if we were escaped convicts. Lights, lights, were everywhere, and so was noise, like some psychedelic rehearsal of an out-of-tune rock band. Everything was deafening.

"I said what the hell are you doing, bub, let me see your license." It was the man. His fingers galloped through Uncle's wallet. "Do you know you can't come all the way down here from Maine and just drive any old kind of way? You can't just drive up Broadway the wrong way because you have a flat tire. Now, look at the mess you've caused. Look at those cars staring at you, wondering what in hell ails you."

"You gonna give me a ticket, officer?" asked Uncle, placing his rough hand on the tip of his Panama and leaning down in front of me.

"Am I gonna give you a ticket! Look at you! Driving an old raggedy-ass station wagon that ain't even made anymore, getting a flat tire, and going the wrong way in

133

Times Square. You are gonna get the biggest ticket of your life! Now, get this trap out of here!"

There, the first time in New York, and a flat on the busiest intersection in the world. Clammy-handed and with perspiration running down our cheeks, we pushed the old Ford west on 43rd Street. Ladies and gentlemen pointed at us, laughed at us, ran behind us, and the lights were bright enough to blind us Maine visitors. We pushed the wagon—Uncle pushed from in front while steering—pushed all the way to the pier and left it at a gas station. And then, backs bent, fingers curled and red, legs needing crutches, we tackled 42nd Street.

"The Theresa's on One Hundred and Twenty-fifth Street, Uncle," I said, whispering from exhaustion, and trying to keep in step with his great strides.

"I just want to see what's going on up here," he said, "where all those lights are. See all those lights up there?"

We reached Eighth Avenue. We were jostled and pushed about in the crowd like sacks of Maine potatoes thrown from a jeep. Momentarily I lost Uncle in the press, had to run up to him, for he hadn't even noticed he had lost me and was still talking to his side, where he thought I was.

"Hey, bro." A black man wearing a Continental suit and shades shuffled up to our side. He raised his arm up toward the sky and pulled down a jewelry box. "Wanna buy a five-hundred-dollar diamond ring for ten bills? A buy of a lifetime, man, I ain't jiving. I may talk trash, but I don't sell it." The ring glimmered like sparks from a train wheel.

"Is it really diamond?" asked Uncle, stopping now, snaking his way between passersby, moving his back against a bookstore window.

"Shhh! Be cool, baby," he whispered. "Don't want the whole world to know. I'm trying to do you a favor. Dig"—snatching the ring out of the box, holding it in two fingers—"this is almost a carat. Amost a whole carat. For ten cents, jack."

"A dime?"

Glancing to his left and to his right. "No, no, baby, how you sound, anyway? Ten papers, ten greenbacks, brother. You like it? You wanna cop?"

"I don't think I need a woman's ring," said Uncle, lifting his brim and sending his hand through his hair.

"All right, dig," he said, this corner salesman, shooting his hand inside his jacket. "How about a nice hundred-dollar Omega watch, huh? Self-winding, waterproof, brand new, used by Olympic wrestlers. I'll give it to you for a five spot because I like your Panama sky."

"I don't know if I need it."

"Well, buy it for your son, man."

"Mitchell's my nephew."

"Well, cop anyway, baby, this is a buy of a lifetime. No sense in being cheap about it. All right, dig," he said, talking faster and going into the other side of his coat. "How 'bout a nice transistor radio for a coupla bucks, huh? I could get busted selling you this stuff, baby. I'm trying to do you a *favor*. The man could come and bust me, I could get ten years, jack. You wanna cop or not?"

"I'll have to think about it, we just got in town," said Uncle.

The Continental salesman took a deep breath, sighed, shook his head and walked away. "You missed a buy of a lifetime, baby. You blew something awful."

We kept making our way up 42nd Street. Uncle had to stop to look at the photos of nude women outside the movie theaters. He had to look in the windows of the stores selling cheap cameras, radios, sunglasses and wallets. He had to stop to buy us burning-hot pizzas and, later, rubber-hard, cold hot dogs. Uncle, old man in Manhattan, was like a young boy at the Chatsworth

Pumpkin Festival. He kept pointing at high, bright signs and lights and buildings, and I looked around to see if we were the object of stares. Sure, this was my first time in the Apple, but I wasn't going to blow my cool. I had done too much reading and studying since Mother and Julius had left to be the starry-eyed kid come to the city. Not me.

We kept moving our way up 42nd Street. At Sixth, we tried to walk through the park but were told by the man that it was illegal. At Fifth, two bums lying on the library steps asked us for money to buy books, and we were almost flattened by a taxi as we crossed on the "Don't Walk" sign.

"I think the tire must be fixed now," said Uncle. Location: across the street from Grand Central. "But I've got to take a leak before I start walking again. Let's go see if they have one in the train station."

Again, we were like pinballs knocked about by hurrying New Yorkers—this time in the dimly lit train station I had heard so much about. So this is where the trains from Portland arrived. Following a sign, Uncle and I—two foreigners from the pine trees—took some wide marble steps down to the men's room. Two in white coats to rent you towels, and men lined up in front of urinals—each one was taken—like theatergoers waiting for tickets. Uncle and I got in separate lines. I looked to my left and right, saw that everyone had his hand on his zipper, ready to pull it down, step forward, straddle his legs. When my line diminished and I got to the porcelain bowl, I saw from the corner of my eye the fat, khaki-wearing man with hair on his arms holding his penis and looking at me. It was as thick as a knockwurst, and he was looking at me with no expression and holding it and weighing it, shaking it, flapping it around, and looking straight at my profile. I pushed the handle on the urinal, stepped away, pardoned myself for bumping into the man behind me, looked over heads and hats for Uncle. He was just stepping up to his urinal, so I went over to the steps to wait for him, didn't even wash my hands. The fat man washed his hands, kept his eyes on me while bent over the basin, then paid for a towel, tumbled his hands through it while watching me. Finally Uncle strode toward me, and the tightness in my throat eased, my heart slowed to normal.

"Some place, huh, Mitchell?" he asked as we went up the steps. I looked over my shoulder like a jockey, saw the fat man in another line. "Some kook asked me if I wanted to go home with him—the damned queer. You know what queers are, Mitchell?"

"Yes, Uncle."

"They say queers are all over New York. Say they have bars here that only let in queers. Say some of them hold hands together in public. In public, Mitchell. We gotta be careful here. This city could wipe us out, Mitchell. I'm kind of scared already. It's bigger than I thought. And they don't even notice us, Mitchell. They just walk right by us, just push us out the way like we don't count. We gotta be careful, Mitchell, 'cause this ain't Chatsworth."

"I know, Uncle," I said. We were nearing Fifth again. "We could get wiped out in this city."

"Feels like rain, don't it?" Uncle wiped a drop from his nose and looked to the sky.

"No. It's just an air-conditioner leaking, Uncle."

True, the Apple is not Chatsworth by a long shot. But walking up 42nd Street on my first night in the city, I was determined that I would persevere, would hold my own in Gotham. I started swinging my arms, I jutted out my chin, carried on an interior half-time, pep-talk monologue. So, marshal your forces, greedy Gotham, I'm laying for you. I'll show you I can withstand your attacks; I'll face up to you and spit in your face if you try to down Uncle and me. Oh, sure, the two of us have had our setbacks before, we've buckled under like ethereal nonentities, like spectral apparitions on too many occasions. But I mean to make my mark here, I tell you. Consider me ambitious and determined as the Dutch who colonized your shores centuries ago. My drumsticks are in the short, and I plan to take some mean solos in the Village, I plan to step out and strut awhile, get my program together. I plan to say, this is me, Apple, and you'd better dig me with my bad self, uh huh.

"Oh, yeah."

"What's that you say, Mitchell?" asked Uncle.

"Oh, nothing," laughing, looking around. "I was just talking to myself, I guess."

At the garage, Uncle peeled off a couple of small bills from his fat wad and put the rubber band around the wad again. Then he dropped the wad of bills in his moneybag, tied the bag up and stuffed it in his pocket.

"We're looking for Pearl Mibbs. She may be in Harlem, but we're not sure, and we're going to stay at the Theresa. Can you tell us how to get there? We've got reservations."

He told us to take the West Side Highway up to 125th, go east until we hit the Theresa. "You sure you want to stay there? It's rundown and full of rats, I hear"—turning away, kicking the new tire and walking to the station office.

On the highway going north, Uncle at his steady speed of forty and cars passing us on our left.

"Look at those lights! Look at all those lights, Mitchell!" Uncle, keeping in the far right lane, was leaning over the wheel and alternately looking past me through the side window at the Manhattan skyline and glancing at the traffic out the front windshield. "And look over there"—turning, pointing at the lights and hills of New Jersey—"more lights."

"That's another state, Uncle," I offered. "New Jersey."

"This is the biggest city in the world, Mitchell," Uncle said, touching his Panama. "Holy cow. Ain't it something?"

He smiled at me, and we took the exit; I listened to the Ford sputter and choke its way up the ramp; I listened with crossed fingers. And we made it.

And Harlem. We broke into Harlem real bad, like our lives depended upon it. Cats were stashed on corners, some were holding up signposts; some buried their faces in handkerchiefs that were already soaked with perspiration. Cats rapping to babes who had laundry carts dragging behind them. Cats were practicing their new steps in front of a record shop for the Friday-night grind. Cats filed their fingernails, adjusted their brims by checking the reflections in store windows, held portable radios up to their ears. Beautiful black cats were everywhere. Their kicks were shined, processes done and Afros combed high, their faces lit by the lights from record stores, furniture stores, clothing stores—all kinds of stores, plus streetlights too.

We saw babes, chicks, janes, mamas, foxes, too. They walked their out-of-sight walks and popped their fingers and kept getting up when cats (corner connoisseurs) tried to jive with them. Plus they looked good, looked foxy as any cat with a reasonable game could possibly hope to handle.

So we came in slowly, cruising like big-timers. Both Uncle and I had one arm resting on a door, and the air was so thick and hot I could almost feel the Ford slicing through it. So, that was how we made our pilgrimage to the Theresa. Through streets filled with papers, rusting cans, newspapers; around double-parked cars; past garbage cans smelling of rotten fish, cats (four-legged) perched on top; past brownstones with women in bras fanning themselves with magazines on the wide steps, beer cans beside them; slamming on brakes so seven-year-olds could run across our path from between parked cars; and so many naked-from-the-waist faces peering from third-floor windows like lonely inmates. And you think Charon had rough going, do you?

"I hope Mother doesn't live around here," I said, moving inside so my voice was muffled, breaking a silence of bewilderment.

"God, this ain't living," Uncle answered, almost choking on emotion, and further, "All these people closed in together. They should move to Maine, where there's space and air." Then, turning onto the strip, and double-parking, he said, "There's the Theresa Hotel. See the sign?"

"Looking for the Theresa?" A man in short sleeves stepped from the sidewalk, his moustache wet with perspiration. He squeezed himself between a parked car and our Ford, rested his elbows on the door. "Allow me to present my card," pushing it past my face and into Uncle's hand. "It's for Tessy's Guest Home, owned by my Aunt Tessy. Listen"——pushing his head of dark-brown skin inside the car—"you don't want to stay here, this place is rundown. Roaches. Mice. Faggots. No hot water. Gone to the dogs. You look like a respectable gentleman who probably remembers the days of grandeur and respectability that surrounded this formerly magnificent establishment, right? That's how come I am taking it upon myself to introduce my aunt's place—wait," jumping backward, pushing out his arms, "I don't want to give the impression that we're hustling or anything like that, now. No sireee. Although I will say that—well, Auntie's down on her luck trying to put me through night college, and every roomer means another part of the tuition paid. That's how come my vocabulary is so proficient, I'm attending City College at night, working on my Ph.D. in anthropology. I figure it'll take me twelve years at night, but hell, man, I've my whole life ahead of me, I'm just fifty. I didn't finish high school, so I have to take these preparatory courses in algebra and geometry. Aunt Tessy's eighty-four, so she's getting along in age, but she can make dumplin's to set your foot tappin', and she tucks a mean sheet. Just two blocks from here. I live nearby. Clean, honest, comfortable. You want to ride up there?" Moving toward the station wagon again. "The address is on the card. She'll be awake—what time is it—near midnight?—oh, yeah, she's awake."

I had almost fallen asleep, Uncle had begun clearing his throat impatiently, tapping his pipe.

"You say the Theresa's all gone to pot?" he said.

"Shot to hell," answered Tessy's nephew. "No joke, square business."

"Okay, then we'll go over to your aunt's." Uncle held the card up, squinted at it, said, "Lives on a Hundred Forty-second Street—that don't sound like a few blocks."

"Well, it's a few minutes' drive."

And we were off. Later for the Theresa, we said.

Uncle had little trouble finding Tessy's boarding-house brownstone. While he was easing the station wagon between two parked cars, my yawning was interrupted when I saw a crowd near the corner. Uncle finally parked, we got out, both of us stood on the sidewalk and stared at the crowd. More trouble, problems, predicaments? Another test? For an instant I wanted to grab my suitcase and hustle up the cement steps, bang on Tessy's door—not ring the bell, understand, but bang my fists on the tall wood-and-glass door—and get to my room. And I'm sure Uncle would have been wasting no time behind me. But we stood, side by side, figures peering down the street at figures, probably thinking, hoping that the other (he, me; I, him) would make the move, begin the night's gambit.

Then I—genius, hero—recalling my earlier resolution of intrepidity and fortitude, sniffed the hot night air, stood on tiptoes, and leaned forward, saying, "Let's go see what the problem is, Uncle. Come on." I took a bold first step, and the others came automatically. Like a wound-up doll, I moved one foot after the other. Uncle followed, striding with hard heels behind me.

It seemed we reached them too soon. I thought I hadn't been walking long enough, yet there we were. A circle of faces—about a dozen were huddled together —turned to run their eyes over us, and their heads snapped back to something down on the edge of the sidewalk. Uncle and I stood on the fringe of the crowd. We stood on tiptoes, we peered over mumbling heads but couldn't see a thing. So I, again recalling my resolution, eased my way between two spectators—and it worked—I got through, stood inside the crowd now. And no wonder they were just staring.

On this hot July night—our first night in the Apple— I had to witness that. When Uncle squeezed through, came up beside me, he put his hands to his eyes, turned his head. But I had to watch. Wasn't it the type of discipline I needed to ensure survival? But what a mess. A black cat scrambling in the gutter. Hopping. Blood gushing and spurting from its mouth, teeth bared. Tail flapping against the asphalt. Rolling over on its back and running, going nowhere, hissing with luminescent green eyes. Spinning on its side. Springing for a second, gasping for a breath of sticky air. Tongue lapping at the dust in the gutter. It had a crease in his side where the tire had run over it, and the fur was matted and pressed, as if he had been dry-cleaned. And there was nothing to do but watch—or not. It gasped a little longer, took great gulps of air, then panted slower, and slower. A few people started moving, backing away.

A woman: "Damned cat shouldn't have been in the

gutter anyway." High-pitched voice breaking the silence like a curfew whistle.

"Where's the driver?"

"I saw the whole thing, it wasn't the driver's fault. The cat was lying there stretched out under the tire, and it just rolled over his stomach—must have broken his back, because I heard something crack. The driver kept going, probably don't know what happened."

Uncle and I got out of there fast, walked briskly back toward Tessy's. Death and suffering have always been bugaboos to me. I have tried to circumvent any confrontation with those specters. But as fate would have it, they have hovered around me like gulls near a ship for all my short life. And what is one to do? Combat them with drumsticks, the love of an old uncle and a dog's friendship? My stomach began quivering, and I had to run between two cars, and bending over, regurgitate against the black asphalt, lumps of sour food landing on my shoes.

"Are you okay, Mitchell?" Uncle's arm went around my shoulders. He pulled me out of the gutter, helped me keep my balance, because I was weak and lightheaded, and he must have felt me totter like an infant. "This is some city, just running over everybody. We only been here two hours, and I'm weary of it already. These things don't happen in Chatsworth. People running over cats. It shouldn't happen to a dog."

My mind flashed back to Larson's visit, and I wanted to tell Uncle nothing in my entire life could happen anywhere—Manhattan, Maine or Kalamazoo—that will equal that night. No, I didn't think the Apple could put anything on me like Chatsworth had. But we'll see.

So, exhausted and hungry, we pulled our suitcases out of the back, and scraping our feet and banging our bags against the stone steps, reached the door. A business card was taped to the center of the glass window, and VACANCY written on it in red ink. Uncle, gasping as if he had crawled to an oasis, rang the bell. Eventually the buzzer sounded, seemed to ring through the entire dark street, and I looked over my shoulder to see—well, just to see what the surroundings looked like. We stepped inside, knocking our bags against the glass, and found ourselves facing another door. I saw steps inside the second door, saw a light at the top of the stairs and a figure near the top.

A voice from the top: "Who is it down there?"

"Melvin Pip."

"Who?"

"Melvin Pip from Maine—Chatsworth. And my nephew, Mitchell. We're looking for a room for one or two weeks." Clearing his throat, fanning himself with the Panama. "Your nephew"—looking at me, shaking my head—"your nephew, uh, uh, uh . . . your nephew, Mister uh, uh . . . "

"Do you know what time it is?"

"Yes ma'am, and we're sorry."

"Did you say my nephew, Benny? Did Benny send you over here? Bless him. I'll be right down."

She opened the door, stood there with a cane, which explains why I had thought I heard three feet plop their way down the steps. Fat like Aunt Ranida and wearing a cape robe. And a scarf over her head.

"Seven dollars a week," holding the cane horizontally, its rubber tip almost making an indentation into Uncle's dress shirt. "No women; bathroom and shower at the end of the hall; and no loud music. First week's rent due in advance. How long you here for?"

Following her up the steps. Someone peeping at us from a cracked door on the first floor. "We're here for a few weeks, looking for a relative."

We fell asleep without taking our clothes off or un-packing. In a room as large as Uncle's bedroom, with two closets and paint peeling, hanging from the ceiling like leaves from a head of lettuce; with one window sending cats' meows, automobile tires' screeching and still, hot air; on a mattress harder than Jeff's back. We fell asleep without saying our prayers and before we could say good night to each other.

In the morning I awoke with a face so wet you could have convinced me Uncle had thrown a glass of water on me. I looked over at Uncle, who, suprisingly, was still snoring; then I got on my feet, nearly staggering from the humidity, bent down to wipe the perspiration off with the end of the sheet. Banging and shouting coming from the window, probably what interrupted my sleep. Machines grinding, steel smashing against steel, machines whining.

Stumbling, almost wading my way through the thick heat of the room, I made it to the windowsill, placed my hands down to look out, and was hit in the eye by a big black—what? Picking it off the floor, I held it by the light of the window. It disintegrated in my fingers. A black piece of disappearing tissue.

"It's incinerator ash," said Uncle. And when I turned, he was looking at me, had been looking at me; had turned sideways and was resting his head on his hands. "It comes from incinerators." I knew what it was, but I gave him the one-upsmanship. And two more black ashes floated in, resting on the floor. "What's all that racket, Mitchell? It scared me to death. Look out the window and see."

I looked down to see men wearing gloves. They hoisted large overflowing garbage cans on their shoulders, then strode barely on balance toward an immaculate white truck announcing in black lettering, SANITATION DEPARTMENT, unloaded the cans in the back of the truck and closed the opening. Then a man would lift a can in the air, its still-silver coating catching the sun for an instant, then drop it, ringing it against the sidewalk.

"It's the garbage men, Uncle," I said. "They're taking up cans from the street. They make a lot of noise, huh?"

"Yeah"—rising from the bed (the mattress squeaked) —"but let's get washed up and changed, put our stuff in the closets and start looking for Pearl. It's ten already; Jesus, I've slept."

Washing our faces in our room's basin, we didn't even mind that no hot water came out from the left spigot. The way we were almost suffocating, the cold water against our faces was an impromptu air-conditioner. Our new wear: khaki pants and undershirts. Uncle wore thick-soled hunting shoes, I donned sneakers. He shaved in front of a cracked mirror attached to a dusty bureau, nicked his face in two places, and, his hands cupped over the flame of his pipe, now lighted, he turned to me with the mouthpiece between his teeth, mumbled, "Let's go, Mitchell. We'll get some breakfast first, then look for your mother."

Going down the stairs was like moving through a man-sized furnace. On the front steps we looked down and up the street at rows of standing and knocked-over steel garbage cans. The sanitation trucks had gone, the street was quiet, and the sunlight made me squint. Like explorers off a ship, we looked this way and that, considered, contemplated, pondered taking the next (actually the first) step, and we still didn't move. The lead was in our feet, the breath had been knocked out of us, our arms were glued to our sides like soldiers'. And so we ruminated, mused, speculated, and still not moving, we certainly must have pushed our minds further—meditating and brooding. We, the two of us, Melvin Pip, Mitchell Mibbs, newcomers from the Pine Tree State, stood like pillars at the top of the steps, in a city larger even than Portland. Should we descend? Turn around and sit in our cubicle for another hour until courage called? Then this thought: maybe I should push Uncle?

Yes, I had done my research on the Apple. I had read about the jazz spots and the action in Harlem and the Village and the upper East Side and Central Park. I knew Peter Minuit had bought this island from the Canarsee Indians for twenty-four dollars' worth of cloth and trinkets. And I had talked to a couple of people who had driven in to Tony's with New York license plates about what was happening here. Plus, had I not read street and subways maps until I thought I knew Manhattan like the palm of my hand? I even read most of the news that was fit to be printed about New York. Yet, we had to take that initial step. With all the information I had, there was still a novice swimmer's reluctance to stick that initial foot into cold water.

But they came bopping down the street from our right, jumped into our periphery as if, like horses, we were wearing blinders. Beautiful black brothers coming down like they owned the street; no, the city; no, they were making it down the sidewalk like they owned the world—the whole damned world.

I had to dig them because their stuff was so tough, they were saying something, breaking out bad down this avenue in Harlem. About a half-dozen, taking the whole sidewalk, walking abreast but moving around and between the lids and cans which formed an obstacle course for pedestrians. Foreheads wrapped in handkerchiefs. Leaning to the side and swinging one arm, the other in their pockets. I mean, bopping. Lips tight and unsmiling, eyes—eyes shifting in all directions. Hair high and busy in Afro style on some, others (two) wearing blocked stingy brims (Dobbs?). In sweatshirts and pressed, bright-colored mohair slacks and black wingtips (Stacy Adams?). Bop on, brothers. I could have been their own one-man cheering section, yelling,

147

"Go on for yourselves, brothers six. Lighten up on your smooth, unacknowledged artistry. Stay in your uptight bags forever and forever." But I didn't know them, did I? I only knew their art, was familiar suddenly only with their beauty. They stopped in front of us, formed an inspection line, looked us over with faces also wet from perspiration. One, the leader, no doubt, scraped his feet, shuffled one foot forward—bopping even in that one step.

"Where you muh fuhs from?" One hand still in his pocket, leaning forward and to the side, the other hand down, its thumb horizontal and behind his leg. Then, bending his knees and straightening his brim, which was cocked to the side anyway—fixing it to the side again and bending as if he were looking in a mirror. Uncle and I turned to each other. "I'm talking to you, home," pointing his whole arm at me, the finger shooting up toward my eye. "Where you from, my man? Speak up, muh fuck!"

My voice cracked; crazy things were melting into my stomach.

"Uh, Chatsworth," I answered, wondering if it sounded real, further adding, "Chatsworth, Maine."

The leader turned to his fellows. "Where's that? You cats ever heard of some kinda Chatsworth? Where's Maine, anyway? I've heard of it; somewhere near Staten Island, ain't it?" Shrugging of shoulders that had dipped with such authority only a moment ago. "You bloods got any bread?" Head cocked again to the side. "We trying to get some vino, can you help us out?"

"We ain't got no money," said Uncle, and I was startled by the sudden clearing of his throat and his snatching the pipe out of his mouth in anger. "You boys shouldn't be drinking wine anyway—too young," glancing at me.

"Old man"—voice shooting to a high, emotional and

angry tenor—"do you know who you talking to? You ever hear of the Sportsmen, the Automatics, the Saber Jets, the Broadway Best? Well, they're some of the baddest gangs in the city, jim, but we're badder than all of those jivetime, pussy muh fuhs. We're the Supreme Lords, and this is our territory, and we cut the shit out of anybody we find from another gang. And if we don't get bread when we ask for it"—slicing his finger across his neck. "Now, for all we know, you cats could be from Brooklyn, and shit, except for that funny-assed way you talk. You splids sound like the British are coming, and shit." Cracking up. "All we ask for is a few coins to get a little taste, just a little Thunderbird. We not asking you to move out of our territory or nothing. We not saying you might get your fuckin' asses kicked if you don't turn us on with some coin."

"We ain't giving you no money for no wine," shouted Uncle, and I didn't even look at him. "You boys ought to be working and trying to make something out of yourselves instead of walking the streets like hoodlums. Why ain't you gettin' ready for college?"

"Awh, you jivetime, old-assed motherfucker, you talk like them social workers. If you weren't so old"—throwing his hand out—"I'd give you a fair one and knock you on your ass." The others shifted positions, were leaning on a parked car. "I can make more dough hustlin' than I can make on a steady gig, so that job shit you talking don't make no sense, jack. You better get hip, and stop talkin' like them paddy boys. Nobody would know we were on this earth if we didn't get locked up or had rumbles with other gangs." Turning, looking at his boys, he added, "I don't even know why I'm wasting my time telling you this shit."

"Yeah, these cats don't know what's happenin'."

"You boys just don't listen to your parents, that's all," said Uncle, and I wondered why he was prolonging the debate, hoped he wouldn't get the leader too angry.

But no, the leader laughed, turned to his fellows, his road partners, who laughed and snorted too, putting their hands to their noses. "Man, I ain't seen my father since I got out the incubator. And my mom's never home. You see these cats here? Ain't none of their fathers lives with them. Now, what kind of parents is that, old man?" Turning: "You hear this cat? Parents!"

And before I could open my mouth to tell them about my father, before I could establish a camaraderie, "Hey, slick, here comes the man—around the corner," said one of them, whispering, sliding down the side of the car, then scrambling on his knees along the sidewalk. And they all scrambled and crawled like that. They disappeared across the street as quickly as they had appeared, so that when the patrol car cruised by, the driver patting his handkerchief on a shiny forehead, there was no sign of any Supreme Lords. I wished I could have gone with them. I wished I could have told the leader before he cut out that I couldn't remember what my father looked like either. Maybe they would have let me join, taught me the art that they knew. Watching them scurry out of sight like discovered roaches, I was so tempted to call, "Take me with you, fellows, let me swing with you." But I would have my chance to rumble. For then, I made notes of their vocabulary so I could rap with the best of them when I got to the Village.

Uncle was working his tool into his pipe, he was emptying the ashes on the steps—no, we still hadn't moved—and saying: "It's a shame. New York really kills you, Mitchell." And suddenly, looking up to the smog in the sky, "I hope Tony's feeding the dogs okay."

But—just New York, Uncle? I think not, but never

told him. They could have been from any city. Even Maine. You can be trampled in any city in the world if the foot is there to step on you.

"Ready to start, Mitchell? Come on, I'm hungry."

I bopped like I was a Supreme Lord—swinging and dipping, working up a sweat.

14

IF YOU HAD SEEN US TAKING TO THE STREETS ABOUT noon every day, Tessy yelling, "Yawl ain't found that relative yet? Well, stay as long as you want, chile, I can spend your money as well as anybody's." In the full heat of Harlem's too hot summer, you might have thought we were drunks returning from a party, the way we stumbled our way along those burning streets. Uncle would be fanning himself with the Panama, unable to walk a straight line and bumping into me. We'd walk up to people—"Hello, I'm Melvin Pip from Maine and I'm looking for a singer called Pearl Mibbs. Seen anything of her?" And the responses were always discouraging. We went all over Harlem asking that question. "Haven't you even heard somebody talking about her? She's a good singer." We even drove to the Village to look. Even took a couple of walking turns around Central Park, and even walked around the East Side (Fifth Avenue!). "They must be in Harlem, Mitchell." No Mother. No Julius. Sore feet, tired, dry tongues, faces constantly damp with perspiration.

One weekend evening, sitting on the windowsill and looking down at a fire hydrant's spray cooling a whole block of kid's bronze backs and listening to all those flat feet slapping against the wet street, and too, hearing the eeks and even seeing smiles, although there was only one streetlamp on. I turned from the fun on the streets to look at Uncle lying on the bed. It was dark except for the red flame of his pipe. I looked at him, stopped drumming on my practice pad, and said, without any forethought at all, as if I had received some mediumistic communication, "Let's take a look in the Village, Uncle, she may be there. I have a feeling."

And Uncle didn't argue, knowing me as he did, trusting me as he did. As he knew and trusted me, so he jumped out of bed, and soon we were exercising our by then familiar knowledge of the West Side Highway, my drumsticks tight in my left hand.

"Where to?" We were in the Village then.

"I think we should just keep on going down Bleecker Street until I get a feeling we should stop," I said, then suddenly yelling, "Stop and park around here, Uncle. Right here."

Just as we slammed the car doors shut a hipster was leaving the Topnote, and he was tipping with his jane on his arm. The door was open for a few seconds. The music came out like a train going by. They were cooking, the musicians. The way the music seeped out just as the door opened and closed, I knew this club had to be our first stop; later for Mother—for a while, anyway. Sure, I had missed her presence since that spring departure, but weren't there other things to find in the city besides a wayward mother? Weren't there poolrooms off the strip, grinds at the YMCA, chicken wings and things at soul restaurants, corner arguments between cats about who was messing with whose woman? These things you don't find in Chatsworth.

See, if she hadn't disappeared to the big city, I probably wouldn't be sitting here now on the last evening of my reading with this wear: boots buckled around the ankle; steel-frame shades; the high-topped and wide-sided Afro-style haircut; an Apache scarf around my neck; and the confidence (yes, I wear that on my face) that I can bop with the best of them. If she and

153

Julius hadn't motored to Manhattan, I might have never become the *hip* genius I am; genius, yes, but hip young smart thing, well . . .

And so, uh, we gathered ourselves together, shrugging our shoulders, scraping our feet, I feeling uneasy that here no one had yet stopped to check out the Ford's antiquity. Although needing only three steps to reach the door, I bopped. Uncle stepped on the heels of my kicks, bumped his chest into my back as I dropped my hand from the doorknob, turned, fell against him and spoke: "Maybe you'd better leave the hat in the car, Uncle?"

"Why?" Someone pushed him against me.

"Well, it might get lost. You could block people's view, too, you know."

"This is my best, this hat, Mitchell. I want to show these people we can get dressed up too in Maine when we have to." Bumping against me again.

Well, this could have continued all night. Bright neons flashing along Bleecker Street, the night and the street alive and crowded with sightseeing couples and teen-agers from Jersey City, Scarsdale, the Bronx; cars inching their way, with horns making an eerie kind of tumultuous musical composition, the whole street sounding like a record run backward. In this din, plus the magnitude of our mission hovering above our shoulders, couldn't we have found a more important discourse than a Panama straw? Why was the scene so much like a pitcher-catcher conference in the sixth inning of one of my Little League night games, the crowd rumbling, roaring, the lights almost blinding us, and everybody in the stadium staring at two white-flannel-wearing figures on the mound?

"Suit yourself, Uncle," I said, turning—but carefully this time—making my way toward the door again.

Uncle, digging into his bag to get the coins, paid the cover, asked who was playing. He scratched the back of his head. "Paul Maley . . . didn't he use to play with Condon? Goodman? Glenn Miller?" Negative answers. "We won't be able to stay too long. We're looking for Pearl Mibbs, the singer. Has she been in here lately?"

I, snapping my fingers and bopping my head, shuffled through the air-conditioned, dark Topnote Café. Uncle was behind me. Tipping our way between chairs and tables and knees we could barely see. The music came from the stage on our left. The lighting was fluorescent green. The quartet was still cooking. I was thinking that our groping was hilariously similar to the time we eased our barefooted way over the rock-filled inlet at Perkins Cove in Ogunquit one midnight. We got chairs, sat, ordered rums and Coke, and I wasn't even asked for an I.D. card. I checked out the cats around me. Most had their lips stuck out, heads nodding, eyes covered by shades, fingers snapping or palms patting out the beat on the table. And, like I said, those cats on the stage were smoking.

All four wore beards—drummer, bassist, pianist, trumpeter—all four wore Continental vines with tapered pants. The trumpeter, spotlighted, was high in the air shooting out notes that ricocheted all over the place, left wall and right wall, high and low. They were on an upbeat version of "My Funny Valentine," and he was blowing as if his sideman were snake-charming him. The drummer was banging and swishing and rat-tatting, and his arms were flailing in the air like a two-handed fencer demonstrating a *puncto reverso*. While taking a roll, he would bend over his skins as if he were sick on his stomach. Then he would lean way back like a driver pulling the reins and—did I forget the cigarette hanging from his lips?—explode into a delicate frenzy of soft brushwork, wrists trembling. The bassist, taller than the others and bending, ran his fingers up and down the strings in one big vertical

155

sweep, while the pianist cooked with fingers blurring horizontally. So they were chasing him, were they? And was he miles ahead or not? He was gamboling over rough picket fences, skimming over choppy waves, bucking through stiff weeds, knocking down all kinds of barriers, getting away clean. He would slow down deliberately and look back at the drummer, who would hustle up alongside, furiously snapping syncopated mileage out of his wrists. But the man on the trumpet would shift gears and glide, soar far upward onto another level. And he would stay up there, sweet-noting himself over grasslands, and beaches, just jetting and accelerating all the time. Running between trees, over fields, past clearings, around meadows. Now, didn't the bassist and pianist combine their forces to intercept him at some distant intersection? And how he skirted around, changed pace, waited for them to flounder momentarily; and then taking off again, spitting musical bullets at every ear in the club.

And at each change he went through, we in the audience who knew the score smiled furtively to ourselves and to each other. Even grunting out loud so the squares around us would suspect some clandestinely exquisite musical communication was taking place. Or did they care?

Soon, still flooded with green lights, the man in the spotlight let his rhythm section catch up with him, so they became escorts instead of chasers. And was he blowing! Also, he had the precisely timed pause where he'd snatch the horn from his lips for a second, scowl, turn his face, and then in a whirlwind of renewed energy, black face shining and frowning in the green fluorescence, attack the horn with his lips again, and blow some more. He would give us a profile of legs and feet together, torso bent almost into a C and horn high toward the ceiling, or he would face the horn's circular end directly at us and smoke. When he went into a deep, muted bag, he would point the horn downward, eyeballs looking up. But always frowning, scratching his ear too, and a handkerchief in one hand. So now, as I say, the rhythm section was up to him. They were like king's courtiers flanking him, supporting him on either side; holding him up, steering, guiding, channeling—and he was advancing.

When he finished his solo, he turned his back to us, tucked his horn under his arm and tipped behind the curtain as softly and delicately as a cat.

We loved it. If he had smiled at us or bowed, we would have kept our distance. But his spurning us warmed us to him; his apparent inaccessibility pulled our collective admiration toward him. Knowing he wouldn't, we begged him in our hearts to lift that horn to his lips for a few more bars, just a few more. Knowing he wouldn't reappear soon (and perhaps even fearing it, for how much could we take of his genius?), we strained our eyes toward the curtain to the side of the stage. And what—some poltergeistlike semblance? The pianist was taking his solo, but I wasn't sure the trumpeter was still not on stage. Some queer sense of his essence filled me, some sensation even as far away from the stage as I was, that he was hovering over the musicians' heads. Presence through absence? It was satisfyingly chilly as sleeping with full cover on a brisk, spring night in Maine, the bedroom window open.

He strutted back on stage like a soldier reporting for inspection and began to blow out the end. I looked around me. With the exception of Uncle, who was dozing with his arms folded, long legs unbent and straight under the table, everybody was digging this cat. He was squealing like an amplified mouse. Furious, demanding. He could have ended on this bar or that one and the piece would have stopped successfully and coherently. But we didn't know when. All we did was listen—everybody was listening, not drinking or talking, and the tension was not unlike that of watching a long-distance runner: positive of his finishing but not sure when or, actually, if. Many times have I seen milers, finish line in sight, throw up their hands, signaling the quit. So he blew. And I looked around at the liquor-filled, starry eyes of admiration and respect and attention, and strangely, I was reminded of the great seesaw record I had made years ago with Tom. Just as my mind was forming the picture of our seesawing, the trumpeter snatched the horn from his mouth, stuck it under his arm, and well-tapered mohair pants shining and sticking to his striding, graceful legs, made for the curtain. End of set. The clapping woke up Uncle, who clapped, asked if I had seen Mother, coughed, cleared his throat, crossed his legs (still unbent), slid his hands in his pockets, beckoned the waiter. I was restructuring the performance in my head, was still reliving that very boss set as the trumpeter disappeared through the curtain. I was thinking of the attention. All of us had come to check him out, and by listening, had acknowledged his magnificent musical existence. We had recognized him for his playing, had aroused the proof of his presence through our contemplation of his artistry. Through his art, he had said, I am. And through our apprehension, we had said, you are, baby—you are indeed, jack.

The pianist and drummer were trading fours.

Winding his way between tables. Wincing his mouth at a spectator, scratching his curly hair, pulling at his ear. He eased past my table, and my stomach got uptight, and I thought my vocal cords had slipped to my stomach when he did an about-face, stood over Uncle and me with arms folded, and spoke, voice raspy: "Is that cat sleep?"

I gulped, ransacked my memory for an appropriately hip remark, brushed tobacco ash from the table, grinned as if I had wet my pants, drew circles on the table with my index finger—all the time he was standing over me—and, thinking of nothing to say, nodded my head. He started to walk away, but I recaptured my voice and rushed to speak. "He's had a hard day. We've been looking for Mother all day and Uncle's been driving. And the heat's so much hotter than in Maine, Uncle gets tired quickly." The most outlandishly incoherent speech I have ever made.

"You cats from Maine?" Eyes big now, forehead of wrinkles collecting, reflecting the green light.

"Yes, Chatsworth, Mr. Maley—just over the border, west of Kittery. We don't get much jazz up there, but I've got most of your sides and a lot of others." I was warming up to the rum and Coke, the wild lights, the feeling of dizzying stupor.

"No stuff?" said the musician, grabbing a chair by its back and pulling it out, then bending and sitting. Uncle and I at the Topnote Café, everybody pinning us, Uncle snoring.

"Uncle and I play your sides at night when we're alone and it's late and quiet," I said. "Uncle's not too hip on modern stuff. He plays a lot of cats like Bechet, Kid Ory, Johnson and Armstrong."

"Don't knock them, baby. Those cats are important. If it hadn't been for them, we wouldn't be where we are now—really." He was sitting opposite me, and we were staring at each other. His arm was stretched before him on the table, his hands were tapping the beat of his drummer, who was taking a solo. "So you cats are from Maine, huh? Ain't that something. No wonder your old man's asleep—all that driving. I used to play in Portsmouth—know where that is?"

I wanted to tell him that Uncle is not my father and that we were looking for a stray mother and that although I was trying to be hip, I was finding Manhattan a tough place to make it in. I could prove that I'm a boss drummer, and I wouldn't have to go back to

Chatsworth, I could make it in the city as a stick man. But instead of rapping like that, I merely answered yes, I knew where Portsmouth is—in New Hampshire. But he put his head down between his hands, rubbed his eyes, ran a hand through his curly hair, and so I took a deep breath and asked him if he were tired. He looked me dead in my face as if I had guessed his age or performed some New England hocus-pocus.

"Lonely, really"—he was sipping his newly ordered drink—"I get so lonely I feel like screaming, I feel like tearing my trumpet to pieces." The suddenness of the outburst caught me with my guard down, I didn't know how to respond. And why me? Did a secret communication perambulate me as some psychological counselor? Did I give the appearance of a natural commiserater? Or did my sitting with a sleeping companion signal our common condition—one of loneliness, groping, insecurity. Whatever the reason, I didn't care. Just listening to him was worth the trip to New York.

"Is that why you play?" I asked, hoping this would be the Ruy Lopez, sparking a spirited exchange.

"I play because I like to feel someone cares, you know? When I'm up there on this or any stage, I know I am in complete command, that people are watching me, digging my every move, trying to figure out just what I'm up to. That's why I don't even acknowledge they're there. I don't like for them to know that I depend on them. Audiences are like babes, man. Once they know how much you care, they start playing games—like not clapping and stuff like that. When I'm blowing my horn and me and the group are cooking pretty nicely, I know I'm beautiful. Sometimes I can just soar all over the room, hit notes I never dreamed of before. Sometimes I'm just way, way out."

"Are you married?" I had become embarrassed by the silence, had to ask that silly question.

"Divorced. I was married to a gray girl—Jewish. It

160

couldn't have worked in a million years—two different worlds. She wanted me to study classical guitar." I squinted my mouth to show displeasure. The cats on the band were wrapping up the piece. "I mean, can you dig that? Here I am a black man with the ability to play music that *we* started, and she wants me to study classical guitar. Jazz is *our* music, baby. Jazz is the black man's art. All the cats who are doing anything are black. All the cats who play tough do it mostly because they have something to say. It's what's happening. It's our way of saying we exist. Every time I take that horn in my hands, I say, I am." The talk was warming me up, but so was the rum. He had bought me two more, and my head was on a slow-motion Ferris wheel.

"I get so pissed off," he said, and without waiting for me to ask for an explanation, continued, "about how the white man has just stolen so much from us. When I told that to my wife, she started making all these sociological explanations. I told her that jazz was our music, and she started coming up with all sorts of exceptions. I told her about how they stole our pieces and recorded them and made plenty of money, of how we don't get paid as much as the white man in the same club, of getting cheated out of union dues. We can't even get as much in the pawn shop! A black man's set of Gretsch drums ain't worth as much as a paddy's. And so every time I play, just about, I'm shouting to her to listen. I'm telling her and everybody else what a bitch it is to be black in America and to be talented too, and see someone else take the bread home. The only way I can shout is through my horn, you know? I'm not a violent man, so how else can I protest? I'm shouting all the time, too—even when I'm playing slow. The only problem is that the people who count aren't listening." The drummer had gone into a Latin beat, the pianist was fading, and the beginnings of clapping told me that the piece was ending.

Looking at my sticks. "You play?"

"A little, I haven't had too much work lately, though."

"You want to sit in for a set?"

And how could I say no? So, I stood slowly, felt the heat of the lights hit my cheeks, pushed back my chair and stepped away from the table. I glanced at a few pairs of eyes digging me, then I made certain I put on one of my best bops as I struck out for the stage, struck out behind the trumpeter.

"This cat's from Maine. Let him sit in on this piece, will you, Jake?"

Soon Jake had left the bandstand, and I, sitting in front of an anthology of pearl-rimmed drums—drums I had never seen so closely, had only imagined from the unexposed acquaintance with a practice pad in this old Ford or the Oriental-rugged living room—felt like a jockey waiting for the gate to open.

"We'll start with a regular 'Bye, Bye, Blackbird', then move up the tempo after the intro," Maley said, looking over his shoulder at us, but still giving only his back. He stamped his feet, snapped his fingers, and I dropped the drumsticks on the snare, they bounced off and clicked against the floor. Silence. People breathing in unison. Ahems. The air-conditioner was working fine. Bartender shaking a drink. Maley didn't even turn around; did, however, allow me an awkward moment to bend down to reach for my sticks (suddenly the most elusive pieces of wood in the world) so that, while dirtying my fingers which scraped around on the floor, my shoulder hit the stand for the hi-hat cymbal, and it tottered while the cymbals clanged against each other. And my foot fell against the pedal for the bass drum, that banging, sounding like the beginning of a military march. How much more suited for these bunglings would I have been if they had dressed me like a Pierrot—with white face, pantaloons, large white jacket? After I finally got myself together and was staring at the honeycomb of fuzzy lights and their halos illuminating the stage, the trumpeter started the piece again.

This time he was shooting rapid-fire, quick notes—eighths and sixteenths—spaced to give the composition an elongation of structure. And we, the rhythm section, had plenty of time to do our thing between notes. We could have drawn legitimate and logical relevancies and ties between the notes. We could have highlighted the differences. We could have indicated a tension between them after the trumpeter would pull the horn from his lips at the end of a phrase. We could have done all these things had I been ready. But I wasn't. I started out pretty nicely on the beginning bars, I was accenting with my left and stroking well on the hi-hat when the bridge came, and I didn't know what to do. The bassist began double-timing, the pianist was running through some block chords, and the tempo was hours ahead of my mind. My hands were sweating, my wrists felt heavy as lead, and the beat was escaping from me like a ball bouncing down the steps. A few in the audience by the bandstand laughing, some were rising, trying to see the confusion they heard. Before coming back to me, the trumpeter nodded to the pianist to take over, then, stalking with his trumpet cradled to his chest, suddenly loomed above me and said without annoyance: "What's the matter, kid—too much to drink?" That was the cue I needed. I shook my head back and forth, started to rise from my round seat, became a drunken driver emerging from his sheen.

"It must be those rums and Coke," I said, holding a handkerchief-covered hand to the side of my head. "Everything is going around, I can't see so well."

"You'd better take it easy, kid, let Jake come in for you. I'll talk to you after this piece."

So I was off the bandstand. Still stumbling and rocking in my steps, simulating a drunk, I shook Uncle's shoulder for a good three minutes before he awoke.

"Is she here?" His eyes were red and wild even in those lights. Uncle, who always rose with the sun, was so tired and disheveled-looking, you would have thought he would never last another day of only five hours' sleep.

"No"—slurring my voice—"but we've spent too much time here. Don't you think we ought to go look elsewhere?" Tucking my sticks in my hip pocket. Tugging at his shoulder.

Finally we were outside, having walked out in the middle of the piece (Uncle hiding me on the stage side). It had rained. The streets smelled good and were shiny, the air had cooled, and we were making it through the Village again.

Since that catastrophic debut on stage, I have practiced and practiced with my drumsticks. Every chance I got, I have rolled and tapped along on chairs, the dining-room table, the cut-up seat of this old Ford—even on Jeff's back. I have practiced and practiced, tried to be a drummer since I saw that acrobat of the wrist who played at the Rialto. I have read books on rhythm, I have listened to the drummer's work on every side I have played, every jazz piece I have heard on radio. But was my failure at the Topnote telling me something? Why couldn't I have shouted out with my sticks as trumpet-player Maley had done with his horn?

Into another club. We sat staring at the stagehand who was setting up the mike. We ordered more drinks. I watched the waiter set up the glasses. Did he have two hands on one wrist? I looked up to see his four eyes staring at me from his two faces, and I knew I was wasted.

Uncle going into his pocket for the change purse. "We're looking for a singer"—reaching into another pocket—"from Maine, southern part"—taking another hand and sticking it into another pocket—"her name is Pearl . . ."

"Sir, do you have money to pay for your drinks?"

"I can't seem to find it—my change bag," said Uncle, looking at me. I was counting pores in my palm, yawning, glancing over my shoulder, smiling as if this were, and praying it was, just some temporary inconvenience.

"Sir, I'll have to evict you if you cannot pay for your beverages."

And Uncle, two rums and Coke downed plus a bottle of vino before we even left Tessy's, stood tall, burped, and said he was from Maine and that he had come all the way down here to look for his sister and somebody had probably pick-pocketed him while he had slept in the Topnote. But he had plenty of money back in his mattress, and would they trust him to go back and get it. Right. Uh huh. Sure. Would they trust Jackie Robinson not to steal? Now standing up, Uncle was going through his pockets for the fifth time—it was beginning to resemble a ritual, when—

"Mitchell! What are you doing in a nightclub!" Mother.

As if she were their cue, the band appeared on stage and a male singer began tilting the floor mike toward him. Mother? She was as fly and gay as a sparrow. She moved toward our table, cruising between the other chairs and tables in the darkness. Her arms were raised, hands were wringing, and she was vined in a plain knit suit.

Uncle said, "Pearl, we've been looking all over for you."

Now the waiter: "This gentleman owes for several drinks."

And the singer on stage: "Just stay by me, baby . . ."

Then Mother, sitting: "What are you doing bringing

165

Mitchell in here—you know he's only fifteen! Look at his eyes—red as beets. My son, drunk. Julius!" Pulling me toward her, my head on her breasts, the breath of liquor spilling in my face.

Mother paid for the drinks, the singer sang, and Julius came up to us.

"Jesus Christ, what's this? Uncle. Mitchell. Well, well. Mutt and Jeff in person. How'd you two get to the Apple?" Teeth flashing and chopping in the dim light. "By the Ford? You brought that old jalopy to the big city! Oh, well, you might as well join us at our table. Come on."

They had a guest, Henry, sitting with them. Mother said that I couldn't drink any more, that she was tired, that she had missed me. She must have picked up a wrinkle or two in her forehead, but she was still lovely, shadows filling-in her cheeks.

Uncle: "Pearl, why didn't you write us? We were so worried about you. We didn't know what happened. We're staying in Harlem."

Mother: "There was nothing to write. A job here, a job there. Nothing spectacular. As a matter of fact, we're thinking of coming back to Chatsworth next week. Things are bad, Uncle. No work."

"What happened to the job Julius lined up for you? What about the telegram?"

Silence. Cutting eyes. Wincing mouths.

Then Julius: "Pearl and her bourbon on the job, that's what. The manager didn't take to a drunken singer."

But Mother: "Awh, hell, I only had a couple before a set," slurring her words even then, squeezing my arm in—what?—inebriated affection or sudden sense of un-balance?

"I've had it," said Julius. "If it hadn't been for Henry here"—patting this thin man's shoulder—"his father owns a club in the Village, and Pearl got a job

166

there a few times. We really would have been up shit's creek—"

"Watch your language!" Uncle whispered, leaning on the table with his elbows and looking to one side, to the other. "Mitchell's just a boy yet."

"You've got some nerve, Melvin"—Mother speaking now—"when you bring him in here to drink hard liquor. You try to get him drunk and then talk about watching somebody's language. Why don't you just go on home, anyway. Mitchell can take the subway. You look like you're about to fall out." Turning to me, she said, "Would you like to say with Mommy for a while? Julius and I will show you around the Village." Her hand rested on my shoulder, she squeezed her fingers into my skin: her signal of affection. The three of them were searching me for an answer.

But Uncle stood, said that he would go home, and for me to have a good time. I thanked him with my eyes for making it easy for me.

"Can you make it back all right, Uncle?" I asked, in my mind seeing him floundering on the Long Island Expressway or the New Jersey Turnpike.

He nodded yes and was gone.

The three of us drank. And drank. And drank. Julius, vined up and clean, complained about the bad breaks, showed me his bare black fingers as evidence that yes indeed he did have to pawn the rings. Mother, almost in tears, lugubrious as any coed without a date for homecoming, bemoaned her age, said that her singing career would never get the break it needed. Henry, almost an outcast conversationally but certainly a member by virtue of his benevolence in procuring work for Mother, was as neat and together as a male model— sitting properly and pensively with arms folded, fingers holding a cigarette vertically, mouth of keyboard teeth glistening. We drank, and they talked until the singer on stage had asked his baby to stay by him for the last time and the waiters had begun sweeping under the tables and the smoke was heavy around us. My mind was buzzing, and we all were reeling from tight heads. When we got outside we squinted our eyes, adjusting to the daylight.

"Mitchell, you ought to stay with Henry for the night. You can't make it back to Harlem by yourself. Mommy wants you to get some sleep. I wish you would stay with Henry—it's all right, Henry? He lives near here, and, Mitchell, you could just fall on the bed as soon as you get there."

To tell the truth, I wanted nothing less than to get on the subway in my condition. My feet were aching, my temples were throbbing, my chin was falling against my chest. I forgot about Uncle's worrying about me. I could have copped my Z's standing in front of the club. My eyes were probably closed anyway when I agreed to accept the invitation.

Mother and Julius said they would see me next week in Chatsworth.

Of course Henry would live on the eighth floor, in a walkup.

"I'll get you some pajamas," he said, unlocking the door to one big room and dancing to the closet, establishing himself in my mind as an outstanding champion of endurance.

"Do you like boxing, Henry?" I was sitting on the couch-bed without invitation and digging his drawings of boxers on the wall. Funny, they wore gloves and shoes but no trunks or jock supports.

"Oh, I hate boxing, Mitchell," his voice from inside the closet, then throwing me a pair of clean-smelling short-pants pajamas and adding, "it's so, so violent. We don't need violence."

"Then why do you have the pictures of the boxers?"

Henry, moving past me now toward the window,

said, "I'll put on the air-conditioner." The__
smiling. "They're great men. Great big men." Well.

So we pulled out the couch, stepped into our sleeping gear (and my pants fell to the floor, since the waist was about three inches too much) and lay on the bed.

"Tell me about Maine, Mitchell." Was he kidding me? Was he a human vitamin? Perhaps a two-legged pep pill?

I turned from my side, sleepily said, "Tomorrow."

"I've never been to Maine. It must be beautiful and clear."

"We'll be happy to have you visit, Henry," I said, turning back on my stomach—a position to which I turn when I mean business about sleeping.

"Do you mean it? Really?" He sat up in the bed. And then a verbal alarm. A question that erased my tiredness as if a healer had waved his clairvoyant hand over my head. An electric timer that set my heart off as if it were a greyhound. A catalyst that set off emotional, chemical and physical reactions separately, then mixing them all to form fear, perspiration and trembling. This question: "Can I feel you, Mitchell?"

I jumped out the bed and scrambled for my clothes as if I were a Strategic Air Command pilot. Henry sat up, exposing his chest. I turned my back to him, stood on one leg and slipped a foot through my underwear.

"Mitchell, don't leave, please. I won't hurt you. I'm gay, that's all. Didn't your mother tell you? I'm in love with you. I'm not evil or mean or anything, Mitchell, I just like men. When I saw you undress, I got so excited."

My knees were sinking in that familiar quicksand. I thought of how I could get out if Henry, all more-than-six-feet of him, tried to stop me. I imagined the police laughing at me if I reported it. I thought of my chances for survival if I went crashing through the window. I

ry putting his hands on me, and my
ow being dragged to the muddy bottom.

hrist, you don't have to act like a damn baby
the thing, honestly," he said, walking toward the
or and—and yes, he unlocked it. I ran down those
steps faster than a fireman.

Outside, the sun was rising, spraying buildings with
gold. The sanitation men were banging the garbage
cans on the sidewalk, the air was close and stuffy, two
women were curbing their dogs, and a milk truck was
coming down the street, a newsboy whistled. But nobody noticed my crying as I walked down the street
with no money in my pocket and 130 blocks to go
before I could sleep safely.

15

<hr>

We are happy to inform you that your application
for admission to the September entering class at Brown
University has been acted upon favorably. In addi-
tion, you have been awarded a full-tuition scholarship.
In numbers and quality, competition for the 600 open-
ings this year at Brown has represented the greatest in
the school's history. We congratulate you for having
those qualities deemed important in our selection process, and we look forward to your having an exciting
four years at Brown.

Enclosed is some information about fees, travel and
other matters of importance to freshmen.

Yours for the Admissions Committee,

T. Newton Hackelbriar

I was holding the letter with quaking hands and
knees as if I were a suitor receiving a long-awaited
billet-doux. Tears were swelling my eyes, I wanted to
shout in the middle of the post office. I interrupted a
man carrying a briefcase, stepped directly in front of
him.

"Sir," I said, "just a minute."

"Yes?" Frowning, incredulous. "What is it?"

Not knowing what to say, scratching my head, I
stumbled over what I did say, which was: "I just got
accepted with a scholarship."

He pivoted around me, stared at me as if I had

propositioned him, and then joined the fleet of marching citizens filing in and out of the Chatsworth Post Office on an April Saturday. I stepped in front of other people, too, but they stepped around me as if I had the sweating sickness. Not one could I get to turn his head in my direction, not one would allow me to move over to him and explain my new victory, my large victory in the face of many defeats. And not a sole soul to share it with? I didn't necessarily want a soul brother, just a sole brother. What a gas. It was after school, so Jeff was still home. Uncle was still home too. And so were Mother and Julius. Everybody was home.

So I started pedaling my way back, past the explosion of buds on tree limbs and gardens, of bursting reds and pinks—past the explosion of spring. I felt that I was blooming too—or was about to bloom, anyway. And wow, wouldn't the dudes in school be uptight! And wouldn't my science teacher, Mills, and the principal, Ralston Emmons. Had it been four years ago—that long—since my talk with Principal Emmons? Four years? A freshman?

"Have a seat, please, Mitchell Mibbs." Emmons's voice had vibrated all over the high ceilings of his dark office.

His back had been to me—I can see those shoulders now, could see them then as I aimed toward home that day with my letter of good tidings. The room was furnished with only one other chair in a corner by the wide, thick, gold-knobbed door. Actually, a bench. The curtains, long and gossamer, had been brought together to cover the one wall-length window. His hickory tobacco was all over, clouding the room like fog, and the thick brown carpet plus the smell of mahogany furniture polish reminded me of so many museums. I sat on the leather bench in the corner. It was chilly—it was early in the morning—so I tapped my toes lightly on the carpet, I was sitting on my hands and wishing I had worn a jacket, especially when I noticed a scarf around Ralston Emmons's neck.

"The heat's off, Mitchell, so we'll just have to bear with it," smoothing a hand over the back of his shining bald head, the hair around the edges forming a horseshoe. He still wasn't facing me, his voice was ricocheting off the wall in front of him, bouncing off the other walls, almost shaking the chandelier. He rocked back in his chair, stretched his arms.

I cupped my hands—he was that far away—and shouted an okay to the high school principal.

"So you're worried about college, huh—is that it, Mitchell Mibbs? Well, that's what my office is here for, to solve you youngsters' problems. Okay, shoot. What's the trouble?"

I had to wait a few seconds for the words to reach me, and then I had to unscramble them, separate them in my mind before the sense of the sentence came home to me and I could cup my hands again, and I thought, would it be hip too if I stood like a sergeant barking an order, saying: "I can't study at nights as often as I'd like, Mr. Emmons, and I was wondering if I could stay after school some days and read in the auditorium, I wouldn't bother anything . . ." My voice was cracking already, although I had just begun, and I wasn't even sure the skin-headed principal could hear me.

"Louder, Mitchell; louder, my boy."

"Then why don't you . . ." My voice cut itself. Better not ask him that.

"Yes? What was that?" But I shook off the impulse to shout, to ask him why the hell he didn't turn around and look me in the eye, at least glance at me, at least notice I was there alive in his office. I became a frustrated spectator: my voice dried into nothingness and I flopped back down on the leather seat. "Well, it's certainly an unusual request, Mitchell, and I doubt seriously that we can honor it. After all, you would be the only student in the whole school doing something like this. Just little old you in that big auditorium, Mitchell; imagine the problems." I saw his arms spread outward in an explanatory gesture.

"But I'll be able to study better," I said, nearly forgetting to hold my hands up to my mouth, half of the sentence never reaching Emmons, probably.

"What's wrong with your home? Everybody studies in their own home, Mitchell. You're supposed to. Why can't you?"

Looking down at my folded hands, I blurted out, fearing that the carpet would absorb most of the volume: "My mother and father argue at nights, or either she is practicing her singing or they play cards all night at the dining-room table. I usually give up doing my homework before they're all done." I rapped fast to keep my voice from falling.

"Well, now, Mitchell Mibbs, understand, you don't want to study too much," he was saying to the wall. "You'll begin forgetting what you read. Look, you must remember that we can never do more than we are capable of. We just do what we can, that's all." He stretched his arms vertically toward the ceiling, flexed his fingers. "Oh, I know, Mitchell, you're worried about college, right? Don't fret, man. Your grades are pretty good, you'll make it. Listen, just the other day . . . what's that?"

The radiator by the window began tapping and kicking, steaming like a locomotive, hissing like so many snakes. It seemed to have too much fire in all its thin, silvery-painted bellies, seemed to want to expectorate any minute now. And the stubby legs—were they actually rocking back and forth, or was it their distance from me that made the legs mobile? Meanwhile: hissss, clink . . . clank . . . rink, dink . . . bong . . . donk, donk . . . hissss.

Almost like a whisper, Emmons's voice floated over

to me, and at the same time, my eye caught his hand flashing a white handkerchief in the air. He was an infantryman in a foxhole beckoning defeat. All I saw was the white linen high in the air, the head bald as an egg, its upper geometry shining above the desk. Then, a magnificent motion downward, and Ralston Emmons was wiping his forehead. "The heat's coming on again, Mitchell." But it was light-minutes before the heat reached me, so I was still shivering with my hands under me. "Now, just the other day—can you hear me with this preposterous banging, my boy?—just the other day Miss Smit was telling me how well you're doing in German. She says you're the best—well, you're the best Nee-gro student she's ever had in her classes, Mitchell. You're probably the brightest Nee-gro in the whole school, Mitchell. What do you worry for, my God? Feel free to take off your jacket and your shoes and socks and loosen your tie if you get too hot, Mitchell Mibbs." (Not a chance of that.) "Why don't you speak a little German for me, let me hear your accent."

"But I'm getting mostly B's. If I had peace and quiet at home or if I could study in the auditorium, I could get A's." I waited for the sentence to make its way through the nose-crippling tobacco smoke.

"Mitchell Mibbs, I am indeed disconcerted to learn about your home problems, but this is out of our jurisdiction, unfortunately. We cannot tax upon ourselves the burden of interfering in family matters. As principal, I must guide my students toward good citizenship. See, we can only help you achieve a level coterminous with your abilities." The fingers smoothing the horseshoe of hair again, the reaching back toward the desk for an ashtray.

"Yes, but I can do better than B's."

"Frankly, Mitchell," raising his voice to megaphone level, "we"—coughing out loud—"we, uh, never expected to see a Nee-gro do as well as you're doing. After all, we don't know too much about your kind, they're so few in Chatsworth. I've read studies, though. I know about how your families have arguments all the time. And I am aware of the tremendous number of broken marriages, violence, cursing, laziness, drinking. But you're doing fine, Mitchell, and I'm happy to say that we have sociable relations within our community. Of course, I'd like to see your mother at a PTA meeting now and then, but, well, I guess she's busy, huh?"

"Yes, but I know I can do better—"

"Mitchell Mibbs, please be more realistic, my boy. Your performance is quite adequate, according to reports I've seen. You could win a scholarship at State."

"But"—my voice was taking on a hollow, mahogany kind of resonance—"I was thinking about the West— Stanford or Reed."

"Oh, my God"—spitting splinters of tobacco to the side—"too big, too big, Mitchell. Besides, you should stay in the East—cheaper."

"What about Amherst or Brown?"

"I should say not. Too small and upper-class. Aim for State, Mitchell Mibbs. That's for you. Your mother will be proud, I'm sure. And I have a friend on the scholarship committee. You might try out for the cheer-leaders. I know you can jump and dance."

"But if it weren't for my mother," I started, shouting through my cupped hands and standing now.

"Mitchell"—he stood also, and I pondered, eyes in back of his head?—"don't live in a fantasy world, now. You are not a genius. You're a little smarter than most Nee-groes."

Um hum. Yeah. Okay. You'll see. I'll put something on your mind, I told myself, you jive-time . . .

So, no wonder that letter, rapture-bringing epistle that it was, shook in my hands like a paper earthquake. Why shouldn't I have grabbed people by the arm to hip them. Victories are hard to come by. And didn't I school all my friends and teachers? Didn't I bop around the school halls like I owned them, carrying a Brown bulletin and schedule of classes for the fall semester? My jaws didn't even get tight when Ralston Emmons explained, vest of a three-piece suit squeezing his ribs like a straitjacket, choked up in a wide, Windsor-knotted tie, "I heard some of the schools with highly selective admissions policies were beginning to lower their standards for Nee-groes." And he said that standing sideways, profiling his pipe and snapping out the words from the side of his mouth.

Never mind. Didn't I dream on a thousand nights of Brown between that April notification and the September morning when I prepared to get my hat? You'd better believe it.

Dig it: the morning I was to stash out for Rhode Island was too chilly already for short-sleeved shirts. And summer hadn't even ended. My two bags were on the porch, and I was out back with Jeff. Blue and Tojo and Plato and the rest were running around in circles. Barking. Claws crashing against the wire. Tongues lapping. Lunging at Jeff, who bounded back and forth, keeping a distance from the fence. I was out there to say my good-byes until Thanksgiving. The sun was streaked with clouds, and the breeze brought up the feathers on the chickens' backs. I put a hand on the fence wire, and Blue jumped up, started slapping a dripping tongue against my knuckles and fingertips. Then a few others jumped up too and licked my fingers, and soon they were growling and snapping at each other to see who would get to lick my fingers. Meanwhile Jeff, jealous possessor of my affection, pulled at my pants bottoms to get me away. He even barked, snapped at Uncle's big hunting dogs.

"Nice boy, Blue, nice boy, Tojo—" and on and on. You have to rap to dogs like that. "I'm going to be gone for a while," I said, awkwardly yawning and stretching my arms because I was as self-consciously affectionate with them as I was with Uncle. But at least I could pat the dogs on their heads and say things they wouldn't understand. But some things they do understand, like: "You guys are going to be good boys, right? Are you going to be good boys while Mitchell's away?" So they started whining and yelping. "Are you going to catch a lot of rabbits when I come back for Thanksgiving hunting, huh?" Then I left, not wanting to run it into the ground.

For almost an hour—this was right after breakfast—I talked to and patted Jeff in the side yard. Then I lay in the hammock (covered with dead leaves) with him, and we just lay there looking through the pear-tree leaves up to the sky. His head was on my chest. Patting, rubbing his firm back, I said, "Uncle will take care of you, old boy, you'll be in good hands, all right. You just be a good boy, huh? Jeff going to be a real good boy while Mitchell's gone?" But Jeff just lay on the side of me, his mouth slobbering over my shirt. And he was simpering through his nose as if he had peeped my hole card and the hammock didn't swing and everything was quiet.

"Mitchell, you about ready to go?" asked Uncle, clearing his throat, hand above his forehead to shield away the sun. His feet were crackling through the dead leaves, a swallow swooped past his face, and soon he was standing above Jeff and me. "Now, ain't this something. A grown dog in a hammock with a human. Nothing but a spoiled mutt." Clearing his throat. "I put your bags in the back of the car. We got a half-hour to make the bus, so, should we put Jeff away now?"

"Okay." But I didn't move.

Uncle showed a half-smile; he was looking skyward at an airplane too high to hear. I looked at the buttons on his red lumberjack shirt, then our eyes met, we both glanced elsewhere, looked at each other again, then glanced away one more time.

"No more pears in the tree until next year now, son."

"Yep." Still lying in the hammock.

"Boy, this summer sure went fast, huh?"

"Uh huh." Jeff snorting in my ear. A chicken cackling far away.

"I guess it'll be warmer in Rhode Island, since it's south of here."

"Yes, probably," I said, swinging my feet out to the ground. Jeff jumped down too. "In the cellar?" I asked, heading toward the gate to the back yard while pointing a finger at Jeff. "Is that where we put him?" Uncle said yes, and soon we were locking the door to the cellar, Jeff was barking, and we could hear claws scratching against the door as we walked away.

"Don't let him hear your voice," said Uncle as we passed through the gate and to the side yard again. "It'll just make things worse. Best thing is to just walk off." When we got to the steps, Uncle stopped, faced me, and spoke: "When you write me, Mitchell, print, don't use handwriting, okay? I can read printing better. Write me as soon as you get there. And if you don't like it, come home."

"Okay, Uncle." We started up the steps, and our feet lifted and fell together, so we smiled at that. "Will you be all right, Uncle? Will you take care of yourself?"

"Shucks, don't worry about me none. Don't worry about me none." At the top of the steps, he turned, pointed to the sun, but his lips closed back up when Jeff's barking began again, this time reverberating from beneath the porch. "He's in the front of the cellar now; he hears our voices." Starting toward and putting an ashy hand on the doorknob, but turning to me before going in and asking, "Where do you think your mother got those two cases of liquor from, son?"

"Two cases—I didn't see any." We were whispering like two in a movie audience.

"I saw two cases of whiskey in the cellar on the side by the water heater," said Uncle, "and I know they cost a lot of money." We went inside. The big clock was ticking, we could hear Jeff's barking in the cellar. We were standing by the door with our hands behind our backs, and although it was bright and brisk outside, the house was as dark as that funeral home in Boston. The curtains were closed. "We're getting ready to leave now," said Uncle, addressing an empty living-room audience. We stood another few seconds by the door, until finally Julius and Mother emerged (rubbing eyes) from their bedroom. "We're leaving now. I'm going to take Mitchell to the bus station."

"Good luck, kid," said Julius, stepping forward with eyes half-closed, moustache needing a trim-up, shaking my hand limply, turning around, sliding his feet back into the bedroom.

Then Mother: "Take care of yourself, Mitchell. Remember, you're my only son." Then caressing me, bringing the warmth of the bed and her body against mine. She kissed me on the forehead. "It's been a long four years of struggling through high school, but we made it, honey."

Um hum. Sure. Just you and I. What a struggle it's been for the both of us, I thought. My waking up late at night after having taken a nap when I finished dinner. At two and three in the morning I would wake up and burn my books by the flickering light in the dining room because only then was it finally quiet. No card playing, no singing practices, no arguments. Only Jeff and I would be awake; so I might read him poetry or we might slide out the back door and go for a cold walk up the half-moon-lit side road. Um hum. Sure. Just you and I struggled, all right. How about, I thought (meanwhile her mouth enumerating instances of overcome obstacles and feigned declarations of love and affection to Uncle, of all people), all those times you failed to attend a PTA meeting. Oh, come on. Struggle hell.

"Well, I guess it's time to go." Uncle looking at his watch. I looked at mine. "You got all your money, Mitchell?"

"No." I looked at Mother, whose eyes were red. "Mother has the hundred dollars you gave me. I asked her to hold it for me." Both of us looking at Mother, who turned into her bedroom. She came out again with her perfumed purse, dainty, polished-nail fingers trembling and working the purse's silver catch open. Pulling out one bill—a ten. My heart flipping out. "I had to use some of your money, Mitchell, but I'll give it back to you in a couple of weeks—isn't it Parents' Visitation Weekend? We'll be up then, and I'll give you your money back. Don't worry, honey."

"Pearl," Uncle spoke as Mother gave me the folded ten-dollar bill and kissed me again on the cheek. "What did you do with Mitchell's money to buy books with? Did you buy all that liquor in the cellar?" His neck muscles were popping. Mother's mouth opening wide, then the lips closing and trembling as if she were in some freezing Maine woods. Uncle clearing his throat, saying, "Never mind, don't answer," and pushing me toward the door. "Let's go." Jeff was barking and slamming himself against the front cellar door; he was whining. I could hear him as we bumped down the front road in this old Ford. I could sense his whining sinking into my memory. And the dogs out back, the hunters of hares and even larger game when Uncle was game to hunt them (deer and bear), were making a racket. I loved it, though. Uncle, meanwhile, was telling me what a good idea it was to lock Jeff up in the cellar so he wouldn't run after the car. But the good-bye. What a peal of uproarious pandemonium. What a woofing and bow-wowing of ballyhoo and bellowing. What a sendoff—perhaps undeserved (by me) but certainly not unreserved (by them). What beautiful circumstances under which to take leave. Okay, so the chorus of canine outbursts was more like a band abandoned by its leader than a Bach chorale. But it's the thought behind the deed, I always say. It's the respect behind the imitation. They gave me a good-bye fit for a monarch.

The clamor was sinking in my ears even as we bore right after passing the circle on the highway. Uncle left me at the curb when we reached the bus station, for he was not good with good-byes. And I think that the din from those dogs—Plato, Rufus, all of them—was following me a week later as I hitched up my pants just outside the auditorium for the start of the freshman dance. I think standing outside, hesitating, unsure, an unsteady hand of unsteady fingers reaching for my dance ticket—I think I was hearing the dogs spur me onward. Even then—one week after I had left, after being on campus for one week. And hadn't they also, just minutes before the start of the dance, screeched in my ear?

Check me out. We had been walking along Brown Street. It had been dark, the sun having set an hour ago, at eight, and we had been chanting old school songs. A horde of freshmen clanging toward the coed hall for the tremendous, freakish culmination of freshman week—the big blast, the big hop. With our brown beanies high on our heads (I was sporting my Afro), we, determined six-day veterans of higher education, marched toward the coeds. And we chanted:

> *Here we come, here we come,*
> *Brown men, Brown men;*
> *Here we come, here we come,*

Brown men, Brown men.
Look out, ladies,
We're proud men, proud men.

And I was shouting as loud as any of them. I was shouting to the lamplights, to the telephone wires, had my neck tilted back when my beanie—brown with a white B—was snatched from my head. I shot out after that cat as if someone had sounded the starter's pistol. He cut across Brown Street toward an alley, but the dark didn't deter me. Then that eerie, echolike barking and bellowing was in my ears; the noise was sending me after that brigand as if I myself were a shot from a rifle. I charged after him uphill, and it was a good feeling to be lifting, pumping my knees and legs again, as if I were in the Little League again, making it from third toward home. My throat was getting dry, though. My nostrils were stinging. We were on a narrow gravel path, and my new cordovan kicks were not exactly sprinter's Adidas. The path was winding and turning farther uphill, but I kept my eyes on the figure of swinging arms ahead of me, kept my eyes on the bottoms of his light shoe soles. New shoes for him, too? And I was gaining now, could hear the siren in my ears getting louder and louder, as if someone had placed a trumpet next to my ear. Smell of ozone filling my nostrils, the calves beginning to ache. And still that bellowing sending me on, pushing me, making a pursuer out of me anyway. So, he leaped with one leg leading over a white picket fence, one leg straight out, his head down and one arm (the hand clutching my beanie) sticking out parallel with his leading leg, and his fleeing was in abeyance for just that moment (a beautiful moment it was, too) as he lay suspended over the fence. But his back toe was not high enough. It tapped a point of the fence, sent him plummeting head first, so that he had to drop the beanie in order to break the fall with his two hands.

I leaped over the fence right behind him and aimed for the beanie, bent to pick it up and was tackled to the wet grass. We were tussling and grunting and pulling on the beanie between us and glaring at each other.

"Come on, give me my beanie," I said, voice cracking, strength dissolving and butterflies having a field day in my stomach—all these reactions after seeing his height and bulky biceps. "It's mine," I said, almost whining like Jeff had a week before.

Flashing of yellow rectangles. A door opening, slamming. Footsteps on the porch.

"Who's out there in my yard? Who's out there? This is private property, who's out there?"

We both jumped up, but I had the beanie, and we were going to the fence, and he hurdled it successfully this time and disappeared down the path, especially picking up speed when the man on the porch said: "If you don't answer, I'll shoot. Who's on my lawn?"

I stood outside the fence. I was huffing, looking at the green stains on my trousers, spitting grass out of my mouth. But I had my beanie. No admission without a beanie and a ticket. I felt for my ticket. Okay. The sirenlike howling had gone, and I felt as if I had successfully stalked my deer. So onward to the auditorium.

I shall definitely have to write Uncle about this, I thought, my face hot from embarrassment as I half-ran down the path toward Brown Street. Five letters already had been posted to him.

On my arrival I dashed off:

Dear Uncle,

The room is pretty comfortable, and the campus is nice. My roommate is from Hartford. We don't talk much. The food is pretty good, and the weather has been fine. Pat Jeff on the head for me. Take care of yourself.

Love,
Mitchell

On the next day I scribbled:

Dear Uncle,

I took tests all day today. I haven't seen another soul brother on campus yet, except for a couple of guys working in the cafeteria. I have six dollars left, so I hope Mother brings me some money when she comes up for Parents' Day, Saturday. Give my love to Jeff and the other dogs.

Love,
Mitchell

With my hand holding down my cap, I tipped up the steps to Coed Hall, presented my ticket, looked over my shoulder, entered the hall. Candles in holders on the walls. Darkness, and I could barely see more than heads moving. I thought I was in a huge shooting gallery, heads as targets. The orchestra, dressed in formal wear, was emitting some strange, slowly rhapsodic notes from the stage. I couldn't believe it at first—Sibelius's *Finlandia*? No wonder people were just stumbling their way acrosss the parquet floor. I took a spot against the wall, I was leaning against it with my hands behind me, palms glued to the cold, vibrating plaster. A couple dragged past me. He was in a bow tie, a tweed jacket, loafers. She had a gown that drooped to the floor, and it was gathering dust like a dry mop. The incense, some East Indian-smelling fragrance, brushed past me as they turned in a swirl, her gown sweeping dust off the floor—dust that twinkled in the candlelight. Then I saw the conductor's baton blur over his head, and the piece was finished. Clapping.

The women of Brown moved to one side of the hall, the men to my side. They inched toward the wall, and I had to scramble away, because a whole line of them was backing without looking, moving to crush me against the plaster. Then the conductor started a Strauss waltz and the men moved forward again to the other side like automatons. I followed behind them. The girls were giggling and switching their torsos back and forth, their arms were behind their backs, ribbons in their hair, roses on their shoulders. We marched by like drill sergeants. One of us would jump out of detail, grab an arm, and whirl her to the middle of the floor. I took heart, closed my eyes, walked over and thrust out my hand. "May I?" And we were sailing. She had a Rorschach of a red birthmark on her neck, her hair was loose and long in its auburnness, and she smelled of a French perfume I knew you couldn't buy at the Rexall store in Chatsworth. Her beauty made my hands perspire. Also, freckles on her cheeks and a small nose.

"Are you nervous?" Her smile faded into the shadow as we turned, moving closer to the wall, and she squeezed my hand. I wasn't afraid to touch her, wasn't worried that I was not worthy of her embrace as I had been with Carolyn that day in the snow. Wasn't this sort of thing done here? Wasn't this a new city? New possibilities? But still, the trembling.

"No, I'm not nervous. Why should I be?" I felt my right cordovan mash her toe. "Excuse me."

"I thought you might be nervous because you're the only Negro in the hall," she said, now limping a little.

"It's so dark, how can you tell," I said, keeping my cool, and wishing I could break out into the twist like Lucy or do the Watusi or maybe even the funky Broadway, dances I had learned in the Apple; and dances that made me comfortable. But this crap: Strauss indeed!

She laughed, then muffled it.

"What's the matter?" I asked.

"Oh, I was just thinking of the funniest thing. I was going to say that you smell like grass. Isn't that hilarious?"

"Quite. It must be my cologne. It has a kind of grassy fragrance, you might say."

"Really—grass?"

"Yes, really," I said, hoping my knees wouldn't stain her dress.

She said, her head going back, trying to dig me under candlelight. "This is my first time dancing with a Negro."

"Where're you from, Miss . . . uh . . ." My eyes were on her feet, and I was double-timing to keep my heavy cordovans off of them and to keep my knees away from her gown.

"I'm Peggy Smidley, and I'm from Greensboro, North Carolina. My father's president of Smidley Enterprises. We have a little summer estate in Seal Harbor."

"Seal Harbor? I'm from Maine."

"Yes. And I prepared for Brown at Squire Country Day School—it's just outside of Atlanta. That's why I don't have a southern accent. I was a member of Heather Club. In the winter I ski." Head bobbing, lipstick shining under the candles, smile as free and unforced as her life must have been. Had our meeting been meant as some romantic reconciliation of opposites?

"I got ninety-eight percentile on my boards. Oh, goodness—I've done all the talking. What about yourself? Why, I don't even know your name yet."

"Mitchell Mibbs, from Chatsworth, Maine."

"I'm glad to meet you, Mitchell," she said, baring perfect teeth that reflected the dull light. "What's your major? I decided to major in sociology, because there's so much you can do with it, you know: law, teaching, social work, so much." I felt the girdled back of some dancer bump into my hip.

"I think I'll take my time deciding, because . . ."

"Yes, you may have a point there. My brother,

Mckinley, who just got out of Wesleyan, which isn't too far from here either, tells me he didn't decide until halfway into his junior year that he wanted to major in history. Mckinley's now an account exec with Fink Brothers, Luther and Company. He lives on Sutton Place. But there I go again. Where did you prepare, Mitchell?"

Overcoming the temptation to say in the bedroom, in the bedroom is where I prepared for life one night. I played it straight and braced myself for her derision: "Chatsworth High School," I answered.

"Um hum. Oh, yes." And when the waltz ended and I realized I had engineered myself successfully through the entire dance without stepping on her toes a second time and we were clapping for the orchestra, she moved closer to me, was facing me and smiling, pushing her freckled nose nearer to my face (meanwhile, panicky, I considered that I was the only one still wearing my beanie, so I stashed it inside my jacket), and whispered, her fragrance dancing around and almost dizzying, at least inebriating my brain: "Mckinley went to Lawrenceville." The clapping had stopped, I was stunned into speechlessness, staring at her: What to do now? When I was in the Apple that summer, I had heard a couple of cats putting down some very tough games to broads on the corner. But could I rap to this chick as they had done to theirs? Could I connoisseur her, blow soft-toned messages of endearment into her ear? My game was uptight, I knew, but was I game enough to present it? Would she listen? Would she hear? I thought not. I began thinking of Smidley Enterprises and that bag she was in. I looked down at my cordovans, which were in, but my eyes ran up my tapered slacks, my Continental suit jacket, which were out. Proper young Brown freshmen were wearing cuffed, baggy pants and long, tweed sport jackets with bow ties. They had gone to Exeter and Choate and

Mount Hermon. Their conversations, I had discovered already through a half-dozen dormitory sessions, were of folk singers and surfing and skiing and politics. Oh, sure, I kept up with them, being the genius I am, but when I brought up jazz or the Village, I could have done better talking to myself. So. Maybe I could do better with Peggy by not rapping at all. Maybe I could save myself an unnecessary losing of my cool. But a glutton for punishment. I blew the baddest game I had. We were dancing again, it was a slow piece I'd never heard in my life, and I whispered the sweetest somethings I could think of in her ear. They had sprayed the room with another round of incense, the auditorium seemed darker and warmer, Peggy's head was nestled on my shoulder while my teeth tickled her earlobes. We barely moved.

At the end of the piece, I expected her to swoon, ask me to take her for some fresh air. But she said she had to get back to her friends, left me. A half-hour later I pulled her from a trio of girls and eased my arm around a waist I thought I was fairly familiar with. "Hi," I said.

"Hello."

"Long time, huh?"

"I beg your pardon?"

"Long time since the last dance."

"I guess so. My name is Peggy Smidley. And yours? Did you just come in?"

I broke off and left her standing on the floor as I walked out with my beanie riding high. Outside, I threw that thing to the middle of the street.

16

I SAW PEGGY SWITCHING HER BERGDORF GOODMAN wear around the campus many times during my first and second years, and she never spoke. My roommate's name is Paul. He talked a lot about his parents, who lived in Hartford, and visited them every weekend, leaving notes on my bed: "Dear Mitchell, please do not bother my movie camera or records or books while I'm gone."

On the weekends, the dormitory members broke out into big bad bashes. They invited janes from Smith and Holyoke and Wellesley. The chicks, throwing their heads back to free the hair from their eyes, slid out of MG's and Jags and Porsches, and they laughed delicate, birdlike laughs, spoke in high tones and wore furs; plus Harris tweeds, too. And out of my league. Peggy had taught me my lesson. I couldn't, didn't even try to rap to these babes looking for upstanding husbands from Scarsdale, Chevy Chase and Lexington who would take them to Europe during the summer and convenience them with fat black maids and cooks during winter and summer. Can you imagine me, stashed against a dormitory wall with a toothpick hanging out of the side of my mouth, sporting stovepipe, tapered pants and rapping as those dudes in the Apple might? "Dig here, sweetheart, I could work miracles with you if you just give me a chance. Why don't you break out of this socialite bag and come down to earth, get down to the nitty gritty with me?" How could I back up my pretensions with a father gone to God-knows-where and a mother like Mother? My social life would be through if they ever checked into my credentials. So I really stopped trying to rap to those broads after one from Radcliffe asked me at a mixer during my second year what my father's occupation was and I looked up to the ceiling, blinked my eyes, felt as if my ankles were covered with quicksand, looked over my shoulder, started stammering.

"You do know what your father does, don't you?" Frowning. Insistent. Small Caucasian face curtained with blond hair.

My lips trembled—"Of course"—and I ran out and struck for my room after fearing she might question me further as to his particulars: height, age, disposition, clothing, complexion. Outside in the October air, I tried to keep my cool by scatting:

> Scat, scat umdoowa
> Shoo bop um bop

But I broke down crying on the college green and couldn't finish scatting.

Back to the big bashes. The entire floor would be empty about ten on Fridays and Saturdays. They would be down in the recreation room doing the Ivy League versions of the boogaloo, the twist, and the monkey. Sometimes I'd stand in the hallway outside my door and shout, "Is everybody here? Is *anybody* here?" My voice would sound against the walls and echo back to me, and I would know that everybody had got his hat, shoved his books under the bed until Sunday night. Then I'd go back into my room, and tapping my drumsticks on the desk to some piece on the radio, try to hold back the tears. Unsuccessful. Soon I'd be coughing and crying loudly. And then I'd throw my sticks down, dive on the bed and push my face into the pillow until my eyes puffed with redness. Uncle and Jeff were far away on these nights.

I personally checked out a few parties myself. I was, uh, leaning against the wall, I guess, when this babe clacked her high-heeled self over to me one night, held out her glass, and said, "Will you fill this, please?"

I took the glass from her automatically, was about to take it to the bar, but then remembered who I was and said, "Wait a minute, I'm not a waiter."

When they paged me over the intercom one of those Friday nights of listening to the radio and tapping with my sticks and hoping that I would be accomplished enough someday to make a comeback playing in the Apple, I thought something was wrong. Why else would I have a telephone call?

"Melvin is in the hospital, Mitchell." It was Mother's voice, slurring, almost indistinguishable as a record playing at a speed too slow. "He wants to see you. Why don't you go see him tomorrow?"

"What's wrong with him?"

"He said he has chest pains, and it's hard for him to breathe. You know Melvin, always complaining."

"I'll catch a train tomorrow. How's Jeff?"

"Look, Mitchell, your schooling is costing me enough money as it is. I don't have enough money to talk to you all night—I'm in a pay phone booth. Just go see your beloved Uncle tomorrow. Can you do that much?"

I caught her mood and hung up, and I have never dug hospitals. Nothing but homes for the aged and infirm, for old people mostly, who stopped living decades ago; whose bodies were shards and gossamerlike; who had been pruned and thinned out upon reaching sixty; and yet, with all their wrinkles and leather skin and canes for legs and bottoms of soda bottles for eyeglasses and out-of-date clothes and unsightly, thick, black things called shoes and veins streaking their arms and legs like miniature estuaries—despite all this, they held on. You walk down a hospital corridor, and you see that only the old are suffering in those rooms.

At the Chatsworth Hospital, you make it up these cement steps meeting a circular driveway. Inside, you think it is no place for cheering. The attendants wear white coats, but their moods are grim, black. There is an information booth you could bump into as you enter; it is the size of a token station in some subway. Two elevators to the right, both groaning and creaking as they take you up or down, the operator bent over, banana-shaped hump back.

I reached the third floor, and not even wanting to bop, dragged my feet down to Uncle's ward. The floors were shiny but the lights were low. People were whispering to patients in their rooms, the patients propped in reclining beds or staring out at me from wheelchairs as I passed by, digging from the corner of my eyes. I walked slowly and cursed my cordovan heels for sounding out down the hall. The alcohol and medicine and drops and vitamins mixed in the air—what air there was—and almost made me sick. So much suffering in a hospital.

"In here, please, Mister Mibbs."

Six men in beds. They all looked at me. I saw Uncle in the middle of them. I walked over to him. If he hadn't been the only black face in the ward, I would have had to ask, "Uncle?" His face had gone sallow, his hair all white. He tried to lift his arm but couldn't.

"What is it, Uncle?"

"How are you, son? How's school, fine? Don't worry about Jeff—Mrs. Dixby is taking care of him." A slow and strained whispering through trembling lips. And Uncle used to be so virile, swinging me in the air and carrying me on his shoulders.

"Don't talk about me, Uncle, I'm fine. What's wrong, does it hurt? Is there any pain, Uncle?"

"They think it's cancer. I've had trouble swallowing, and it hurts here," touching his chest, "and here," pointing to his throat. "They may have to operate, Mitch. The other people in this room can't talk, their vocal cords have been plucked out like you draw the innards from a frying chicken."

"Have they been treating you all right?" I meant Mother and Julius.

"Nothing but pain. Haven't had a good night's sleep in months. I'm so glad to see you, you don't know." Frowning, jerking a hand and drawing in his breath. "Excuse me, the pain comes like that. Last week they stuck some kind of broncho tube down my throat. It was like a long, steel pencil, and they pushed it all the way down to my stomach, seems like, until I couldn't breathe." I turned my head, took a deep breath, but there was no stopping my heart, pumping so fast my temples throbbed. What to say to that?

"The food is good, though, and they treat me better than those two at home. One night I was screaming out in pain and"—trembling—"and they locked me in the closet for a half-hour because they couldn't sleep. And I took care of your mother since she was a little girl. I used to take her to the circus, Mitchell. I changed her diapers. But she made Julius lock me in the closet. I never did anything to Pearl, I love her."

"That's more than I can say," clearing my throat.

"Now, Mitchell, remember: judge not lest ye be judged." But I had some biblical phrases to throw at him, if I cared to, like *lex talionis*. "I made plans to have the insurance man come in first thing next week. I'm making you the beneficiary so you can finish your schooling, and I want you to have the car and the house and the dogs. The car's been sitting there since Julius cracked it up last year. I haven't been able to do any work at all on it. There's some savings bonds and money I have hidden in my room under the mattress. You get them before Pearl does."

"But, Uncle, you have to hold on, you can make it, champ. You have to be the champion, remember? Hunting season's coming up, arm wrestling, drinking wine at Tony's."

"Tony's dead, had a stroke. That's why I took Jeff to Dixby's. That old white codger, Tony, one of my best buddies. Heart attack. And I'm next to go. I hid some poison in the box where the records are in the attic. In case the pain got too much, I was going to put it in my wine."

I saw the nurses come in for dinner. They asked me to leave because they had to feed the other patients with tubes and the men would become embarrassed at an outsider's watching. I could go to the solarium until dinner was over.

"Why do you have my uncle in here?" I asked. "He can eat from a plate by himself."

The nurse smoothed out her starched apron and locked her eyes to mine, testing my reaction. "Acclimation," she said. "We want him to see how easy it is to be fed from a tube." Again my heart racing. My eyes cruised away and swelled. I hustled out.

And why did she send me to the solarium? Testing my reaction again? Trying to overwhelm me with terror or trying to cultivate a courage already flickering like a candle flame on its way out? Perhaps searching for a participant upon whom she could thrust, if just momentarily, a share of her everyday experience? My hand was on the door. The first man I saw didn't have a nose; the second was minus an ear; the third lacked a tongue. They were reading in wheelchairs, the sun had been long gone, the music was soft.

"Come on in, we're just trying to get the last bit of sun," said one, churning his wheels toward the door, his magazine thrown down on the floor. And smiling. The others looked up, threw down their mags and raced over to me. Three of them staring at me, who couldn't look at them. One smiling without a tongue. Deformed but glad to be alive. Staring at me.

"Maybe I'll come back," I said, turning. "I thought my uncle was in here." In the hallway I pushed my back against the wall to steady myself. I stood there for an entire half-hour, waiting for the end of dinner. I saw the nurse come out of Uncle's ward and scuttle down the hall toward me. Her arms were swinging, and her little feet were kicking, and she was looking downward as she pulled up and stopped in front of me.

"You can go back in, now, Mister Mibbs. Why are you standing against the wall?" Nodding at a passing nurse. "You may have noticed some missing features on the faces in there. No need to be alarmed. We grow pedicles from other parts of their bodies to replace the missing features which were removed to get at the cancers. If you go into ward twelve"—pointing down the hall—"you will . . ."

"I don't think I want to see any more," I said, almost gasping.

But insistent. Hands on hips. "You will see, Mister Mibbs, examples of the remarkable strides surgery has made in the past few years. For instance, in ward twelve, some of the pedicles—pieces of flesh, if you will—are almost two feet long. We have one patient growing flesh from his shoulder to his neck. Remarkable. Doctor Farley is performing most of these operations, and he's certainly doing some beautiful work. What he'll do is cut off the flesh and shape it into a nose or ear or what have you. Beautiful work. Did you see the old Jewish fellow with a pedicle growing from his throat to his abdomen yet? He walks through this hall quite frequently."

"Will you have to do this to my uncle?" My voice faltered.

"Oh, we can't tell, sir, I think Doctor will start by—the operation is next week, you know—by removing his larynx and pharynx and part of the esophagus, and maybe some other odds and ends, and maybe . . ."

"Thank you," I said, moving around her, and thumping heels breaking the silence in the hall, walked back to Uncle's ward.

"You're all we have left in the family, Mitchell," he said, Adam's apple riding up and down his throat, and his eyes were closed, his lips were tight. "If you don't make something out of yourself, Mitchell, all of the family will end up as nobodies. You've got to finish college and become something. Don't be an old lumberjack who can hardly read and write. Make people say, 'There's Mitchell Mibbs,' when you walk down the street. Make people stand up and take notice of you, Mitchell. Get that education, Mitchell, you only got two more years."

I told Uncle I would—make him proud of me, that is. I wanted to grab him and squeeze him against me, wanted to hold his hands, wanted to touch the stubs of gray hair about his face. "Uncle, I'm proud of you," I said, and then started humming to myself and shooting my eyes left and right to see if anyone had heard. And rallying, feeling amazed at my comfortableness, I stepped closer to the bed (the paint on its iron post chipping), bent over, and whispered to Uncle: "I love you, Uncle." Did it really sound right? I wasn't sure if I had used the correct tone, but afterward, seeing the thin smile form, hearing his little legs move under the sheets, I felt as if I had swum up from fifty yards under water, had reached the top, and the pressure had diminished. "I really do, Uncle," I added, losing my inhibitions but still shuffling my feet in a self-conscious kind of awk-

197

wardness and humming to myself. I patted his hand—hand mostly of bones and long, unclipped nails with dirt beneath; and his hands were trembling; and light as a dog's leash. "I'll be back to see you next week, okay?" He nodded, and I turned for the door.

It was raining hard when I went down the hospital's front steps. I waved a cab away, took off my shoes, and walked down the sidewalk. It wasn't too cold out. I slopped through sidewalk puddles, and the rain was beating against my face because I was walking into the wind, my head was down, and I licked the water from my lips. Once Uncle and I had walked from the circle, up the highway, up the road fronting the house, and to the house during a thunderstorm. We had no raincoats, no boots, no rain hats. And we took off our shoes, and disregarding the soda caps and rocks, we stuck our feet in the mud as if it were the thing to do. We laughed, hearing the thunder; we squinted our faces, seeing the lightning flash blue and die. We shouted to each other, and Uncle sang old songs, outsinging the thunder.

"You might catch a cold, Mitchell; get in the bed and out of those clothes as soon as we reach the house."

"Aw, I won't catch a cold, Uncle," I had said, about eleven years old and walking in that summer-afternoon storm.

And he had cracked me up with: "Liar, liar, your pants are on fire, your nose is as long as a telephone wire."

Having left the hospital in the rain, I was thinking about that day with Uncle. Now I was tramping in the rain by myself, headed toward the old homestead. I wasn't bopping, I had my hands stuffed in my pants pockets and I heard frogs in the woods along the sidewalk. The streetlamps were few and far between, sometimes a car wouldn't come for minutes. It was fine for me; the way I liked to be alone when I am trying to get myself together. I moved into the outskirts of the city, and the gravel road turned to a stone-laden course of mud. The hemlocks and burr oaks were hurling shadows across the road, and the wind was howling, everything smelling green and fresh. Soon the rain slacked up. I was standing at the traffic circle, and I decided to put on, tie up, my shoes. A cab came into the turn. I hailed it. I was out of breath and dripping when I told him, "To the bus station, please." I wasn't ready to go to the house yet.

At school I sat around all week working on the practice pad, and I stopped attending classes. I stayed in bed and read, getting out three times a day for meals. I looked through my wallet, pulled out pictures of Uncle in his big blaze-orange cap standing beside a deer he had just shot. I have another of Uncle and me with shotguns aimed high at nothing but clouds and looking straight ahead, smiling for the camera. Then I have another of Uncle looking down, pointing at the tracks of a black bear like some big-game hunter. I had brought a couple of his 78's with me, but had never played them because Paul had warned me about working his superuptight stereo set that had a labyrinth of knobs and switches and outlets and inputs and indicators. He never played a record on it.

So on Friday, I pulled out the two sides, one by Jelly Roll Morton, the other by Kid Ory, and had placed one on the turntable when my name exploded over the hall intercom. The phone call. Should I go? I looked out the window, then smoothed my bed blanket. I started the turntable, placed the needle on the record, dusty and scratched. I arranged my books on the desk, was about to arrange my roommate's too, when my name came over again, this time the voice demanding. So I tipped down to the first floor, stepped into the phone booth, held the warm receiver to my ear, spoke: "Hello?" Some sweet voice from the hospital told me that Uncle had died that morning. Kicked the bucket. Done for. Through. Uncle. No more.

Whistle blowing in my head. No, it wasn't the sound of a kennel of dogs, but more like our tea kettle screaming of boiling water. The phone booth was disintegrating into four separate walls. I heard the telephone box clanging like a fire truck. The floor was collapsing into melted tile, and I was sinking through the bottom. Walls slippery as oil, and I couldn't grab on to anything, and I was losing my balance. Devastating odor of decayed flesh jamming my nostrils. I banged and kicked on the door, I was trying to escape the flames growing up from the phone-booth floor, trying to get my balance and falling and slipping. Had someone locked me in, or what? A telephone booth going mad and taking me with it?

"Turn the handle, crazy, turn the handle." They were outside—the voices—and I could see the eyes, noses, lips of so many faces revolving around the little glass window of the door. "Turn the handle—how else do you expect to get out?" Their hair and ears were separated from their faces, and these features were still circling in front of me, moving closer to the glass door, retreating so I could barely make them out.

I turned the handle, fell out, was perspiring madly and ignoring the band of first-floor residents standing in front of the phone booth.

"Uncle's dead," I said, running down the hall toward the stairway. Then up the steps, then bursting through the door of the room. Paul standing, frowning over his turntable, my record on it. "My uncle just died," I said, out of breath.

"Did you put this record on my turntable?"

"Yes." I was getting my underwear, shirts and socks together and throwing them in a bag. "My uncle just died."

"I don't care about your damned uncle," he yelled, "you shit-faced schizo. Don't touch my record player again, you crazy kook, lying around playing with drumsticks and daydreaming. Why don't you see a psychiatrist or something?"

I was packing my bags and moving like thirty, and he was screaming at me, calling me names, and I didn't even have enough anger in me to start a fight.

"Good-bye, Paul," I said over my shoulder, dragging my bag of belongings behind me, making it.

"Crazy kook," he said.

Moving across the college green with my suitcase. The grass was fresh and just cut, the clock on top of Alumni Hall was ordering the end of classes. My bag was banging against my thigh, and I was chucking across the campus like a quarter-miler. "Uncle, Uncllllle," I shouted as if I were swinging through the trees, as if I were a town crier. I kept running, off the campus and down the hill to town toward the bus station for a bus to take me to Chatsworth, Maine. Nobody even turned his head as I flew past.

When I got off the bus, the sky was a sinking canvas of red claret. I ran again, dragging my bag behind me, scraping it against the asphalt, against the muddy edge of the road. I turned into the road fronting the house. The haze was thick and getting thicker, a rabbit's eyes glinted, and the two streetlamps weren't on yet. It was getting darker. Up that road with its miniature gullies and bumps, rocks and bird feathers. Coming closer to the house, whose roof loomed above the mist like an iceberg on water. Home again. Crickets on my left and right. I saw the sports car sitting outside the fence like a giant, crouching mouse. Uncle's Ford, propped on two wheels like a leaning wheelbarrow, was across the road facing me. But I saw no dogs barking, heard no dogs' barking. I went through the front gate, closed it without a click, and tipped through the side yard to the back. The hammock was turned inside out. The pump in the back had its handle sticking out, caked with rust. And farther back, standing by the dog kennel with a banged-up tan suitcase at my side and listening to the mutter of the chickens in their hut, I saw the evidence of Tojo's and Plato's and Blue's absence: upside-down tin water pails, no dog waste, straw from inside the houses strewn all over their yard, the kennel door wide open and no mush in their food plates.

"I guess they got rid of the dogs," I said out loud. "I'd better watch my step," tiptoeing to and up the back steps. Cousin Samuel's voice stopping me. Yellow light from the kitchen window, and the sky had turned black.

"Pearl, you ought to get most of the money, because you're his sister. You ought to get all the life insurance and just give Ranida and me the cash and some savings bonds," he said.

"What about the house, who gets the money from selling the house?" Ranida's voice was loud.

"Who lives here?" said Julius, and I imagined him staring at Samuel.

"How we gonna find out where the money is? We been looking all day."

"Before Mitchell goes to school, I'll tell him that he'll have to get some cash from Uncle's savings because I'll be broke on account of the funeral," said Mother. "I know Melvin told Mitchell where the money is."

"He had some nerve trying to change the insurance-policy benefits," said Ranida.

"Beneficiary," came Samuel's correction.

Julius continued: "He probably wouldn't have tried that if you hadn't made me lock him in the closet, Pearl."

"Well, he can't change the title to the house, and I got that right here. Those people who want to buy it and the land too will be coming around next week to sign the papers."

"I'm gonna open a bigger garage right on Commonwealth Avenue," Samuel said. "Whatcha gonna buy, Ranida, a girdle?" Loud laughter.

"Don't be playing with me, damn it, Samuel. You know I got a little more weight than Julius. I may joke and kid, but I don't play."

"We can really make it now, Pearl. I'll get back to the Apple and tell those agents that we got money to back us. They have to get us some engagements then. We'll be on our way to the big time!"

"Whatcha gonna do about little Mitchell and his dog?"

"He's almost grown," said Mother. "I can't take care of him forever. It's costing me enough money now to send him to school. He'll just have to get a job or something. Running around with drumsticks and that crazy dog."

"How much you get for Uncle's hounds?"

"We didn't get much," she said. "Enough for a case."

It was getting blacker. I felt my way down the steps, bumped my bag against the steps, and thinking I heard them stir, froze like a ballet dancer. They didn't hear me. I took one step at a time, feeling with my toe for fear that I would go slipping into the air from some chicken droppings. No moon was out. I eased through the gate, went to the hammock, sat on it. Opening my bag, I pulled out my drumsticks and beat out an accompaniment to "Take the A Train."

My head was being pierced by an electric sidewalk drill. It was being pounded by steel mallets. My temples were thumping, puffing like abscesses. It was the worst headache in the world that was drowning my thoughts, my sense of stability. I kept drumming, but the pain was increasing. I was close to tears, yet I had to keep playing, keep shouting out my protest as that trumpet player in the Village had done, even as that drummer at Boston's Rialto had. So, there I was fighting the pain with all my resolve and all the rhythm I could squeeze out of my wrists, and the mallet was hitting me harder and harder, enhancing the pain until I thought my skin had been broken and the hammer was cracking against my cranial bones. I was on an assembly line, was being transported along some steel road of ball bearings and was being pounded, pounded systematically by timed machinery going up and down, up and down on my head. Would I be pulverized into dust? Perhaps my counterattack was not potent enough. Perhaps I would have been annihilated had I not stood, dizzy, from the hammock and decided that this was no way to protest. This stick-playing, with all its art, its necessity for order and precision, was not what I needed to protest. And already the pain was easing, my eyeballs had stopped aching—easing at just the thought of a new strategy. A new strategy. Fight back? Melt the damned steel mallets into lumps of unforged metal? Pull the cord of the electric drill from its very plug? Spit and curse and froth and jab and feint and stab, kick and punch and gouge. Okay. Violence. That was the way. Become a Supreme Lord. Sure, practice, keep playing the drumsticks, but don't expect to make it at the Topnote. Become a Supreme Lord. That was the way to protest, to show your game.

I threw down my sticks, and head light and floating— floating on a pillow, seemingly—bopped through that sideyard toward the front steps.

I banged on the door as if I were a police officer. Mother opening it and looking lonely and lofty in a plain white dress and ice cubes clicking around the glass in her hand. Sweet, open-mouthed smile, arms embracing me. I dropped my bag.

"Mitchell, my son, I'm so glad to see you. It's

Mitchell, everybody. Come on in, take your coat off, cold, huh? Ranida and Samuel from Boston are here." Sitting down, picking up a handkerchief and pressing it against each eye. "We were . . . we were talking about the funeral arrangements, Mitchell. I'm so upset I don't know what to do," she said, taking a taste. "My only brother is gone."

"Try to stay calm, Pearl," said Samuel, hands on his belly and stomping in from the kitchen. "Hello, Mitchell," coming toward my hands. "Keep the faith, my boy."

Julius and Ranida came in, she sniffling and he steadying her with an arm around her shoulders. "Uncle's gone," she moaned, "but we gotta keep going, my boy. The Lord's ways are strange, but just." Falling into the couch.

My eyes shot over each face feigning grief. Mother dabbing with a handkerchief; Ranida's brow pinched into frowns; Julius's head down and he patted his hair; Samuel shaking his head back and forth. I stood there like a director waiting for the next line of dialogue and then opened my mouth: "Where are the dogs?"

"They ran away, Mitchell," said Mother, belching and putting a hand to her chest. "Excuse me." Then rubbing her nose.

"They must have been looking for Melvin, huh?" Ranida putting in her two cents. "They must have run away looking for poor old Melvin."

I lifted my bag and started through the room. Samuel and Julius jumped up, each reaching for my bag. ("Here, let me help you. No, let me help you, I got it.")

"I can take it myself, thanks," I said, eyes toward Uncle's bedroom. In his room, which smelled of alcohol and so strangely like the third floor of the Chatsworth Hospital, I sat on the bed.

"Mitchell, how's school?" Mother's voice from the living room.

"Fine," I said.

"I hope I can scrape up enough money to keep sending him," she mumbled (loudly) to Ranida.

But Ranida stood up and began stomping her feet, humming, clapping her hands and starting: "Come on, children, let's sing for Melvin." And then:

> Oh Lord, help us on our way,
> As we go along the lonely way.
> Lord, keep our souls with thee,
> So our life up there is free,
> Oh, free, so free, my God.

Four choir members now, huh? They were all singing, Ranida leading and Julius's voice squeaky, Mother's syncopated and jazzy, Samuel's basslike and toneless. Singing to their beloved old Uncle Melvin, who had kept dogs and taught me how to hunt and left me the car he loved. I eased to the other room, and shoes thrown on the bed and Uncle's long, six-battery flashlight in my hand, took the steps to the attic. I didn't turn on the light. In the box where his records were, I saw the three-ounce bottle, a black skeleton face and crossbones on the label. They were still singing downstairs. Holding the bottle, I made my plans. I stood up and flashed my white circle of light over the cobwebs and other dusty boxes. Taking a deep breath, my hands perspiring as if I were delivering a three-two pitch, I said, "Okay, this is it. This is it, all right." I placed the bottle in the bottom of the box and bopped toward the steps, dipping my knees and thrusting my shoulders forward in my best imitation yet of a Supreme Lord. I was ready to take care of business. TCB.

17

BEFORE LEAVING FOR BOSTON THE NEXT MORNING, Samuel drove me to lady Dixby's pad, where we picked up Jeff. He jumped and twisted and licked my face. We came back toward the house doing sixty, and Jeff was thrown around in the back seat from one window to the other. He and I jumped out, listened to Samuel beg Ranida to get in the car. She was on the steps saying good-bye to Mother and Julius, and Samuel was revving the engine above all the talking. His Jaguar was kicking dust through the weeds and jerking forward and backward as if on a horizontal Yo-Yo string. Finally Ranida crashed down the steps, lifted her leg up and slid, tumbled down and inside the sheen. And Samuel got rubber (startling Jeff) shooting away from our so-longs and skimming down the road.

"See you at the funeral."

Jeff and I went over to the Ford to survey the damage. I heard footsteps crunching through the needles behind me: Julius. I was glad he hadn't caught me talking to myself.

"Think you can fix it?"

I tried to catch an intonation of deceptiveness. And even after the words had been spoken into and disappeared within the air, my ear was sampling the stress he had placed on each word. Was he smiling? No. Completely serious? Not sure. I attempted a verbal reincarnation and tried to fix his phrasing of each word in my mind again while balancing the various inflections and nuances. So, I would have to carry it further to pinpoint his game, huh?

"I think so," I said, poker-facing the trees beginning the woods just on the other side of the station wagon. Let him do something with that, I thought.

"I guess Uncle Melvin left you the car for yourself."

"I guess so." I stamped on the ground to warm my feet.

"Mother got the home, you know. The deed's in her name. She also gets the insurance because she's the closest of kin, and the agent never did find out that Uncle wanted to make you the beneficiary."

"I don't want the money anyway," I said, still trying to make my mood difficult. "What do I need it for?"

"Well, you might could use some extra money for college."

"I'm quitting," I said, still facing the Ford and the trees but straining to glance at his expression. I saw his face turn toward mine, and using peripheral vision as if I were a pitcher eyeing a runner leading off first, watched him without facing him as he stuck out a stiff arm to hold on to the roof of the Ford with black leather gloves, and his legs were crossed.

"Quitting? Well, maybe that's good, Mitchell, because I don't think your mother was going to help you out too much. Your scholarship doesn't cover everything. I don't see why you want to do so many things for her."

So he was starting to cop his plea now. "What do you mean—I'm not doing anything for her." I leaned over to pat Jeff on his back.

"You're going to show her where Melvin hid his savings bonds and cash, aren't you? She's going to leave me and you, probably shack up with somebody else.

Now that she's getting all that money, she's going to think that she won't need me as her manager." I listened to his voice shake and knew then what his angle was. He was perspiring.

"I might want to go to the Apple with her," was my reply.

"She don't want you with her, kid. You should hear some of the things she says about you—and Uncle. But look, kid," moving closer to Jeff and me, his gold teeth glinting, "if you want to stay with your mother and you don't care about the money, why not show me where the cash is hidden so I can get myself together. I've put a lot of time in grooming your mother, and I ought to get something for it—right?"

"Will you leave tonight if I give you the money?" My mind was putting together the makings of a plan, my mental machinery was racing ahead of my words and taking me hours ahead of where I was, what I was doing then.

"You're damn right I will. She don't care about me at all. You know, she's been seeing a white cat named Carl? He's got a big sailboat and lots of money, and I think that white devil's been trying to get her to leave me for years."

I scratched my head, trying to focus in my mind a picture of a boat, a muddled conversation, a white skipper, a trip on the seas.

"And Samuel is always telling her to leave me. He never liked me anyway."

"Don't you and Mother get along?"

He scraped his shoes over some dirt, dug a pattern with his sole and stared at his feet. Jeff yawned and lay down, watching Julius's foot move.

"I can't satisfy that woman. When she gets in the bed, she never wants to get out—never." He walked away from us toward the gate; his shoulders were hunched as if he were pushing against a winter wind.

Inside the yard and a foot on the first step, he turned, said, "What time?"

"After dinner," I said. "I'll show you where it is after dinner. Do you want to leave then?"

"Okay, I'll get my things together right now."

Jeff and I sat in the tough old Ford for most of the afternoon. I was tapping my sticks on the steering wheel and talking with my only trusty companion. I knew my answer was not in the music and rhythm that the sticks symbolized. But the attachment to them; the feeling of something in my hands was assuring, so I tapped on, knowing that later in the evening I would have to relinquish momentarily my quest for musical notoriety.

"Big night, this night, Jeff," I told him as he climbed all over me and licked my chin and nuzzled his face between my legs. "This is a very big night for us, old boy," patting his head. Jeff was beginning to gain weight, and I noticed for the first time the two gray whiskers sticking from his nose.

At dinner, we spoke little. I dropped my knife twice, and Julius knocked over his coffee cup.

"What's the matter with you two tonight? Seen a ghost or something?" Mother asked, rubbing her nose.

I kept snatching glances at her as if she were about to embark on a long trip and I had to photograph her face in my mind for remembrance. She was clearing her throat and coughing from a cold, holding from time to time a linen handkerchief up to her nose—holding with long, thin, lovely, tan fingers with painted fingernails. And casually wearing a robe. When she finished eating, Mother asked us to wash the dishes for her because she would lie down for a while.

So it was in the kitchen with a dish towel around his shoulders where Julius whispered to me: "I put my bag on the side of the front steps. While she's sleeping is the best time to go, huh?"

"Yeah, I guess you're right," I said, leading him from the kitchen to Uncle's bedroom, then switching on the light. The sun had gone down during dinner, and now the Hawk was beginning to act up. For a split second while standing in Uncle's doorway before hitting the switch, I thought I heard the Hawk beginning to whip down the road. Now, with the light on, I knew it was he, gusting down the back road, for I heard the back gate smash against the fence, heard the pump handle slam down. He was out there, all right, no doubt about it. I slid my hand under the mattress and pulled out a stack of bills and bonds.

"Under the mattress—of all places. We never thought to look there. Under the mattress. Ain't that a gas."

"All the bills are hundreds—"

"Hundreds? Let me see," snatching the pack from me.

"They're all hundreds, and the savings bonds are signed already."

"Okay, Mitchell, look, I'm gonna get going before the storm starts, see. I'm gonna try to catch that seven-thirty Greyhound from Boston to the city, so I'm gonna cut out." Stretching his calfskin belt, he stuffed the lump inside his waist. A whiff of after-shave lotion from his face; hair shiny and waved; pants pressed, kicks glossy, the tip extra bright from a spit shine. He was breathing hard.

"You won't be at the funeral, then?" Keeping my fingers crossed.

"Oh, no," tipping into the other bedroom and emerging with a stingy-brim and shaking his shoulders to adjust his cashmere. "I'm in the Apple for a while, and then I think I'll try to make it to the coast. I hear things are pretty loose out there." And he was tiptoeing toward the door, putting his hand on the doorknob, lifting his coat collar up to his cheeks, opening the door, whispering, "Good-bye—and thanks—see ya, Jeff," and into the night to lean stiffly against the Hawk and the Maine storm. Jeff was whining and sticking his nose near the bottom of the door.

"Yes, he's gone for good, old boy. You won't miss him, will you? Come on, let's go check out the radio." Sitting on the rug in the dark, we gave our attention to some talk show until it went off, and then I stood, listened toward Mother's room, heard nothing. The floor creaked, reminding me of a groaning barn door as I inched toward the bedroom where the attic steps were. Up to the top, then pushing the wooden two-by-four door open—and having to push with both hands too, because the draft was working against me—pushing it and rising upward to the floor of the attic. Jeff came up behind me, his legs working like a swimmer's: first the forelegs, then his hind legs (sometimes slipping, stumbling and hesitating on those tricky steps). Momentarily I felt for my life as I stood in the attic's blackness and groped with one hand for the light string, while holding the other out, ready to catch my fall or to ward away some attempt to knock me off balance. Standing, straining on my tiptoes and in all that darkness with a draft blowing against my face, the Hawk whistling and my hand waving back and forth for a string. Anything could have happened. Jeff bumped against my leg, and I almost yelled out. Finally I found, pulled on the string, and the fat 150-watt bulb was white with light.

I pulled a side-by-side shotgun from the wall and pointed it at a spiderweb in a far corner. Rust was eating into the barrel, the triggers were hard to pull. Next I rummaged through that cardboard box full of records, scratching my fingers against the records' edges until I reached the bottle. Jeff came over and sniffed. I placed the shotgun back in its stand, held the bottle up to the light. Okay, half-filled. Then pulling out some balled-up newspaper from a bucket, I reached in for the almost-filled pint of bourbon sitting in the middle. Stolen from Mother's closet. The walls were cracking from the Hawk, and my hand was unsteady as I poured the whole bottle of poison down the mouth of the liquor, placed the liquor bottle on another cardboard box, threw the poison against a far wall. Now. Downstairs.

I sat at the dining-room table with Jeff at my side for about a half-hour—until Mother woke up. She came out of her room yawning and rubbing her nose.

"What time is it?"

"Almost midnight," I said.

"Sounds like the storm is here. Why do you have all the lights out—put some lights on around here," she said, going from a lamp by the sofa to one by the big chair and then by a window and pulling the curtains apart. "It looks like a storm, look at that hammock flip-flop. Where's Julius?" Her bedroom slippers slapped across the rug as she came into the dining room with one arm around her stomach to hold her robe together, blowing her nose.

"He went to the store to get a bottle. He said he left some bourbon for you up in the attic because he didn't want Samuel to find it."

She took a chair opposite me. Perfume was all about her; Mother's hair was in a bun. "Silly man. Of all the times to go out to the store. He'll probably get back drenched."

My hands were perspiring, and the veins in my wrists were pumping. I kept my eyes on her arms. Could she change my mind? A kind word, a smile, a touch from her soft fingers—would they stamp out my urge, my plans? I gritted my teeth, pushed my toes against the bottom of my shoes. I had to stay firm.

"We'll have a little money now, Mitchell, since I'm going to sell the house, so you won't have to apply for a scholarship next year. Won't that be nice? And the three of us will move to New York and live in an apartment there. Come upstairs with me while I get the bottle. I don't know why Julius had to go that far to hide it. We never talk much, do we, Mitchell? Come on, the attic is nice and still." And she was rising from the table, and then she was standing up straight, the lamps in the living room silhouetting her hips against the robe. "Let me get a glass first."

I watched the muscles in her legs flex as she took the stairs. For the first time in my life, I saw the birthmark on her thigh.

"Here's the bottle right here, Mitchell," and she grabbed it, undid the cap and poured a full glass.

My knees were so weak, my breathing was coming so laboriously, I could only stand there dumbfounded.

"You shouldn't drink that straight, Mother," I said, and am surprised even today that she heard me, my voice was so lifeless. And what was that act of benevolence for—to offer her one final grasp for a life preserver? But I couldn't help myself. I even added, "You ought to mix it with some soda," saying that, hearing the words come out and trying to ascertain at that precisely similar moment, why? Why was I saying these things, acting like some white slaveholder of old offering manumission and knowing he didn't mean to give it. If my mind kept on this crazy course, I might end up telling her that I had put a whole bottle of poison in the bourbon.

She had the glass of beer-brown bourbon up to the neck level, was raising it to her lips, but pulled the glass back to waist level and said, "You never did like Mother to drink, did you, honey?" Moving forward and running her hand over my hair and then bringing her hand down the back of my neck. Chills. "I don't blame you. Sometimes I do some silly things when I'm drinking, but I know you understand. I don't mean them. I love you too much to hurt you, Mitchell." She took a healthy drink in one swift motion while I watched, standing one foot away as the Hawk wailed and the shadows below her eyes and nose were black from the harsh, direct light of that big bulb. "Awfully strong," she said.

We stood listening to the wind. I had my hands clasped behind my back, and my tongue was tied. Mother rambled on for about two minutes, and I don't know what she was talking about, my mind was such a blur. I saw her standing, felt her hand press down on my shoulder and saw another hand hold her forehead. She leaned toward me like a falling red oak, then wavered backward, dropped the glass near my toe, grabbed at her stomach, and began to sink forward to her knees. Groaning. Gasping. Perspiring. The tongue was hanging out, the face was wrinkled, the mouth turned down like an unsmiling Janus. She looked up at me from her knees, reached for me with two hands, fingers clutching toward my belt, her eyes dancing in her head like loose marbles. Soon she was pulling at her hair with her fingers and then falling back, the robe opening while her knees knocked together and the breathing came slower and slower and slower, until she was lying spread-eagle with her eyes open. Now smiling.

Jeff sniffed, blew, snorted. Then he licked her knees, stuck his nose between her legs.

I leaned down to drag her by her neck to a far corner in the attic. Just as I dropped my mother's body on its side, face against the wall, and had covered it with some old army blankets, the bulb went out, thunder began, and I was ready to call it quits. It was a time for losing one's cool. Jeff was barking at the noise in the sky, so I crawled on hands and knees toward his barking, bumping into old clothes and dusty boxes on the way. Where was the flashlight? When I reached out and felt the hair on his back, I wanted to thank him but didn't have time. I pushed him in the direction of where I thought the steps were. He finally understood, went down in his inimitable cloppity-hop manner, and I followed feet first, going down backward.

At the bottom, I burst out crying and laughing. Strange collusion of fear and relief, as if I were frightened, being chased by a black bear but comforted by the fact that I could run. Frightened at the enormity of the deed. So quick. The picture of her lying there flashed before my face. A thought came to me, and I took two steps near the bottom of the stairway and shouted up the entranceway louder than the thunder or the wind, "Mother? Mother, are you okay?" No answer. So I grabbed Jeff around his neck and touched my nose against his. Now we were sitting on the floor by the steps. I pushed and pulled him back and forth, and he snapped playfully at my hand, and I was still half-laughing, half-crying. "She's done for, Jeff. All gone, baby. I just did it." I got up and ran into Uncle's room and began screaming out my laughter (the crying had stopped) as loud as I could; laughed, I thought, as a companion with the screaming Hawk and the thunder. Jeff began to howl, sitting on hind legs and sticking his face up like a coyote, sending a religious wail throughout the house. It was the first time I have heard him give a dog's mournful signal that a human is dead. He howled most of the night, too.

18

I WAS BLINKING MY EYES, TRYING TO FIGURE OUT
who those people were in the funeral home. Some
doings of Ranida and Samuel, no doubt. I had come in
late and was part of the viewing line when I looked
back at the faces in that crowd of mourners sitting,
hands folded. I was looking for a familiar face—
Morris's, Jake's, Herman's, Sadie's—and couldn't recognize one pair of eyes, one wide nose, nor a single set
of lips. Ranida and Samuel were sitting up front because
they were family.

The organ music was "Rock of Ages," and there
were two pots of flowers sitting on either side of the
white casket. We moved sideways along the dais in time
with the music. They poked their faces in as if they were
looking at a newborn. Shaking their heads. When I got
to the casket, I ran my fingers along the silk lining, my
eyes were closed, and I was trying to steady myself. I
was the last in line, so I could take my time, could hold
on to the edge of the casket as long as I wished. I
opened my eyes. Uncle was lying there in his best bow
tie, white-on-white shirt, black tux. No, not Uncle, I
thought, and I was glad for an instant at this discovery.
This is not he. I backed away from the casket, turned to
Ranida, whispered, "There's been a mistake, this is not
Uncle. He must be still alive in the hospital. This is not
my Uncle Melvin."

They stared at me. Ranida in her knitted veil, Samuel wearing a suit—they both stared at me, and the music was still going, everybody had taken his seat.

"But that man's a midget in there, it can't be Uncle," I said, and my voice was splitting into different tenors, my hands were shaking.

They still stared at me, then looked down at their feet.

"He's so little," I whispered. "It can't be Uncle," turning to go back, stepping up the dais, looking again at that tiny man in the little five-foot casket. I touched his face, and the makeup colored my fingers. His Adam's apple was large as a fist; his fingers reminded me of painted bones. Face shaved without nicks. Hair white as Jeff's paws. Farther down, Uncle's ankles looked thin as shotgun barrels. I stared at his face—a spotlight from the ceiling shone on it—and reluctantly acknowledged it was Uncle. No mistake.

We were outside, and you would have thought we were fifteen sets of twins the way our black suits, black dresses, black hats and black faces blended. A convention of penguins? I was standing by the door and watching them carry the little casket, lift it up ("one, two, three") and ease it into the back of the hearse. Ranida and Samuel came up to me as the men slammed the Cadillac door.

"Where's Pearl, your mother? Where's Julius?" We were surrounded by passersby, and my mind was not yet completely clear, roaring was all around.

I said, "Julius said he was going to the coast, to California."

"Well, where is your mother?" Samuel was panicky.

"She went to New York," I said.

They looked at each other. The mourners were filing for the other cars parked behind the hearse. These cars had their lights on. They were slamming the doors and saying how beautiful he looked, just like he was sleeping so peaceful, and oh, didn't the mortician do a good job, I mean he looked real, chile, and I was standing on that sidewalk in Boston, I was taking all this in and keeping my fingers crossed that I wouldn't slip with the tongue, that my two relatives would go for it. Samuel held his stomach as if he had been shot through with pain.

"I just made a down payment on a new Jaguar," he said.

"You mean they left?" Aunt Ranida's cheeks were twitching. "They ran away? Took everything with them?"

"They said they were never coming back," I answered, "after I showed them where Uncle had hid his money."

"Shit, I'm not going to the damn burial," said Ranida, pulling her hat off her head, a stickpin catching a bunch of hair. "He ain't no relative of mine."

"I'll be damn if I'm going either," rasped Samuel. "I'm just gonna go to the wake and start drinking," pulling off his hat too and slapping his knee with it.

"Might as well tell everybody to come on over to my house right now," said Ranida, waving her arms at the parked cars, "since we paid for them to come anyway. Don't nobody want to see no burying anyway."

So it was just the three of us in the gray upholstery of the Cadillac hearse. The other cars had pulled out ahead of us like drag racers and were sheening for Aunt Ranida's. They had cut in front of us, had almost crashed into our side. And it was just this one long limousine sitting in front of the funeral home. Quiet. So we cruised finally, cruised with Uncle's casket in the back, going to the cemetery, and the two men on each side of me not saying a word. I wanted to lean back and tell Uncle that I had taken care of business, wanted to tell him that I had made something of myself, that I had used my education to spark the genius responsible for my act of courage. The car's windows were up, I couldn't hear a darn thing. Winding up the road to the cemetery. The landscape looking like a golf course destroyed by granite tombs. I watched from the car as the two got out, and hands on the polished-metal lifters, stumbled with the casket to the newly dug hole. Then putting a long steel bar between the lifters and dropping the box, dropping my good-doing, wine-drinking, tobacco-smoking Uncle Melvin Pip from Chatsworth, Maine, U.S.A. into that hole. THUMP. And then they were shoveling from the mounds of dirt on the side of the rectangular hole, throwing dirt over Uncle's casket. The dirt was so hard it sounded like rocks hitting the box. They took off their black suit jackets and shoveled in their shirt sleeves while wiping the moisture from their brows with their hands and shaking their hands and stopping to stand up straight so they could rest, bend their backs. They shook their shoulders too and knelt, holding the insides of their thighs. And staring at me in the quiet hearse. So I went out to them and asked if they needed help. But they didn't have an extra shovel. So I scooped up dirt with two cupped hands as if I were building a sand castle at York Beach and threw it on the casket. It was hours before we finished, it was dark. I declined a ride back to town.

"I think I'll stay with him for a while," I said.

"Your father?" asked the tall one.

I thought for a second, held up my intended answer, and said instead, "You might say so."

Then it was just Uncle and I. The red taillights disappeared down the road and melted into the highway, and I stood still for a minute, made sure they weren't turning back, made sure no one was around, and then I ran back over the gravel path to the grass, fell to my knees, and started digging with my hands. I wanted to see Uncle's face one more time.

And it is night again, and it is raining, and Jeff is getting impatient. Tomorrow is the big day, and uh . . . what else can I say? I guess it's time to check out and get myself together, huh? Yeah.

Other SIGNET Books of Special Interest

More SIGNET Bestsellers You Will Want to Read

☐ **A RAISIN IN THE SUN by Lorraine Hansberry.** Winner
of the 1955-59 New York Drama Critics' Award, it tells
the compelling story of a young Negro's father's struggle
to break free from the barriers of prejudice.
(#T4262—75¢)

☐ **THE LONG JOURNEY: A BIOGRAPHY OF SIDNEY
POITIER by Carolyn Ewers.** You're handsome, talented,
wealthy, adored by millions of women—and you're
black. You're the Academy Award winning star of Lilies
of the Field, To Sir, with Love, Guess Who's Coming to
Dinner, For Love of Ivy and In the Heat of the Night.
(#P3790—60¢)

☐ **THIS STRANGER, MY SON by Louise Wilson.** A moving,
harrowing account of a mother's determined struggle
to raise a child who is a victim of paranoid schizo-
phrenia. (#Q3731—95¢)

☐ **IN WHITE AMERICA by Martin Duberman.** Text and
supporting documents of the moving off-Broadway play
about the American Negro's centuries-old legacy of pain
and discrimination. (#P2758—60¢)

☐ **THE SONG OF DAVID FREED by Abraham Rothberg.** A
poignant and evocative story of a young boy's coming
of age. Abraham Rothberg writes with warmth and
humanity as he turns the events of childhood into
dramatic and meaningful art. (#T3740—75¢)

Current Bestsellers Now Available in SIGNET Editions

☐ **LOVE STORY by Erich Segal.** The story of love fought for, love won, and love lost. It is America's Romeo and Juliet. And it is one of the most touching, poignant stories ever written. Will be a major motion picture starring Ali MacGraw and Ryan O'Neal. (#Q4414—95¢)

☐ **JENNIE, The Life of Lady Randolph Churchill by Ralph G. Martin.** In JENNIE, Ralph G. Martin creates a vivid picture of an exciting woman, Lady Randolph Churchill who was the mother of perhaps the greatest statesman of this century, Winston Churchill, and in her own right, one of the most colorful and fascinating women of the Victorian era. (#W4213—$1.50)

☐ **SAM THE PLUMBER by Henry Zeiger.** Taken from volumes of verbatim conversation overheard by an FBI-planted bug, SAM THE PLUMBER screams louder than The Valachi Papers in revealing the shadowy power of the Mafia in our lives. It is the incredible real-life saga of a Mafia chieftain who is a successful businessman with a thriving plumbing and heating business—but also is a Cosa Nostra boss with a controlling hand in gambling, labor racketeering, shylocking, political fixing, hijacking and murder. (#Q4290—95¢)

☐ **FLASHMAN by George MacDonald Fraser.** His scandalous pursuits in battle and bed make FLASHMAN ". . . the most entertaining hero in a long time . . . one of the real finds of the season."—*Publishers' Weekly.* Rave reviews, sassy story . . . the appeal of this novel is almost limitless. (#Q4264—95¢)